LEVELLER

A.R. LERWILL

Also by A.R. Lerwill

War for Humanity: The Wrath of Black Scar
War for Humanity: The Heir to the Order
War for Humanity: The Return of the Promised One

Publisher: Independent Publishing Network
Publication date: 24.05.24
ISBN: 978-1-80517-394-6
Author: A.R. Lerwill
Book cover by Book Design Stars
Email: arlerwill@gmail.com

ISBN 978-1-80517-394-6

Join the mailing list community for news and special offers. And receive a free book!

Listen to the theme song, 'Blink and You Will Miss It'

Scan here:

I dedicate this book to you. Accept this reality for what it is. Be kind to yourself. And do your best.

"Chaos is the law of nature; Order is the dream of man."
- Henry Adams

Part One
Retribution

One

I remember the day it happened—opening my eyes for the first time.

But here I am, sitting within the confinement of these four walls—a small room with dreary, grey decor, an imposing low ceiling, and a sticky floor. There is a lingering, dank smell. An overhead lamp showers the scene with clinical white light, illuminating the swaying flow of dust particles.

To my right is a large mirror, which, I suspect, is two-way for others to spectate whilst maintaining anonymity.

Why is that necessary?

There's a metal table with chairs positioned on either side. Sitting across from me are two people. They've refrained from disguising their identities, features partially covered in shadow, with neutral expressions and intense stares. They're wearing plain, white clothing. It's hard to deduce anything about their origin or motives—this rouses suspicion.

They're positioned rigidly, clenched hands resting on the table. Intently, they read every nuance in my mannerisms, hoping this would reveal subtle clues about my thoughts and general state.

But I remain still, sitting in silence. Fatigued, slumping in the chair, my arms folded and legs spread out—purposefully relaxed yet guarded. I look off disinterestedly into the distance between where their shoulders meet.

No restraints?

I've been in these situations before. Because of years of training, I know how to handle myself—focused under pressure. No impulses. Depending on whatever these interrogators are looking for—and how adamantly they need it—I'm prepared for waterboarding or other imaginative means of torture. I will accept it passively. When subjected to pain, I have a high threshold.

Disconnection. My body feels drained, like a hollow shell—symptoms of withdrawal.

I remember the memory of the park pond.

I'm staring at the door on the opposite side of the room. At standing eye level, there's a small, rectangular window with a thin crosshatch pattern. I suspect the glass is bulletproof or resistant to heavy collision. On the opposite side, I see the silhouette of a guard standing, facing in the other direction. Because of the limited visibility, I can't tell what they're wearing. But I notice one shoulder slightly slumped. It might be supporting the weight of a strap—they're possibly bearing a large firearm.

Are these two interrogators also armed?

To my left, the one person, a man, who I suspect is in his late forties, clears his throat—the emphasis expresses impatience. The other person rustles in their chair, tightens clenched fists, and swallows. It's a woman, possibly in her mid-thirties, just a few years younger than me. In my peripheral vision, I can see them exchange exasperated glances.

I'm smiling inside. For the interrogators, this is monotonous, but for me, it's amusing. I lost track of time a while ago. It pleases me to waste theirs.

'Mr. Blake,' the woman announces.

That's my real name. My eyes momentarily twitch. But I resist the urge to look at her, instead keeping my focus on the crosshatch pattern.

How're they aware of my personal information? Despite the cliché methods of interrogation and laughable security measures, this disclosure suggests there is some credibility to my captors.

She continues: 'Do you know why you are here?'

At present, I can't be sure. To throw off my interrogators, I subtly start chewing my lip to convey false anxiety. They can see the muscles contracting in my face—all to give off the illusion that they're slowly cracking away at my impenetrable disposition.

She unclasps her hands and reaches over to the side of the table. There is an unmarked, beige folder. It looks relatively new. I suspect it contains classified information.

Why would they go to all this effort to take me captive? Are they aware of the consequences if I'm to retaliate? What exactly got me here in the first place?

Although the room is still with an uncomfortable silence, my un-tethered thoughts go running wild. Despite the exhaustion and with-drawal, I retrace my steps through the endless corridors of memory.

Then the exact thought appears, hurtles towards me, and related imagery floods my mind's eye—everything about the mission that opened my eyes for the first time.

An all-consuming feeling.

Despite it being a covert operation, do they know what happened? Were they part of it all?

For the first time, my eyes, which had become unfocused, gazing absent-mindedly at the window, now avert to my two interrogators. They appear to stare right through me.

I have the impulse to externalise my thoughts. My lips move to form a word. But, again, I refrain and continue to perform the chewing act. Although my body doesn't convey, I pull myself back into that calm, balanced state.

There are spasms in my limbs that I keep at bay.

I look down at the folder, contemplating what is inside.

My mind wonders. I think back to how this all started. It was not the most conventional of places. But some unforgettable experiences can begin in the most unexpected ways.

My two interrogators sit watching me. The woman begins to open the folder. They're unaware that I am starting to relive all of what happened whilst remaining in the same position with the same neutral expression.

And for a moment, my eyes avert to the right-hand corner of the room. There, I see something misplaced—a single white feather. Delicate. Curved upwards and frayed at the edges.

Two

Like most agents that operate on an ad-hoc basis, I'd been waiting restlessly for something to happen—preoccupying my time with things that aren't good for me.

The phone call, from a withheld number, was brief. I didn't know who I was speaking to—the person's flat tone was indistinguishable, probably a case officer or an AI-generated voice. I can't tell the difference these days.

They supplied a location and time—a bar in Chelsea at twenty-one hundred hours.

The area was busy, but I found a parking space nearby. I looked out for oncoming traffic before getting out, crossing the street, and casually walking towards the entrance. I would merge effortlessly into the crowd, dressed in dark, understated clothing.

My hands twitched. That stubborn itch. Withdrawal.

The outside of the bar had large windows, purposefully flaunting what was inside. It was a sophisticated, overpriced hotspot for the area's most affluent social climbers. There were finely upholstered sofas, grand chandeliers adorned the ceiling, a glass bar with a mountain of liquors on the back wall, and a golden glow illuminated the room.

Joining the queue, I could see an array of people in front, shaking off the spring breeze, excitedly waiting to go inside. More money than sense. Most probably oblivious, or at least indifferent, to the hardships most of the population was experiencing. What with the rising cost of living, strikes and protests. You can't sense that tension here amongst this crowd.

On the door were two bouncers, both steroid-built, wearing earpieces. This establishment kept a vigilant level of security despite the supposedly civilised clientele.

I didn't know what to expect inside. It wasn't my first time at a place like this. The standard practice for someone on my level was to receive the most minute information. Each strand of the web gets just enough to do its part without potentially derailing the whole operation if compromised.

After the lofty bouncers had patted me down and granted me access, I walked through. Thanking the overly polite door attendant, I entered the bar.

Inside was the smell of an expensive fragrance, champagne fumes, and pretentiousness. The wall of noise from the chatter wasn't too overbearing. I could hear chilled house music playing in the background. To my left was the DJ booth.

Looking at my watch, I was punctual. I would check the place out before twenty-one hundred hours struck. Taking a clockwise route around the bar, I subtly gazed at the room's corners for security cameras.

There were trust-fund socialites, z-list celebrities, social media influencers and business deal celebrations. Servers manoeuvred through the crowds, answering every request, ensuring no glass was left empty.

Then it happened—the all-too-familiar sensation.

At first, I ignored it, but, as was often the case, it took my undivided attention. Perhaps being in this environment or anticipating the operation, something gave me the urge to self-medicate.

No amount of mindfulness practice could work. I couldn't resist. It was time to freshen up.

Checking I still had time, I searched amongst the crowds for the toilets. And in the distance, I could see the human silhouette symbol upon a door. Calmly, I paced through the bar, collecting a glass of water given by a waiter.

Once inside, a few men were at the marble urinals. One toilet was available. Feverishly, I walked inside, closed the door, and put on the latch. I lowered the toilet seat, placed the glass onto the tank cover, and rummaged inside my jacket pocket for the bottle. I pulled out the translucent plastic container. Inside were the tablets that I wanted.

They're called Statera. And are still in development; they don't have a street name.

You're probably wondering why a professional of my calibre would have a prescription drug dependency. These were initially given to me by doctor's orders—and higher authority's approval—to help enhance performance and regulate mood. I found that more than the recommended dosage heightens your mood and senses. Over time, I've grown a liking to them and now have a high tolerance. Instructed to take them, they don't flag up on mandatory tests. Sure, the amount I consume might be against medical advice, but it helps me to function.

To deal with a lot of thoughts and feelings that I don't know how to handle otherwise.

I opened the container and poured a small handful of the tablets into the palm of my hand—more than the daily recommended amount. Replacing the sealed container into my pocket, I took the glass of water, heavy-handedly threw the tablets into my mouth, closed my eyes tightly, and drank the glass dry, swallowing hard. With the back of my hand, I wiped away excess fluid. I could feel the drugs seeping down my oesophagus and into my stomach. With relief, I placed the glass down, straightened up, and took a moment to compose myself.

Suddenly, the irritability was gone. I felt comforted, focused, and in control.

Why can't I have more self-restraint?

I flushed the toilet and walked out to clean my hands. Drenching them in water, I scrubbed meticulously using lotion before looking at my reflection in the mirror.

Although I maintained myself—a chiselled jawline and well-groomed—I always focused on the tired, wrinkled eyes. I scarcely looked at myself properly in the mirror because that look revealed a vulnerability, although subtle only to me. A sadness that I had buried deep inside.

I dried my hands and adjusted my jacket. Returning to the bar, I checked the time—it was nearly twenty-one hundred hours. Instead of standing around, looking like a rabbit in headlights, I walked over to the illuminated glass bar. Chancing upon a spare seat, I smiled at a couple who moved aside to allow me to sit down. Perching, I felt the suspension momentarily adjust to accommodate my muscular frame.

I looked to either side, spectating the merrymakers, and caught the glance of a bartender who came forward. I ordered a slimline tonic. Resting my hands on the bar, I contemplated when the Statera would kick in—I was always an expert in priority. And self-deprecation.

At that moment, gazing listlessly along the endless rows of liquor, I sensed someone was looking at me. Resisting the urge to be too abrupt in my movements, I slowly looked to my left at the gathering of people.

Standing a few metres away was a young woman with striking features, strong posture, and elegantly dressed.

The bartender returned with my drink. I presented my credit card for the contactless payment. Thanking him, I sipped the tonic, feeling the liquid tantalising my tastebuds.

The couple walked away.

A fleeting glance.

Suddenly, she picked up her cocktail glass and a clasp handbag before walking towards me. At first, I thought nothing of it, conscious of the time, but sensed her presence behind me.

'Do you mind if I take a seat?' she asked. There was self-assurance in her tone.

I turned around to face her at eye level. She looked at me cautiously.

'By all means,' I said casually.

At that moment, I saw someone standing nearby. I turned forward to continue enjoying my drink.

'Thank you,' she replied.

Easing forward, she lowered onto the seat, putting the glass and handbag down onto the bar.

'What brings you here this evening?' I asked, looking at her.

'Oh, you know—after-work drinks.' She smiled, rubbing her neck in a somewhat nervous manner.

I decided to be straight with her: 'First time?'

'I beg your pardon?'

We maintained eye contact for the fleeting moment of awkwardness. In the background, the DJ introduced a new song that roused appreciation from some of the crowd.

'As soon as you came over, I could tell.'

'Oh, really?' she said dryly, reaching into her handbag—a sleight of hand.

I received a folded slip of paper and slowly placed my hand under the bar without trying to attract attention. Pocketing the note, I looked up at her. 'Couldn't this have been sent to me electronically?'

She smiled sarcastically. 'Sometimes, the simplest methods are safer.'

'Gone are the days of meeting on a park bench with a briefcase,' I said whimsically, looking forward. Swirling around the ice in the tonic, I took another sip.

'Simpler times, indeed.' From my periphery, I saw her eyeing me sceptically. 'I bet you would like it if I wore a mac. *Suggestive.*' I nearly spurted out the mouthful. She leaned in closer. 'I know your type— You don't know what you want but you know how to get it.'

She lifted her left hand—an indentation from an engagement ring removed to protect those closest.

The thought cut into me—the memory of the park pond.

I wanted to feel the effect of the drugs.

'I suggest you watch your back on the way out.' My eyes averted over her shoulder. She followed their path toward where a man was standing by a pillar, trying to enjoy a drink without drawing attention to himself. 'He tailed you here.'

She collected the bag and stood to leave. 'I know how to look after myself.'

'I wouldn't doubt that for one moment,' I said sincerely, looking up at her. 'Although brief, it has been a pleasure.'

'You never know, we might bump into each other in the office by the water cooler. Good luck.'

I momentarily looked over her shoulder. 'Same to you.'

'Good evening,' she said. I returned the gesture, watching as she left the bar, slowly tailed by the man.

Facing forward, I sank the last few drops of my tonic. Standing, I adjusted my jacket, nodded toward the bartender, and made for the entrance. On my way out, I thanked the overly polite door attendant.

Once back in my car's safety, I withdrew the folded note from my pocket and looked inside.

Ascribed were a name and two addresses.

Now I knew the operation—an extraction.

Three

It was a twelve-minute drive, taking a route southward until turning onto Grosvenor Road and heading east along the riverside. The orange glow of streetlights illuminated my view. Beyond the segmented tree line were distant silhouettes of buildings on the opposite side of the river.

There was traffic at the junction as I turned south onto Vauxhall Bridge. Driving over, to my left, was the headquarters of MI6. And to my right, the extraction point—St George's Wharf. An apartment complex consisting of large, tiered buildings at the water's edge, surrounded to the right by skyscrapers. The building's lighting cast blurred reflections upon the water's surface.

Approaching, I questioned why an overqualified agent needed to extract someone from what appeared to be a low-risk environment—this seemed like an entry-level assignment. Of course, I preferred field work instead of being a pencil pusher behind a desk all day. This mission appeared straightforward on the surface. But from years of experience, I've learnt not to make assumptions.

I had no idea about the importance of the target.

On the opposite side of the bridge, I had to follow the one-way system, circling Vauxhall train station before swerving right onto Wandsworth Road. Indicating, I entered the apartment complex's semi-circular driveway—this passed under one of the front buildings. Despite it not being a designated space, I parked the car at the end facing the road. After the extraction, I would have to drive around the one-way system until heading southwest, towards the second address ascribed on the note—the rendezvous point.

Turning off the engine, I looked around for a few moments. Using the mirrors to inspect the scene, I watched traffic passing and pedestrians walking by. I looked around to get a bearing of the surrounding buildings, surveying possible hiding places for sharpshooters—a few too many.

Once assured there was no tail or no one had reacted to my arrival, I reached into the glove compartment. Revealing a concealed handgun, I loaded and harnessed it. I pulled my jacket closer to hide the weapon. Finally, I put on thin, black leather gloves before getting out and closing the door. I waited for the automatic locking mechanism to signal before pacing forward. There was a cool breeze. I walked northwest through the complex, past a seating area framed by trees, towards Hamilton House.

I entered through two glass doors into a small reception area. To the right was a tall, wooden desk where the concierge was sitting, looking half asleep—eyes averted. I suspected he was playing on his phone. Instead of going over to feed him an alibi, I marched through, casually smiling and nodding in his direction. He reciprocated, unfazed.

I walked towards the lift and scanned the list for the floor where apartment five-hundred-and-sixty-seven resided. It was on a higher level. From my recollection of surveying the building upon approach, this was one of the larger apartments.

When the lift arrived, I entered, pressed the button, and turned around. As the doors closed, I scanned the corners to ensure no cameras were watching me. Withdrawing the handgun, I took out a silencer, which I screwed onto the end of the barrel, before re-harnessing the weapon.

It was a precautionary measure to keep a low profile in case things got, how shall I say—out of hand. It was crucial that our activities went unnoticed by the general population. I had to blend seamlessly into the background. We conducted everything with utmost secrecy beyond anything you can imagine.

You've probably heard that before. But this was no ordinary agency.

As the lift arrived, I readjusted my jacket. The door opened, revealing the corridor. My immediate observation was there were only two apartments at each end. Expensive, contemporary artwork hung against the opposing wall. Cove lighting illuminated the scene.

Immediately, I knew something was untoward—the neighbour was standing in their doorway looking in the direction of five-hundred-and-sixty-seven. Surveying the door, I saw it was ajar. Someone had broken the lock. It was too risky to enter that way. To avoid attracting suspicion, I pressed the button to close the lift door while avoiding the neighbour's eye contact.

To reach the target, I would have to take a different route.

Less than a minute later, I knocked on the door of five-hundred-and-sixty-nine. It opened. A tall man stood, wearing a turtleneck jumper, brandishing a large glass of red wine. His eyebrow rose, looking me up and down.

'Yes?' He sounded displeased.

'Sorry to bother you,' I said in a friendly tone. 'Maintenance. Do you mind if I come inside? I need to gain access to your balcony.'

It wasn't the best story, but I had limited time. The resident looked me up and down again, not concealing his smug dubiousness. 'You don't seem appropriately dressed?'

I opened out my hands in a non-threatening manner. 'The service charge pays for the best.'

He frowned momentarily. 'Right. Very well.'

The door drew open, and he allowed me inside. The lounge area was like half a spear's head: to the left was a long, straight wall. Curving inwards from its end were ceiling-high windows looking out over the Thames. To my right, there was a large partition. Behind this stood the kitchen. I noticed a laundry basket with two large towels on the heap.

I was taking mental images because the target's apartment below would be the same layout.

The lounge area looked like a showroom, everything almost brand-new. In the foreground was a long wooden table with leather chairs. A horseshoe-shaped sofa was at the centre of the room. Here, a guest casually reclined. Seeing my approach, he pushed upright, glazed-eyed, intoxicated.

'What brings you here this evening?' the man asked, closing the door behind him.

'Other residents raised complaints about noise issues,' I said, looking at a space between the wall of windows and the kitchen. There was an entrance onto the balcony.

'I did notice some peculiar sounds. Perhaps coming from downstairs? It was like…gunfire?'

I stopped, turned to look at him, and said in a restrained tone: 'Really?'

He came forth with one arm folded under the other, slowly twirling the liquid in his wine glass. 'Yes, only minutes ago. I was about to call the concierge, but you arrived.'

'That's why I'm here. I shall look into it straight away.' Forcing a smile, I turned to the guest sitting on the sofa. He smiled suggestively, raising his wine glass to toast.

I realised the Statera was kicking in.

Despite the warm reception, I had no time for further small talk. Quickly, I made for the sliding door opening onto the balcony.

'Now you are here; I have an issue with the shower curtain rail,' I heard behind me. 'It was, ah, accidentally ripped off earlier.'

'All in good time,' I said over my shoulder.

Unlatching the lock, I swung the door open, walked out, and closed it behind me. Knowing what I was to do next, I had little time before these lovers would report me.

From here, there was an unobstructed view of the river below. Other than the hum of the city, I could hear the water surging by. In the minimal light provided by lamps in the gardens and walkway, I could see a black mass of liquid moving hypnotically.

Right below me was the balcony for five-hundred-and-sixty-seven. Refraining from looking back, I paced forward, grabbed the metal handrail, and jumped over. Still holding on with my left hand, I pulled hard, swung around, and threw my right hand out to catch the rail. My arms and face slumped against the glass barrier whilst my legs dangled freely.

Holding on tightly to the rail, I looked down past my right armpit towards the target's balcony. I would have to calculate this with minute precision.

By now, I could feel the full effects of the Statera.

In most situations, the circulation of adrenaline would put me on edge. But I felt calm. A recommended dosage produces restrained symptoms. But I felt a sense of euphoria. It wasn't the proper sensation to complement my current circumstances. My body felt warm. But I wasn't sweating. I took a few deep breaths to oxygenate my body because I enjoyed the stimulation.

Heightened awareness. Finely-tuned senses. Reduced amygdala activity—no fear.

In front of me, I could hear the balcony door sliding open. Not wasting another valuable moment, I let go.

My body started falling. In that split moment, I saw the balcony disappear, followed by concrete, followed by darkness.

I reached out with my hands and caught onto the metal railing of the next balcony. As this happened, my face and torso slammed against the glass barrier, and my legs flayed wildly. A sharp sensation ricocheted through my arm sockets and shoulders.

Resisting the discomfort, I held onto the rail, catching my breath. I hoisted up and over onto the balcony, landing lightly in a kneeling position. The sight ahead caused me to reach for my handgun.

There were two sets of sliding doors on either side of a wall. The one on the right was open. There were no lights on inside the apartment. I was staring into a dark void.

Bullet holes riddled the glass. The cracks adjoined, trailing in a correlated line, too precise for an automatic. I looked at the wall. Some markings weren't from exit holes but appeared from where bullets had hit it externally. Below this were decking chairs. Shards of glass and wood were scattered everywhere.

I turned to look down towards the Riverside Walk. From this high up, it wasn't a feasible angle for someone to aim at from the ground level, either side of the river. The glass barrier in front of me wasn't damaged. Bullet holes peppered across the surface of the curved wall of windows to my left.

I edged towards the right-hand doorway. It was open just enough for me to ease through sideways. Once inside, I instantly aimed my handgun out into the darkness. Moving forward, I knelt and took cover in the kitchen. I listened intently for any sounds. But all was silent.

After a few moments, assured that my eyes had adjusted, I glanced around the partition towards the lounge area. A blue glow from lights emitting below painted the room. Furniture, smashed ornaments, a large flat-screen TV, and the contents of bookshelves lay in a sea of debris. I presume the sounds of this, and the gunfire, were what the wine-swirling neighbour had heard.

I stood up, cautiously inspecting the scene. There were no bodies or signs of altercations. Whoever had been here was either looking for the target or something else.

Had I arrived too late?

Moving through the apartment, I made sure to be light in my movements and concise in my footsteps. Holding tight the grip of my handgun, I searched the apartment for any clues.

My heart was beating calmly. Eyes intensely focused.

I walked through the opened double doors into the main corridor. To my left was the main bathroom. It was in a similar condition. Next, I circled into a bedroom that housed the other sliding door—this was relatively unscathed.

After checking another smaller bedroom, all that remained was the main bedroom near the entrance. The door was wide open. I walked inside, ensuring to check every corner, my eyesight strained by the darkness. Slowly, I checked under the bed, which was clear. The en-suite was empty. The only thing left was the large walk-in wardrobe. The door was ajar.

I expected I wasn't alone.

Drawing closer, I reached out with my spare hand for the handle. But the door suddenly burst wide open before I could grab it.

Out came a man screaming, frantically swinging a golf club. In-stantly, I knocked his attacking arm out of the way, sending the weapon out of his grasp. He fell forward. I curved around, dropped my handgun, and embraced him in a bear hug. For a moment, he continued to scream, arms immobilised and legs kicking widely. I held him, standing back against the door.

'Get the *fuck* off me!' he shrieked, sweat trickling down his cheeks, fingers clawing into my thighs.

'Please listen to me,' I said calmly.

But the man repeated more aggressively. I pushed him onto the bed.

Reaching for a lamp, I turned it on. Picking up my handgun, I held it by my side.

As he turned around to face me, I could see the look of terror in his eyes, thinking that his attackers had returned to finish him off. He looked towards the golf club and doorway, presumably contemplating the likelihood of escape.

'Are you Doctor Bachira Aditi?' I asked, walking over to take a seat nearby.

He looked at me in shock.

'Who are you?' he replied, brushing away the sweat.

'My name is inconsequential. I'm here to take you to a safe place. I presume you contacted us because you are at serious risk?'

He straightened up, clearing his throat. 'Yes, yes, that is correct.'

'I know nothing about who you are or what attracted this trouble. I'm here to ensure you get to the rendezvous point. Where are the other people who live here?'

'My wife and children are visiting her parents. I had to stay to oversee a project at work.'

'What happened here?'

'They were here a short while ago,'—he started shaking—'I hid in a secret compartment in the wardrobe when they broke in looking for me….'

'Not looking for *something*?'

'No. Well, I don't think so. I think the intruders were only looking for me. They already have what they want.'

When someone says something like this, I'd want to question them for more details. But could only ask for specific information relevant to my part in the mission.

'They came here to kill me.' Hysterically, he looked up at me. 'Just like *you*!'

'Doctor Aditi, I'm here to protect you.' Standing, I walked over to the bedside. He looked up at me, eyes widening in terror as my tall frame loomed over him. 'Here, you can have this.' I tossed the handgun onto the bed. He looked up at me suspiciously, flew forward and grabbed it. The weapon momentarily slipped into his hands. He pointed it at me.

I retook the seat. 'Doctor, I'm giving you the handgun as reassurance that I don't intend to cause harm. The sooner you accept that I'm here to help you, the quicker we can get out of here.'

The grip on the handgun loosened as he processed my words. His body continued to shake with fear. 'Where are you taking me?'

'To a rendezvous point. My colleagues will escort you into hiding or whatever you need. If necessary, we can arrange a full relocation and identity change for you and your family.'

'How are you going to take me there?' The change in his tone of voice conveyed newly founded openness.

'My car is parked outside.'

For a moment, he remained there, the handgun still aimed at my face. But eventually, he rationalised, lowering it. Moving over to the end of the bed, he sat on the side, threw down the handgun, and buried his head in his hands.

'I'm sorry for the outburst…pointing that gun at you.'

'You don't need to apologise. I should have been here sooner to ensure the intruders never got in,' I said reassuringly, looking at the wardrobe. 'Do you have your phone?'

'Yes.'

'Did you call the police?'

'No.'

Good.

'Is your phone charged?'

'Just about. I will need to call my wife.'

'That can wait—my colleagues will provide instructions when we reach the rendezvous point.'

'Okay. Can I bring some of my belongings with me?'

'Only the essentials. I want to get you out of here at once.'

He looked up at me. 'I will get my things together.'

I stood, collected my handgun, and walked to the doorway. 'I will wait by the entrance.'

He nodded.

I inspected the front door—the broken lock had been a professional job.

Moments later, now dressed in activewear, the doctor walked past and into the lounge carrying a canvas holdall bag. Vocalising shock, he approached an overturned cabinet and pulled out a few documents. He stuffed them into the open bag. Turning to me, he could see the curious expression on my face.

I resisted the temptation to ask, but he decided to say, 'I specialise in advanced quantum computation.'

That detail confirmed why I was on this assignment. It wouldn't have made sense to extract a regular medical doctor. He couldn't afford a place like this on that salary. Whatever he had been working on needed the agency's input.

'Oh, right,' I said casually, masking my concerns.

I walked forward, intending to escort him out of the apartment. But suddenly, the room erupted with a loud noise as bullets showered it.

Instinctively, I leapt forward, pulling the doctor to the ground. Shielding his head, he screamed in dismay. As I lay over him, fragments of furniture exploded around us. Briefly, I looked towards the balcony but couldn't see anyone standing there. Rolling over, I signalled for us to scramble towards the doorway. He nodded frantically, following me. All the while, the chaotic barrage of gunfire continued.

Eventually, making it to the front door, I got to my feet and pulled it open. Looking around to ensure the corridor was clear, I walked through. The doctor was close behind. We both started running towards the lift.

'Where was that coming from?!' he questioned.

I stopped and pressed the lift button before turning to look at him. 'I don't know.'

Four

Entering the reception, I harnessed my weapon and slowed to deter any suspicion from the concierge. Doctor Aditi walked by my side, flustered, clutching the holdall strap with a shaking hand, the bag swinging with his movements.

Passing the reception desk, we both smiled at the concierge as he went to receive a phone call. Moments later, as we neared the entrance, I could hear him vocalise astonishment. I suspected other residents had reported what had happened in apartment five-hundred-and-sixty-seven.

Anytime soon, the police would arrive.

We had to get out of there.

I felt the stress hormone cortisol flooding my bloodstream, whilst the effects of the Statera overpowered this, maintaining a potent high —an internal boat on choppy waters. Energised—ready to fight, I had to take a few deep breaths to ensure I wasn't too overzealous in my mannerisms.

Before opening the entrance door, instinct told me to avoid walking out. I sensed something wasn't right, troubled by thoughts of whatever had attacked us in the apartment.

Abruptly, I stopped, turning to face the doctor.

'What's the matter?' he asked.

'As soon as we walk out, I will provide cover. We have to be very careful getting to the car. The door will be open.'

He nodded.

I took his holdall and threw the strap over my shoulder. Withdrawing my phone, I held down both volume keys. It would send a signal to my colleagues at headquarters, informing them I was performing the extraction.

Behind, I could hear the concierge shouting in our direction.

'Are you ready?'

'Yes,' he replied confidently.

Pocketing the phone, I opened the door. Walking out, I withdrew my handgun, surveyed the area, and started moving forward.

He followed on my heels. I provided a shield, feverishly training my handgun on the surrounding apartment buildings. They loomed over us. There were numerous windows, ideal for concealment. As we passed each corner, I expected confrontation. Our heavy footsteps and fast breathing perforated the deathly silence.

When we reached the semi-circular driveway, I gestured for him to walk around to the very end. The car's locking system registered my approach. The doctor ran forward, opened the passenger door wide, jumped in, and slammed it shut. I quickened my pace to reach the driver's side of the car.

Suddenly, I could hear a buzzing sound coming from behind, echoing against the surrounding buildings. For a moment, I ignored it, but it got louder. Nearer. When I reached the driver's door, I opened it and threw the holdall onto the back seat.

I looked toward the corner of an apartment building. A large black drone appeared. On the underside of the body was a mounted machine gun.

Turning in our direction, it registered, opening fire with a loud cacophony, peppering the car with bullets. I knelt for cover. Thankfully, there were perks with my work: a vehicle customised with reinforced bulletproof windows and plating.

Civilians walking along the pavement ran in fright. I launched inside the car and closed the door. Exchanging glances with the doctor, he was wide-eyed, panting heavily.

'Well, that'll explain things,' I said dryly, harnessing my weapon. 'You'd better hold on—this won't be an easy ride.'

He nodded anxiously, attaching his seatbelt. I secured mine and switched on the quiet, hybrid engine.

The drone had flown ahead and turned around to face the car. I pressed down on the throttle, released the handbrake, and instinctively pulled down hard on the steering wheel, sending the vehicle on a hard right in the opposite direction of the traffic flow.

The tail end of the car swerved outwards before straightening. The doctor gasped. Several vehicles were driving in our approach, beeping. I manoeuvred past them. Some swerved to avoid a collision. Overhead, the drone vaulted ahead, showering the car with bullets.

We drove towards a junction. I originally intended to head straight down Wandsworth Road, but traffic surged from the one-way system to our left, blocking the way.

Looking to the right, I saw no traffic approaching from Nine Elms Lane. I pushed down on the throttle. With the engine roaring but barely making a sound, I pulled down on the handbrake and sent the car in the new direction, again in the wrong lane.

We started driving down Nine Elms Lane. To our right was the apartment complex. In front of us was the river, which this road snaked alongside. The car momentarily shook as it straightened. Vehicles were coming in our direction. Evasively, I drew over the verge and onto the left side of the road but had to slow the speed as we neared other cars.

Looking in the rear mirror, I saw that the drone had circled and tailed us. It recommenced a barrage of bullets that smashed against the vehicle's surface, the sound muffled by the thickness of the windows.

To prevent civilian casualties, I meandered through the cars ahead, jumped the next set of lights, and pushed down hard on the throttle to create distance. Ahead of us, the road was empty. The U.S. Embassy was to our left, surrounded by a mountain range of modern skyscrapers, office blocks, and apartment buildings. To our right were smaller buildings overlooking the Thames.

Behind, in the far distance, I could hear bellowing police sirens. They were heading for the apartment.

'Are you going to try and out-run that thing?' the doctor asked, looking over his shoulder at the barely visible aircraft camouflaged in the darkened skies.

I looked in the rear mirror, watching the drone gradually getting closer. 'Not likely.'

The drone stopped firing at us. The operator must have realised it couldn't pierce the bulletproof material. It accelerated forward, circled to our right, and started firing towards the wheels. Although these were run-flat tires made from heavy-duty rubber, unlike the rest of the car's exterior, they were vulnerable to constant bombardment from machine gunfire.

Training my eyes on the road ahead, I swerved to avoid a collision. The drone maintained its aim, pelting the right-hand front wheel. It wouldn't be long before the material obliterated, causing the wheel to burst and a possible loss of steering.

We met traffic. I took the pressure off the throttle, manoeuvring the car through like water passing stones in a stream. All the while, the drone had continued its pursuit, edging nearer.

'How far are we?' the doctor asked.

'Depending on traffic—less than twenty minutes,' I said, looking to my right as we passed Battersea Power Station.

Suddenly, and most inconveniently, two more drones appeared in the distance, flying in our direction.

When something like this occurs, affecting civilian lives, I obviously can't take it lightly. It was a well-planned attack. And especially right out in the open. Something like this does not happen every day. Our operations are usually done in the shadows, away from the public. We typically stop these things before they happen.

Who was operating these drones?

As we drew past Battersea Park station, the drones surged ahead, shooting at a dozen vehicles under the bridge and beyond at a junction.

The audacity.

Panicking, the drivers all reacted by putting on their brakes. Some swerved, and others crashed into each other, ploughing into a cyclist and creating a barrier ahead of us. Civilians started to run and scream.

There was no alternative but to continue forward. Thankfully, there was a small gap to manoeuvre through, narrowly missing a double-decker bus.

The doctor breathed a sigh of relief. I held control of the car, pressing down hard on the throttle, pushing it to its limits.

I was in the moment. My heart was still beating calmly.

We continued down Battersea Park Road past a residential area. Once again, I had to weave between both lanes to avoid oncoming traffic. Meanwhile, the three drones continued to pelt us and other vehicles.

Drawing towards another junction, at the last moment, I applied the brakes, causing the car to grind to a halt. The hydraulic suspension-assisted seats cushioned us. Meanwhile, the drones flew onwards. Deciding to take us away from my intended trajectory, I drove forward, pulled up hard on the handbrake, and twisted the steering wheel, forcing the car to swerve to the left, causing the back end to swing around and the tires to screech. As this happened, I drew down my window, withdrew my handgun, aimed at the drones, and fired. A few hit their mark, but the aircraft were undeterred and turned around.

I dropped the gun into the footwell, released the handbrake, and used both hands to retake control of the steering wheel. We surged southwards onto Falcon Road. The car momentarily wobbled before I was able to stabilise it.

Twice thrown off my original route, a few valuable minutes added to the journey. Thankfully, I knew these streets intimately. But I knew we were entering busy Clapham Junction at the end of this road.

'Doctor, would you mind doing something for me?' I asked, looking in the rear mirror.

'Yes.'

One of the drones was drawing nearer. I couldn't see the other two.

'Can you reach into the backseat and pull up the lower cushion? Underneath, you'll find an assault rifle.' He proceeded to unbuckle, twist around, and lean back. As instructed, he pulled up the cushion, revealing the weapon. 'There are two ammunition clips. Take those as well.' He unlatched both and brought them forward. 'Thank you. Just hold onto them for me.'

We came to a junction. Opposite us was the old Arding & Hobbs building. I took a sharp right, avoiding vehicles from every direction, and drove up St John's Hill towards the train station. To no surprise, two other drones appeared ahead. They started shooting at the front wheels of the car.

'There is another one!' the doctor exclaimed, looking back.

Fully aware, I looked in the rear mirror but corrected my presumptions. Drawing behind us was the original drone, along with a new counterpart. As the original started firing at the car's back wheels, the newer aircraft was better equipped—it launched a small missile that narrowly missed the side of the vehicle and smashed into a nearby lorry, which exploded in a thunderous ball of fire and smoke. Civilians started running frantically in all directions.

Nothing is ever easy—the memory of my son's face.

As I swerved around other vehicles, we made our way onto a bridge across the train tracks. All four drones circled, positioning themselves at each wheel, continuing to bombard the car with bullets and missiles. The latter missed. I veered through the oncoming traffic.

'Doctor, hand me the rifle and clips. You must take the wheel.'

'What?!' he questioned.

'I will keep my foot on the throttle,' I said, loading the rifle before activating the window. The doctor reluctantly leaned forward and took hold of the steering wheel.

I produced the rifle, aimed at the drone to my right, and released a volley of gunfire. It had the desired effect of smashing through the drone's plating, which I deduced wasn't made from metal. Moments later, the propellers malfunctioned. The drone exploded onto the concrete, fragmenting across the pavement.

Meanwhile, the other drones spotted me leaning out of the car. They directed their fire at me. Instinctively, I leaned back in for safety, closing the window. I passed the rifle to the doctor and retook the steering wheel.

The road tightened. We continued down St John's Hill past houses, shops and restaurants. Civilians ran for cover. Debris exploded around us.

Eventually, coming to a turn on the one-way system, we followed this south on the A3. Snaking around, Wandsworth Common was on our left. Once again, heading westwards towards the rendezvous point.

We continued, jumping lights at a junction, gradually heading to-wards Wandsworth. The newer drone drew forward, faced us and launched a missile at the front-right tyre, this time hitting its target. The wheel was blown to smithereens, causing the car to shudder. Shrapnel propelled into the air, hitting the windscreen. The exposed wheel hub crunched against the ground, spraying sparks in all direc-tions.

The doctor vocalised his shock, hugging the rifle close to his chest. I tightened my grip on the steering wheel to ensure I wouldn't lose control, narrowly missing an oncoming car.

I could no longer drive at top speed. We continued on Wandsworth High Street, now taking a downhill trajectory, only a minute away from the rendezvous point.

How was I going to shake off this tail before getting there?

The steering wheel gyrated in my grasp. My arms spasmed. But I was in control.

Approaching heavy traffic, I swerved through. There was no choice other than to mount the pavement. Doing this, I punched the horn repeatedly to alert oncoming civilians. One manoeuvred, riding an electric scooter. Ahead, the lights went red. I evasively drove out past the parking traffic. We narrowly avoided collisions from other angles.

Eventually, I took a hard left onto Buckhold Road. In the distance, I could see the rendezvous point—a grey multi-storey car park.

I swung left onto Neville Gill Close. As this happened, I heard another explosion. The rear-left tyre also burst, causing the car to gyrate violently, slowing its trajectory.

I turned left under the low-hanging barricade entrance. Overhead, the front two drones flew away to avoid colliding with the building. The remaining drone, surveying the steep bank inside the car park, refrained from following us and flew out of sight.

I breathed a sigh through my nostrils. The car continued to struggle.

We needed to get to the second level—not ideal.

Getting to the top of the ramp, it curved past the guard station to the left. As the car smashed through the barricade, he stood up, looking on in dismay.

We drove through the first level and approached the next ramp. Despite the reinforced windows, we could hear the screeching of the wheel hubs echoing against the walls of the car park. I contemplated getting out and running the rest of the way, but I could see the drones circling the building. I didn't want to take the risk.

I could feel the car struggling on the incline as we drove up the final ramp. Ahead, over the lip of the new level and a short distance away, I hoped my colleagues were waiting for us.

As we reached the top of the ramp, I instructed the doctor to grab his bag. We drove around to the right. There was clinical, white lighting. At the top-right of the level was a single white van. As we wobbled forward, the back doors to the vehicle opened. Out climbed two agents brandishing rifles.

I didn't recognise either of them.

The car came to a grinding halt as I applied the brakes. Taking the rifle from the doctor, I reloaded it, surveying our surroundings.

'Ready?' I asked.

The doctor nodded anxiously.

Opening the door, I instantly aimed it further down the building whilst the doctor hesitantly got out.

But just then, standing only a few metres away from the rendezvous point, I saw something appearing in an opening. Before I could act, a bright light illuminated the level. A missile was hurtling toward us.

At that moment, I turned to face the doctor.

Suddenly, I felt the unbearable sensation of my body blowing through the air. The missile collided with the underside of my car, sending it spinning into the air in a blinding ball of flames.

I landed on my back, my head connected with the floor and arms splayed outwards, losing hold of the rifle. For a few moments, everything went dark. I fell unconscious.

When I came to, my eyesight was blurred. I was overwhelmed with a high-pitched ringing sensation in my ears. Reacting, I used my hands to push up into a sitting position. Before me, the car was over-turned, still ablaze and blackened. I looked to my right, watching deliriously as the two agents fired their weapons at the drone.

I scrambled, stumbled forward, and ran around the car. There, I found the doctor lying on the ground, blood dripping from his mouth and ears.

In my disorientation, I couldn't fully process what had happened. I drew forward onto my knees. By the doctor's side, I looked down at him. Resisting the temptation to touch the doctor, I remained still.

Suddenly, his eyes, bloodshot, opened. He looked up at me.

'Doctor, I…' I managed to utter, shaking.

The ringing was intense.

With his burnt hand, the doctor ushered me closer. I leaned forward, putting my ear close to his mouth.

'I must…pass on…information,' he rasped. I looked into his eyes, glazed with tears. And then, he said that fateful word, which would change my life forever, leading to my eyes opening for the first time: 'Leveller.'

Five

'Are you okay?' a muffled voice asked. It was only a short distance away.

I drew into the moment—the sounds of gunfire and an engine. I was sitting in the back of the van, my head buried in my hands, eyes closed. I was trying to block out the horrific image of the doctor's burnt face. His body lay nearby in a black sack.

The female agent repeated herself. This time, I looked upwards and into her eyes. She looked younger than me—less corrupted. Her hair was short. The expression on her face reciprocated the concerned tone in her voice.

In a state of shock, unable to vocalise anything.

I'd failed to get the informant safely to the rendezvous point.

'What is your name, agent?' she asked, leaning forward.

'Blake,' I managed to say, my throat damaged from smoke inhalation.

I looked leftwards to the rear of the van. Another agent was standing, pointing a rifle out of the smashed right window, firing at what I suspected were the drones, unrelenting in their pursuit. He released a final spray of bullets before stumbling backwards, out of firing range, to replace the ammunition clip. Turning to face the female agent, he said: 'Carroll, why are they still chasing us?'

She'd maintained focus on me. An eyebrow rose. 'Because the informant passed on intelligence to Blake before he died. Am I correct?'

I averted my gaze, nodding.

'But he can't come with us?' another voice announced from the van's front seat.

I turned to face the man. He was steering the vehicle, addressing his colleagues in the rear mirror. He suddenly made an abrupt left-hand turn. There was the distant sound of car horns blaring. The van increased in speed.

'Webb, we couldn't have just left him there!' Carroll protested. Meanwhile, the other agent had returned to aiming his rifle out of the window. Carroll looked at him. 'Penrose, how many do we have left on our tail?'

'I can't shake this last one,' he shouted over his shoulder.

The van overtook another vehicle. I looked back up towards Webb. He was swerving erratically, glancing in the wing mirrors, trying to shake off the drone.

I looked at Carroll, confused. 'Where are we going?'

She sat there, clearly contemplating whether to tell me. I sensed there was something troublesome afoot. It was common for agents within the organisation never to cross paths. But there was something about these three which seemed—for the lack of a better word—different.

'We are going to a safe house,' she finally replied, looking back at Penrose. 'And ideally without that drone following us!'

Moments later, the van took an aggressive right turn. The drone continued its pursuit, firing at us.

'How close are we?' Carroll shouted over the racket of the gunfire.

'Twenty seconds,' Webb replied.

Carroll looked back at me, her eyes searching mine. We remained there, looking at each other in uncomfortable silence.

The van took an abrupt right turn. It continued, curving leftwards, down a new road.

Moments later, Webb pulled up on the handbrake. The van skidded rightwards, wheels screeching, the back swinging around. I held onto the bench, bracing myself.

We stopped. Without hesitation, Carroll stood, withdrew a handgun, and loaded it. She ushered me to stand up. I pressed against the bench for support. My body was in agony.

Penrose kicked the backdoors wide open, jumped out, walked around to the left, and continued to fire at the approaching drone. I followed Carroll, landing on the tarmac.

The van sat diagonally across the road, facing in the direction we came from. Nearby streetlights illuminated the scene. To my left was a complex of single-storey business units entered via a metal gate. I walked to my right, around the opened door.

There stood an industrial building. It was two stories high. There was a large, retractable loading door. Above this were three small windows. On the ground level, to the left, was a door. Security cameras looked down at it. The unit had an attached twin to the left. It mirrored the layout. Grey metal coverings encased the whole structure. At the centre and either end were three vertical green stripes. To the right was a small driveway, accessible via an open metal gate.

'Where are we?' I asked, looking back at Carroll.

'Lydden Grove,' she replied, taking cover with Penrose by the other opened door. I was unfamiliar with the name but suspected it was south of the rendezvous point.

Carroll and Penrose started shooting at the drone while signalling me to head towards the building. All the while, the aircraft continued its slow advance, out of sight, bombarding us with gunfire.

I ran around the side of the van. The passenger's door was open. Webb had jumped out. He gestured to a door at the end of the driveway. I followed him.

But as this happened, the drone spotted him nearing the building. It drew higher, adjusting its aim. A burst of bullets riddled Webb's body. Blood splattered against the wall. He crumbled forward onto the ground.

The others screamed. Running forward, they offered me covering fire. The drone responded, flying backwards.

Without hesitation, I ran forward to assist Webb. Kneeling, I turned the fallen agent over onto his back. Looking up at me, his pale face awash with fear, blood seeping from his lips. Even though my body was weak, I leaned forward, wrapped my arms around his abdomen, and pulled him onto his feet. Webb passed me a key and threw his arm over my shoulder for support. We stumbled towards the door.

I inserted the key, unlocked the door, and pulled hard on the handle. It opened. The hinges creaked. I took Webb inside.

Looking back, the other two agents approached. They ran inside, firing once more at the drone before quickly shutting the door. The aircraft continued to pelt the side of the building.

Minimal, orange light seeped through a window to my left. Glass shattered.

Carroll turned on a switch, drawing forth to assist Penrose with taking the wounded agent. I let go. They took Webb under the shoulder and walked further into the room.

Overhanging lights eventually flickered on. My eyes adjusted. We were in a large room. At the far end was the retractable loading door.

Unexpectedly, something else drew my attention.

In the centre of the room were three reclined chairs, their headrests facing each other. White, domed objects rested on top of them. There were various leads. Some ran towards a large, black box: a computer—on a nearby table.

'What is that?' I asked, stepping forward, mesmerised by the device.

The pair ignored me, sweeping items off another table, lying Webb down, applying pressure to his wounds, and giving him reassurances.

My gaze returned to the seats, domed objects, and computer.

Distracted, I didn't fully acknowledge the distant, muffled screeching of tires. Only moments later, when the drone stopped firing at the building, I regained focus on my surroundings.

Webb's heaving perforated the long silence.

Suddenly, I heard the thundering sound of the retractable door lifting upwards. Behind me, the door kicked open.

I looked towards both. Entering the room were numerous masked intruders bearing arms, wearing black overalls and bulletproof vests.

Unsure what to do, I stood firm. One of the intruders advanced towards me. Instinctively, I launched for them. But they reached around with the butt of their rifle, smashing it into the side of my head.

I couldn't register the pain. The world turned to one side.

Vision blurring, my head hit the floor.

Six

When I eventually woke up, my eyes focused on a brick ceiling instead of the warehouse's interior. I could hear a heart monitor's frequent, quiet beeping to my left. Cables attached to me dangled towards the floor. There was a clinical smell in the air.

Confused by my new surroundings, I pushed down on my elbows, leaning upwards into a sitting position. It made me aware of a throbbing sensation on the side of my head—I remembered the masked attacker.

I was lying in a medical bay surrounded by brick walls. There was a translucent glass door and wall to my left. Outside, I could see the silhouettes of people passing by. In front of me, my blurred eyes registered a medical professional walking out of the room.

I lay back for a few moments to process everything. Then I heard someone else entering. Looking forward, the view before me was surprising. Standing at the opposite end of the room was a statuesque man, impeccably dressed. He looked down upon me with a concerned, cautious expression.

'I'm glad you're finally awake, Blake,' the man announced in a restrained, friendly manner.

It was the director—the national head of the agency. That is the most I ever knew about him. We had only met on a superficial basis. I usually reported to one of his subordinates when debriefing after an assignment.

What was he doing here?

I tried to speak, but my throat was sore from smoke inhalation and dehydration. Noticing this, the director walked around to a bedside table, poured a cup of water, and gave it to me. Accepting the drink, I sipped, gagged, and drank the contents. I waited until my throat lubricated before uttering: 'I didn't expect to wake up…here. Headquarters?'

The director placed the cup on the table. 'Correct.' He usually had a reserved demeanour. But I noticed a subtle change. As expected, he questioned me demandingly: 'What happened on the mission?'

There was an unmistakable hint of agitation in his voice. I'd never witnessed this before.

'The informant was compromised when I delivered him at the rendezvous point.'

He eyed me meticulously. 'And did the informant disclose any intelligence before he died?'

'Yes, sir.' I paused, recollecting the image of the dying doctor's burnt face—the look of impending death. And the peculiarity of what was said. 'One word: Leveller.'

For a moment, he stood there in silence, digesting. 'That is all?'

I nodded, trying to deduce a reaction from his neutral expression.

'Do you know what Leveller is?' I read his eyes, but he stayed static. For a few moments, there was an uncomfortable silence. 'When the other agents took me to the safe house, we were ambushed?'

'Those were reinforcements called in to take out the final drone. Because you weren't supposed to be there and displayed hostile behaviour, they had to respond accordingly.'

I wasn't going to receive an apology.

'And, in the safe house, there was this…I don't know what you'd call it. A device,'—as I said this, his eyes widened—'three chairs with dome-shaped headsets, like MRI scanners, all attached to a large computer. Do you know what—'

'Speak no more of it, Blake,' he exclaimed, leaning closer. We were now at eye level. Then, he spoke almost in a whisper, firmly enunciating every word. 'I want you to process every word I am about to say. What we have just discussed, I want you to forget. You will mention nothing outside of these four walls. Do I make myself clear?'

'Yes, sir,' I answered submissively, although this was an automatic response—I was sceptical.

He stared intensely into my eyes. 'Good.'

'I feel guilty for the doctor's loss.' I averted my gaze toward the bed. Maybe, in another life.

I remembered the memory of the park pond.

'Are you baseline?' the director questioned.

Self-conscious, I looked up at him. My jaws clenched. 'Yes, sir.'

'Very well.' He nodded, standing upright.

'Have the drone operators been found?'

'As of yet, no,' he replied bluntly.

'The remains of the drones—were there manufacturer serial numbers?'

'There is no lead. The drones and weapons were 3D printed. But that is nothing of your concern. You did what was necessary. Now, I want you to take further rest.' The director smiled warmly and walked towards the door. 'You'll receive another call in due course.' Before opening it, he turned, looking at me. 'Remember, Blake—no mention.'

'Fully understood, sir,' I said confidently, watching as the director left the room, drawing the door shut behind him.

I looked listlessly into space for a moment. My mind was racing with questions. We had never interacted like that before. The doctor's information was clearly of great concern to the director.

And why didn't he answer my question about the device?

I felt irritable. My first response was to find comfort and quieten my mind. I looked at the bedside table and saw some of my belongings there. Besides my smartphone, wallet, and keys, there lay the drug bottle looking near-empty.

I looked at the door before shifting over, pulling the bedsheet aside, and placing my bare feet on the floor. I remained, allowing the blood to circulate into my limbs. Taking a deep breath through my nostrils,

I applied weight, stood up, allowed myself a moment, and staggered over to pick up the bottle.

Later, once given further checks and the all-clear, I put on supplied clothing: a t-shirt, jumper, joggers, and trainers. Collecting my belongings, I made my way out of the room.

In the corridor, it was hard to figure out where exactly I was in the headquarters. Most had low ceilings and the same brickwork throughout—an endless labyrinth. I had limited access to a few areas around the facility.

I could see the doctor standing close by, talking to her colleagues. I caught her eye. She pursed her lips in a smile, nodding at me. And with that, I started walking down the corridor to find an exit.

Strolling further into the headquarters, various agents passed me, preoccupied and somewhat oblivious to this wreck walking amongst them.

Eventually, I reached an open workspace. People sat on comfortable sofas, avidly typing away on tablets or in deep discussion, probably about bureaucratic particularities and office politics.

That was unless there was another rousing subject of conversation.

Overhead, large, flatscreen televisions played various news outlets' lunchtime headlines—fresh, filtered information. I walked forward and stood looking up at one of the screens. They were displaying images of the aftermath from yesterday evening: aerial footage of overturned vehicles and destruction along a street.

Standing here made me feel self-conscious.

'You put on quite the spectacle last night, Blake,' I heard someone announce whimsically from behind.

I turned around. There stood an agent I'd worked with on a reconnaissance mission in Budapest. Her name was Felicity Tomlinson.

I sighed through my nostrils. 'It wasn't exactly what I had in mind.'

'Well,' she said, walking forward to stand by my side while looking up at the screen, 'you're now famous.'

'How do you know I was involved?'

'I oversaw last night's mission.'

'Couldn't the clean-up team get there before the media?' I asked, following her trail of sight.

'Because of the scale of what happened, there were too many witnesses to process everyone through the re-perception program. Civilians took footage on their smartphones.'

'Did they manage to share it on social media?'

'Yes. Thankfully, there is no footage of you. However,'—Tomlinson pointed to a screen on our right,—'there are always a few who complicate matters.'

On the screen, there was a young woman. I guessed she was in her early thirties, dressed in hipster clothing. She was sitting in what appeared to be a makeshift studio, talking to the camera.

'Who is that?'

'Elina Wells. A self-proclaimed independent investigative journalist. What we are watching is the latest video uploaded onto her channel. She's grown in popularity across various social media platforms. You can always expect Wells to open her mouth when something irregular like this happens. It's a shame; she would do well in our ranks if not driven to uncover how we operate.'

'Is she aware that the agency exists?'

'No, but she knows something is going on beyond public knowledge. She doesn't have the evidence to cause serious concern. Most of what she sprouts is baseless speculation.

'The media department is already on the case with this video, spreading disinformation on social media to tarnish her reputation. Hopefully, the platform's moderators will remove this video for pushing misinformation.'

'I'm surprised she can be this vocal. I presume she is under heavy surveillance?'

'Yes. But we need to promote freedom of speech. If we steal Wells' research, send her threats, or resort to other means, it would be obvious she is onto something. Her work has gained traction, but thankfully nothing substantial.

'We are playing people like her at their own game—all part of maintaining the narrative.'

It's the way that things have always been. Well, since I can remember, anyway.

When first recruited, I learned about the agency's founding: Over several decades since the Second World War, meetings continually happened behind closed doors between most world leaders (some nations not invited for obvious reasons), multilateral organisations and multinational corporations. They aimed to create a unified, planetary community to propel economic growth and prosperity—settling differences, making compromises, and enacting new legislation and trade agreements. It was an unprecedented feat of cooperation.

There was a secret pooling of resources to uphold this reorganisation. And our agency started operating. The deeper state. Invisible. All sovereign, publicly-known agencies unknowingly work for this unnamed agency. It is small in operation, orchestrating everything without disturbing general perception.

The agency had power and influence that transcends borders, laws and governments. Questionable? No doubt. But it had to operate covertly without restraints to function optimally. It was for everyone's benefit. And a small price to pay—since its founding, there has been a gradual decrease in war, transnational organised crime and human trafficking. Religious extremist groups were infiltrated and dissolved. There was an unofficial regulation of the illegal drug market.

Despite various conflicts, the uprise of unorthodox political figures, and destabilising referendums, humanity had never experienced such times of safety and security.

There was a fragile balance in the world. And we were there to maintain it.

'What have you been instructed to do?' Tomlinson asked.

'As usual—wait until I'm called upon again.'

'You haven't been castrated or demoted for this little public display?'

'It wasn't like I intended for this to happen,' I said dryly, eyeing her.

'You still prefer field work?'

'Compared to being in this place all day long.'

She faced me. 'Good to see you, Blake.'

'You too,' I said, watching her walk off.

I looked up at the screen. There was something about how Elina Wells carried herself that, admittedly, was captivating to watch.

I felt a vibration in my pocket. Reaching into it, I withdrew my ringing phone. I was surprised it still had a charge. And signal underground. The call was from a withheld number.

Walking away from the workspace, I looked over my shoulder to ensure nobody could hear before accepting the call, placing the receiver to my ear.

'Good afternoon. Is that Ridley Hewitt?'

'Yes, speaking.'

Seven

'Is it okay to speak right now?'

I recognised his voice.

'Yes, no problem, but I might have signal issues.'

'Okay, I'll be quick—I'm calling regarding the cyber-security work, checking to see whether you've finished the report?'

I straightened up, started walking down the corridor, and said relaxedly, 'I'm just on the way back to my apartment. Once there, I'll send over the finished document. You have the instructions explaining how to decrypt it?'

'I do.'

'Then you'll hear from me shortly.'

'Excellent. Thank you, Mr Hewitt. Bye for now.'

'Bye.' I cancelled the call, pocketing the phone.

Preoccupied with the mission, I'd forgotten about my cover work.

Every field agent led a double life. After serving for over a decade in the special forces, receiving a calling for selection, and going through a vigorous recruitment process under heavy security, I committed myself to the agency, stepping away from my old life, disowning distant relatives (my parents are both deceased) and what little friends I had (they were all monitored to prevent our paths from crossing). The agency wiped Jackson Blake from every government, medical and financial system—I was effectively dead.

I would receive a false identity, including a new name, birth certificate, national insurance number, passport, bank account, living and holiday expenses, accommodation, thorough backstory, and a fictional job.

As Ridley Hewitt, I spent most of my time pretending to be a regular, upstanding member of society whilst sporadically called in by the agency to partake in operations.

Retaining my original name was acceptable when used within the context of agency matters. It gave me a semblance of identity other than simply being an asset.

Sometimes, I lost track of who I was.

I worked as a freelance security consultant with minimal training. Most of my output came from the agency's security department. When I received commissions and gained access to clients' systems, this enabled my colleagues to hoard data, building a greater under-standing of business and black-market security. Instead of protecting themselves, the clients were unknowingly becoming vulnerable. Their feeble measures couldn't match the highly advanced computers in the security department.

All I had to do was relay documents. One was on my laptop, ready to send.

There were assurances that a new car would be delivered. For now, a driver would chauffeur me home. He was another organisation mem-ber I'd never encountered. After asking for directions, he said nothing else. I stayed quiet during the journey. Looking out the window, I tried to forget all that had happened.

My apartment was inside Global Wharf, a warehouse conversion complex on Rotherhithe Street. It was in a quiet area next to the river, with easy accessibility to the headquarters. Of the few options given, I'd chosen this because, over time, I'd appreciated being alone, away from the over-stimulation of the city centre. Here, I found a sense of calmness to decompress.

The driver delivered me outside. Thanking him, I got out, closed the door, and stood there as he drove off.

It was a chilly Thursday evening. Streams of fading sunlight broke through the cloud line. Birds circled overhead.

I walked into the building. My apartment was on the third floor.

Letting myself in, I dialled the code on the security panel, checked for intrusion alerts, and walked down the corridor into the main living area.

The lounge and kitchen were conjoined. I always kept it immaculate. There was exposed brickwork on the walls. I'd done my best to furnish the place, but it looked like a bland holiday home. Always on the move and never settled, I didn't want to invest too much time projecting my personality here.

For me, home wasn't a place—it was people.

The dining area had windows with red frames. Double doors led onto a small balcony. By now, the sun was setting to the west, seeping through, painting everything in a dark, grey glow.

Sitting down at the dining table, I opened my laptop, logged in, opened my emails, and checked my inbox. I opened a new draft, wrote a subject, pasted it in a pre-written message, attached the encrypted document, and then sent it to the client. It was all part of the performance.

Closing the laptop's lid, I pushed back the chair and stretched, looking out at the river. On the opposite side was Limehouse. I could see flats where people were turning on lights and socialising.

Normality. A concept I no longer understood.

I stayed there looking out over the vast body of water, my eyes blurring, comforted by the silence.

Sometime later, I went to the bedroom, undressed, threw the clothes into the laundry basket, and walked into the shower room. After turning it on, I stood under the hot, steaming water. Closing my eyes, I felt the liquid trickling over my bruised, muscular frame, running my hands through my hair. The pain in my head had subsided.

Afterwards, once dried and wearing a bathrobe and slippers, I walked back into the lounge. I turned on the lights, put on some background music and walked over to a counter housing a collection of spirits. All were standing in order of country of origin and year—

a consequence of my increasing OCD. Taking a tumbler, I poured myself a large scotch. Walking over to a reclining chair, I sat down, rested my feet on the stool, and took a large sip.

Doing this, I looked out the window. It was dark. All I could see was my reflection. It felt like a stranger looking back at me. Or someone familiar.

It was then, whilst looking at my reflection, the memory of the doctor's dying face eclipsed my internal view. Don't get me wrong, I have witnessed many people losing their lives. But when it happened due to my negligence, it was unacceptable. Taking another large sip, I allowed the liquid to rest, the bitterness pulsating in my gums.

Who or what was Leveller?

I tried to stop my mind from drifting. The memory of the doctor predictably led me spiralling down a path of thought until I reached that same unavoidable conclusion—the terrible feeling of losing another person.

And it appeared—the memory of my son, Charlie. The dwindling image of a four-year-old boy. Full of joy, vitality, and curiosity about life.

I swallowed hard, my throat burned. Hands were trembling. I averted my eyes from the window, faced forward, and closed my eyes tightly in a vain attempt to suppress it—a distorted, fragmented memory from times when I had managed to create a balance between work and personal life.

A semblance of normality. Fleeting happiness.

It happened on a Sunday. After a pub lunch, Charlie, myself, and his mother, Julia, casually strolled homeward through Victoria Park. We stood by the pond. Charlie, typically excitable, wanted to run around the waterside to look at greylag geese nestled in high reeds nearby.

We allowed him to go whilst standing there in quiet contentment.

But we were momentarily distracted.

When we called out to him, there was no response. Instinctively, we ran around to the reeds. But he had disappeared. Staying calm, I searched for him whilst Julia, understandably distraught, called out his name.

I will never forget her echoing screams of despair.

But he had vanished—gone, just like that.

It was the realising of a parent's worst nightmare.

The police arrived and thoroughly searched, including sending divers into the pond. But it proved unforthcoming. In shock, I reassured Julia that I would do my best to find our son. She was married to Ridley Hewitt, unaware of my occupation.

In the ensuing days, there was a full-blown media out-cry for witnesses, a national campaign plastering Charlie's face across the headlines. I asked that our identities be kept anonymous. We conducted no interviews. Julia didn't object. There was unease within the agency because it could have compromised my cover.

The kidnappers announced their ransom fee. Did I suspect it possibly had something to do with me being a secret agent? Of course, but their motives were never made clear.

The organisation used their resources, eventually finding the kidnappers. Upon contact, they were hostile and neutralised.

But in the crossfire, the unthinkable happened.

Charlie, my little guy, was lost forever.

The memory of the event was buried, like his body.

Over time, the inability to deal with emotions changed me. Grievance counselling didn't work. I couldn't help but mentally replay what happened, fixating on alternative scenarios—how I should have done better.

Because of my incompetence, I failed them.

Eventually, regrettably, it broke down my relationship with Julia and destroyed our marriage.

The past three years had been hell.

I recollected all these memories whilst pouring myself another large glass of whiskey. Sinking the contents in one, I went to serve another, emptied that, and downed another. Walking over to the kitchen counter, I opened a drawer and withdrew a new bottle of Statera. Erratically removing the lid, I poured several tablets into my mouth and sipped the whiskey to help swallow them down.

All of these chemical reactions. Reward systems. Bittersweet distractions. Lifetime subscriptions.

Slamming the glass and bottle onto the counter, I staggered to the dining table where I'd left my phone. Picking it up, I searched the contact list and found Julia's number.

Seeing her name on the screen felt disorientating—a stark reminder of a reality I didn't want to accept.

I sat down on the reclining chair and tried to call her. My eyes started to glaze as I heard the ringing tone. It seemed to go on indefinitely. She wasn't going to answer. We hadn't spoken in months.

Frustrated, I cancelled the call, let my arm slump onto my torso, and stared listlessly into space. I could feel the warm alcohol immersing my body. Soon, the drugs would kick in. I would find comfort.

But before this could happen, my eyes became heavy. I closed them for a moment and fell into a light slumber.

Eight

Felicity Tomlinson had meticulous attention to detail, her finger on the pulse of every aspect of her life. Whether conscientiously career-driven, predicting stock market investment fluctuations, deliberating over which food-delivery service had the most sustainable waste model, or even knowing the optimum formation for her youngest daughter's Sunday morning football team.

Many called her anally retentive. But Tomlinson prided herself on being acutely aware of everything.

It was natural for someone of her disposition to rise through the global clandestine organisation's ranks. But Tomlinson found it frustrating not being able to share her true successes with her family. As far as they were aware, she provided for them, fictiously, working for a hedge fund.

Like any morning, she woke up on that fateful Friday at zero-six hundred hours. Robotically—without fail, she subtly pressed the alarm button before its third chime.

Brushing her teeth, she always worked around her mouth, clockwise, then made an espresso (with the finest, sourced beans), before spending thirty minutes in the basement on the rowing machine. As she showered, her husband and three children woke up. He prepared them breakfast. Tomlinson kissed them all goodbye before leaving for work. This strict routine always helped prepare her for whatever happened at headquarters.

Outside, there were clear, blue skies. Tomlinson's family home was on Church Road. It was in a quiet, suburban area of Richmond. Very unassuming. They always tried to socialise with their neighbours.

Whilst her husband—equally self-sufficient: home-working (but oblivious in his own right)—took the children to and from school, she ensured to be a proactively engaged member of the Parent-Teacher Association. When possible.

It was a seven-minute walk to Richmond station. Her family believed she took the District Line from here to the office in Monument. But she was heading in another direction.

The tube was busy. But as people waded in, she chanced upon a seat. Along commutes, Tomlinson usually read a news application or listened to audiobooks, portraying a semblance of everyday existence. She decided to check out a new, popular self-care podcast. But losing interest, instead referring to a music playlist, reminding her of university days in Durham.

At approximately zero-eight hundred hours, the tube stopped at Westminster. Here, Tomlinson switched to the Jubilee Line. It was only a short journey before she alighted at Waterloo, close to the agency headquarters.

In the early nineteen-sixties, during the Cuban Missile Crisis, at the height of the Cold War, metropolitan boroughs in the city were to build underground bunkers. Lambeth, grouped with neighbouring Southwark and Camberwell, would make up civil defence region 53a. They negotiated over where to build their control centre. Initially, they considered building the facility underneath Jubilee Gardens, by the riverside, interlinking with unused Waterloo tube station tunnels. But after the building started, financially constraining, they abandoned the operation, instead opting for a more viable strategic location: an area in Gipsy Hill to the south of the borough, protected by hills, designated for a new housing estate.

During the agency's founding, they chose the undisclosed, half-built, abandoned bunker, repurposing it for their operations. It meant they were near—and easily connected via tunnels—to Whitehall, Downing Street, Westminster, and the publicly-known agencies—MI5 and MI6. There were various unassuming surface entrances around Waterloo, County Hall Apartments and Southbank Place.

Exiting the station, avoiding traffic, Tomlinson walked across the street and would enter through the latter. Once inside one of the large luxury buildings, she walked into an lift—ensuring not to be followed—inserted a key into the panel and pressed the basement button.

When it arrived, there stood guards bearing semi-automatics. Exchanging pleasantries, she had to walk through a biometric scanner that measured her DNA.

Given clearance, Tomlinson walked further in and entered the changing room. Here, she changed from her finely cut suit into standard black attire for case officers. From there, Tomlinson proceeded down the corridor until reaching a door requiring another biometric scan. Once accepted, she walked into her real office—the control room.

It was large and semicircular, with ramps leading down to either side. In the centre were rows of workstations for all the case officers. Adjacent, the wall accommodated countless screens, surrounding a larger one in the centre: these displayed live surveillance feeds, satellite positions, flight routes, and data reports. At the back of the room, looking down upon the dimly lit scene, was a viewing platform where a coordinator sat at the main desk.

Tomlinson walked down to her workstation, comprising a computer with three suspended screens and a headset illuminated by a lamp. From here, she had only a few days prior coordinated the extraction of Doctor Aditi.

'Morning,' a voice called from her right-hand side.

She looked over at a colleague who was leaning back in his chair.

'And to you too.' Tomlinson smiled, taking a seat and brushing her hair back. She would have indulged him with small talk about life outside the office. But all case officers were contractually obliged not to discuss their covers.

Turning on her computer, she looked at the wall of animated screens. 'I'm glad they've fixed the glitch on B-sixty-four. It was off-putting yesterday.' She faced him. 'What's on the schedule?'

His index finger trailed down a clipboard containing a list of each case officer's daily tasks. 'You're overseeing the Arctic mining operative.'

'Just another day's work,' she chuckled, receiving the clipboard enthusiastically.

Her colleague stood, stretching. 'Coffee?'

'I'm good for now, thanks.'

'Gotcha.' He walked off.

Reading the reference number, Tomlinson typed it into the computer. The screens came to life, streaming information about the case. She leaned forward, reading recent entries. Around her was the clicking of keyboards, quiet discussion, and the occasional cough.

Several minutes later, she'd read the updates. Her colleague had returned with his drink. Tomlinson took a moment to process the operation before making the necessary arrangements.

It was zero-nine-hundred hours and ten minutes.

Sitting back in the chair, Tomlinson took a moment away from her work to look up leisurely at the wall of screens. It was a spectacular of collective, focused effort.

Her colleague sat there, contently slurping his caffeine fix.

But then, something caught her eye—B-sixty-four was, frustratingly, glitching again near the bottom left-hand side.

Tomlinson leaned forward—resisting putting the microphone to her mouth to speak to the coordinator—when something on the screen seemed different. It was CCTV footage from the southern end of Exhibition Road, a desirable area and tourist hotspot full of restaurants, cafes, and seating, between South Kensington Station and the Victoria and Albert Museum.

There seemed to be an irregular, erratic movement of civilians.

Due to the pixelated screen being several metres away, Tomlinson had to squint. But couldn't determine what it was. She drew the microphone to her mouth. 'Good morning, this is Tomlinson. Can you bring up B-sixty-four on the main screen?'

'Morning. Is it glitching again?'

She noticed a tone of indifference in his voice. 'Yes. But there is something else.'

'Okay.'

Moments later, the image expanded onto the main screen.

Looking at what was unfolding, Tomlinson gasped. She stood up, wide-eyed.

Nine

On the screen, people were scattering from what appeared to be a giant water fountain spurting outwards. But this liquid-like substance was grey, thicker—growing—flooding—consuming everything in its path like a lava flow.

Spitting out his coffee, the colleague asked by her side, 'What the hell is that?'

Tomlinson was speechless.

The other case officers noticed the pair, averting their attention towards the large screen, vocalising their shock. Meanwhile, behind them on the viewing platform, the coordinator picked up a phone and pressed a speed-dial button.

Instantly, someone spoke: 'Yes?'

'Ask the director to come down here at once. Code Red. Suspected terrorist attack in the city centre. Repeat—a suspected terrorist attack in the city centre.' He slammed down the phone and frantically commanded the wall of screens to display all CCTV footage from the nearby area.

When this happened, he gasped in disbelief. Everyone looked on in horror as the tsunami of grey matter engulfed surrounding roads and buildings. Civilians dispersed, some abandoning their vehicles, all trying to get away but were eventually overwhelmed.

A few moments later, the coordinator heard the main door open. The director paced forward, stood on the platform, and without an utterance, put his hands on his hips, gazing at the scene unfolding.

He marched forward to address all the case officers: 'Alert the government, all hospitals, everyone. I want all available police and military personnel to help with an evacuation. Scramble all helicopters. Inform all our national offices and international headquarters of possible attacks.'

But as he said this—and the case officers got to work—the grey mass consumed the Natural History Museum, increasing in size, moving at an accelerated rate.

The director looked on in despair.

'Sir,' one case officer addressed her superior. 'I'm not getting any biological readings. That thing is synthetic. Electrical.'

The director remained silent, his hands twisting tightly on the balcony rail. The coordinator noticed this. 'What is it, sir?'

'Those are self-replicating machines. Programmed to consume all biomass as an energy source to build more of themselves.'

'Nanobots?'

'Yes.'

'There are restrictions to stop development beyond bio-engineering purposes. I thought this was a low-probability scenario?'

'If it can happen, it will.' The director frowned. 'There weren't adequate preventative measures.'

The coordinator looked on in despair at the horrifying sights. 'They are going to spread too rapidly to be stopped!'

The director stood there in silence, surveying everything, helpless. Overhead, small screens showing CCTV footage went black. Those remaining showed the machines surging outwards, making their way towards Hyde Park, Chelsea and Buckingham Palace, rapidly consuming everything and everyone in their path.

As word spread, panic rippled through the city. Civilians were desperately trying to escape its clasp. There was heavy congestion.

'Sir,' a case officer said from below. The director, who had lost track of time gazing at the screens, looked down at him. 'To contain the spread, we could release an electromagnetic pulse. That might fry their circuitry?'

'We can't do that!' another objected. 'Dependent infrastructure would be compromised.'

'But soon there won't be anything left to power!' the first case officer rebuked before facing the director. 'Sir?'

All eyes averted toward the director. Momentarily, he acknowledged the devastating effect of bringing down electrical systems. But he knew what was necessary before these machines spread across the city.

The director turned to the coordinator. He revealed a chain bearing a set of keys. Taking it off, he sifted through them until he found one disk-shaped. Meanwhile, the director walked to his side, presenting a matching key. On either side of the black desk, there were identical holes where they were both inserted. Instantly, part of the desk's surface drew back, revealing a variety of buttons and switches.

'Initiate the sequence, concentrating the pulse on all grid systems in the immediate vicinity,' the director commanded whilst looking up at the screen. By now, the self-replicators were moving towards the Houses of Parliament.

'Locked and ready.'

'You have my authority.'

'Yes, sir.'

And with that, everyone's eyes averted to the screens as the electromagnetic pulse was released. From their standpoint, the only indications were building lights and telephone lines sparkling or exploding in the surrounding areas. But to their dismay, it didn't have the desired effect on the large mass of self-replicators. Instead, they were intensifying their replication.

'Sir.' The coordinator swallowed hard. 'It looks like the nanobots have absorbed the electromagnetic energy.'

Below, all the case officers shared horrified looks, accepting that it would only be a matter of time before the spread would reach the headquarters.

But looking on helplessly, they saw that the self-replicators stopped surging towards the water, instead continuing along the north bank of the river, now adjacent, heading towards the Embankment and beyond.

'Sir, shall we consider a nuclear weapon?' the coordinator asked.

The director looked on as the nanobots began to swallow Somerset House. 'It will only do the same—these machines are unstoppable.'

For the next ten minutes, he stood there watching the devastation unfold. It drew east, devouring thousands of people, sweeping under its synthetic flood Saint Paul's Cathedral, the Tower of London, and Wapping. Reaching Canary Wharf, it enveloped the gigantic skyscrapers, effortlessly reducing them to grey rubble.

But as it finished obliterating the Isle of Dog, the unexpected happened: the self-replicators suddenly stopped in their growth and spreading. As the matter was consumed and transformed, the wave of nanobots lost momentum, cascading downwards, falling onto the earth in an avalanche, no longer causing destruction.

'What's happened?' the coordinator questioned.

'Can someone give me a reading?' the director ordered.

The same case officer, who had looked at the data readings, turned and announced: 'Sir, the nanobots no longer show any indication of electrical signals.'

'They've malfunctioned?' the coordinator asked.

The director stood rubbing his chin before finally replying: 'Or were programmed to turn off.'

They were now looking at aerial footage provided by circling helicopters. Indistinct chatter and the camera operator's crackling cries perforated the sound of the rotating blades.

In less than twenty minutes, the nanobots had consumed a ten-mile expanse along the north side of the river, going inland by approximately two miles, reducing everything to a flattened, grey mass.

As this unfolded, Tomlinson had been frantically searching through recorded CCTV footage. At first, she rewound through B-sixty-four's footage before meticulously working across cameras in the local area and underground network. Finally, after painstaking effort, she paused the last video, stood, faced the director, and announced: 'Sir! I have managed to track down the culprit who set off the nano-bomb.'

Abruptly awoken from a numbed state, the director heard Tomlinson's voice, and saw the case officer on the floor. He walked over to the rail. 'What did you just say?' Tomlinson repeated herself. Everyone standing nearby looked on in amazement. 'Come up here!'

Tomlinson ran from her workstation down to the front and up the side ramp until she reached the coordinator's main desk. The director gestured for her to take control of the main computer.

Moments later, CCTV footage appeared on the main screen of a disguised individual walking onto Exhibition Road and discreetly putting a small object inside a bin before leaving. Tomlinson then activated a sequence of sped-up footage—it showed the individual making their way out of the city centre using the underground.

'They took the District Line from South Kensington to Victoria. From there, the Victoria Line to Stockwell. And finally, the Northern Line to Morden.' Tomlinson produced satellite imagery that showed the terrorist, but in real-time, riding on a motorbike.

'Where are we looking at right now?' the director asked.

'Currently heading south on Brighton Road, just past Tadworth. Held up by evacuating traffic.'

'Brilliant work, Tomlinson.' The director patted her on the back. He walked forward again to address the other case officers: 'Dispatch a task force to capture the terrorist—alive. Bring them in for questioning.'

Nodding, they went to work. But one turned around, announcing: 'Sir, one of our helicopters is nearby and will engage momentarily.'

The director stood for a few minutes, avidly watching. Satellite footage showed the helicopter surrounding the motorbike and landing, blocking its path on the congested road. Armoured soldiers disembarked, their rifles held to engage the target.

'What do you think their motive was, sir?' the coordinator asked.

The director was lost for words, unable to answer.

Painstakingly, everyone looked on as the soldiers managed to contain the situation, tackling the individual to the ground. There were a few cheers amongst the case officers. But the atmosphere inside the control room was sullen. The coordinator received word from the task force detailing their intention to deliver the terrorist to the headquarters for questioning.

'Sir, are you sure it's safe bringing the terrorist here?'

'I would prefer interrogating them here under our tight security,' the director replied.

The satellite images showed the helicopter taking off, heading northwards.

And there, in the briefest moments, the director closed his eyes tightly—digesting the circumstances. Necessary breath after self-reflecting breath.

He couldn't face the possibility of who was committing it. But he remembered one conversation about history with someone who should have been dead.

Suddenly, the entrance door sounded.

The director's eyes opened.

In walked Okoro, his assistant. She was a tall woman with fierce eyes and a shaved head. Turning to acknowledge her, the director at once knew by her expression that something possibly unrelated was bothering her. He ushered Okoro to the doorway, following her, ensuring no one could overhear.

Meanwhile, Tomlinson and the coordinator watched with suspicion.

'Yes?' the director said, standing before her.

'Sir, there is something you need to see.'

'We have just caught the terrorist who released the nano-bomb. Can't this wait?'

'I understand, sir, but something is transmitting to…the branch.' Her eyebrow rose as she uttered these final words.

He whispered: 'What do you mean something is "transmitting?"'

'Somehow, the quantum computer has picked up what appears to be a live stream. The video is about to start.'

Without saying another word, he gestured to the door. Okoro nodded. They made their way out.

Ten

They marched down a long tunnel stretching across the headquarters, taking them southward until they reached an unassuming door. There was no sign showing what was inside. It could be mistaken for a cleaning cupboard. The only clue was a contraption above the door, which was unnoticeable, camouflaged in the same colour as its surroundings. It was a biometric scanner.

Approaching, the director hastened in his step, stood below the scanner, and waited until given access. The door automatically opened, allowing them both inside.

They drew into a small room. To the left was a wall of screens above a large bank of computer terminals behind a Perspex screen. In front of this was a wide desk with keyboards, various switches and gauges, and a telephone. Sat in front of this was the other assistant called Alejo. Opposite to the main door was a corridor leading off into shadow. And to the right, hanging from the wall, was a prominent symbol like a trident—the Greek letter psi, in lowercase.

Seeing the director enter, Alejo looked at him with grave concern. Okoro walked forward, retaking her seat at the desk. The director stood behind them, undid his blazer, and placed his hands on his hips.

'Can you explain what you received?' the director asked.

Alejo turned to address him. 'Sir, five minutes ago, something came up on the computer. We ran diagnostic reports. But that didn't resolve the issue.' He leaned forward, clicking a button. 'And then this appeared.'

The central screen displaying readings went blank, replaced by: 'LIVE VIDEO STREAM TO BEGIN—LESS THAN ONE MINUTE'

The director stood looking at the image, perplexed. 'You're convinced this has come through the quantum network?'

'Yes, sir,' Okoro replied.

Suddenly, the words disappeared to be replaced by an image. It was of a man in his mid-forties sitting at a table. He was well-groomed and smartly dressed.

Seeing him, the director instantly felt a cold shiver dispersing across his body. He couldn't believe it.

'Good morning. I hope the director is watching this. But I will introduce myself. I am Rufus Miller, a variant of our founder, George Fielding.

'He was once an operative for your agency. After an unfair dismissal and an unsuccessful assassination attempt by your colleagues, he went into hiding. As you can imagine, being badly mistreated can have a detrimental impact, especially after serving the organisation loyally for many years.

'It took a long time for him to accept how corrupted the agency truly is, how it is there only for the benefit of the few.

'And here I am, speaking to you through a video transmission. You're probably wondering how. Well, as my counterpart was once a member of your secret little team of dimension-jumpers, he got his hands on a quantum computer and has beaten you at your own game.

'The original intention was for him to contact you directly, in your reality, but now, having been caught, he cannot conduct the rest of the plan. Variants in other dimensions also conducted similar attacks. You'll be pleased to hear that they have all either been captured or killed.

'As such, I am the only one left. This video is a contingency plan.' He paused.

'Everything is built upon deception and manipulation. Order at the expense of civil liberties. It is time that the world knew the truth about this great injustice.

'I demand that your organisation announce its existence to the world within twenty-four of your hours. Otherwise, I will unleash an unstoppable nano-bomb. It will be released at different times into different realities, depending on when the countdown runs out for each world.

'To show that I am not bluffing, you can check the metadata of this video file. There is nano-code embedded that can be activated to produce self-replicators. I could have quite easily timed this file to be the next nano-bomb, but I didn't want to give you a chance to decode it.

'It is time to take centre stage and reveal yourselves to the world.' He smiled wickedly. 'Do the right thing. Goodbye.'

Suddenly, the screen went blank before a twenty-four-hour count-down appeared.

The director and assistants remained for a few moments in shocked silence.

'If we meet his demands, the repercussions would be unprecedented,' the director announced.

'It could cause an international scandal?' Okoro looked at him with unease.

'It would destabilise the world order,' the director huffed. Both assistants looked up at him in dismay. 'The global community is flourishing because of this organisation. This exposure cannot happen. Alejo, was he telling the truth about the embedded nano-coding?'

He nodded nervously. 'Yes, sir. I have also run a further analysis of the metadata.'

'What did you find?'

'It was heavily encrypted, even for our quantum computer to decipher. I have never seen anything like it before—this variant must be using far more advanced technology. I couldn't determine the video's origin because there was no embedded location information. But I did get a time—'

'Well?' the director questioned impatiently.

'It states that the video was recorded in the future, sir.'

'That tells us this wasn't a pre-recording made by our variant?' Okoro asked.

'It seems that is the case,' Alejo replied.

'Sir, we can search the quantum network for dimensions with this time signature?' Okoro suggested.

'Good idea. Get to work.'

'Yes, sir.'

'Can you rewind the video?' the director asked Alejo.

'No, sir. But I duplicated it.' He typed a few commands into the terminal. The recording appeared on the screen.

'Put it on mute,' the director asked in a repulsed tone. 'I don't want to hear his voice.' Alejo followed the order. 'Run a check—is that a deep fake? AI-generated?'

Moments later, Alejo responded: 'No, sir—it's his real face.'

'And the voice?'

'Yes.'

'And the backdrop?'

'Also, authentic.'

The director leaned forward, squinting his eyes. 'What is that place? It looks like a dining room?'

'That's what I thought, sir,' Alejo replied.

'The textiles and wallpaper are a lead. Get to work.'

'Yes, sir.'

Suddenly, the phone started ringing.

Taken aback, Okoro picked it up and listened to the person on the other end before replacing it.

'Who was that?' the director asked.

'They have just brought Fielding in for interrogation.'

The director nodded, turning towards the entrance.

Alejo asked: 'Sir, shall I contact the other national directors?'

'No, we can handle this.'

'Just in case—shall we start drafting a press statement?'

Okoro also looked up at him.

'That won't be necessary,' the director said sternly over his shoulder.

Eleven

Unlike most interrogation rooms, one stood underneath the headquarters. To get there, the director walked into an lift, ordered other personnel to leave, pressed the '-1' button, and had to dial a code onto a separate touchpad, granting permission.

Once this happened, the doors closed. It gave the director a few moments to prepare himself. Usually, he remained stoically calm. But at this moment, he could feel his heart racing and hands moistening. Taking several large breaths through his nostrils, he adjusted his blazer, raised his chin, and looked forward. Conflicting thoughts clouded his mind.

The lift stopped, doors drawing open. In front of the director was a long, metal corridor with clinical lighting. There stood the captain of the task force.

'Sir, we arrived a few minutes ago,' the captain said, walking alongside his superior.

'What happened when you approached him?'

'Once we surrounded the target, he was submissive, allowing us to restrain him. He had this weird smile on his face.'

'Did he say anything en route?'

'Nothing, sir. During the helicopter ride, he looked relaxed.'

'You made sure he is able to speak?'

'Yes, sir.'

'You checked he wasn't carrying any devices?'

'We conducted a full-body search—nothing found.'

They reached the end of the corridor where other task force members stood. To the right was a station where a guard was sitting in front of screens showing footage from inside the heavily secured interrogation room.

The director addressed the guard: 'I want all cameras and microphones turned off while I'm in there.'

'But, sir, the safety precautions?'

The director responded in a stern tone: 'It's fine. I know how to handle this.'

'Yes, sir,' the guard said reluctantly.

The director walked towards the reinforced door and waited for another biometric scan. Once approved, the entrance automatically opened outwards, revealing what lay within.

The large interrogation room was spherical. On the walls, metal panels had cameras and gun turrets. A single catwalk in front of the director led towards the centre, with a platform.

The director walked forward onto the catwalk. His leather-bound soles echoed against the metal pathway. The door closed. His eyes fixated on a large, metal seat where Fielding was sitting. Holding him in place were thick straps across his forehead, torso, and limbs. Surrounding him was a bulletproof glass case.

'What a lovely way to be reunited,' Fielding announced, his voice echoing against the metal walls.

'Indeed,' the director said dryly, walking forwards. 'Were you planning to be caught today?'

'On the contrary, I thought I would have died before coming here.' Fielding smiled. The director stopped in front of the case. 'I bet you never thought you'd see me again?'

'I didn't,' the director said with a neutral expression.

'They should have done a better job trying to assassinate me. I was able to escape without a trace. Invincible now that you thought I was dead.'

The director hesitated. 'It wasn't personal, Fielding—'

'But it was. You *know* it was. I was the best agent you ever had. And because of our disagreement, you decided to strike me off.'

'It was for the preservation of the Convergence Protocol.'

'It was for the preservation of your *reputation*.' There was a moment of uncomfortable silence as they stared into each other's eyes.

'How did you manage to gain access to a quantum migrator?'

'You always knew I was resourceful.'

'Was it Doctor Aditi?'

'Not exactly.'

'What is Leveller?'

'So, the doctor *did* extract information!'

'What do you mean?'

'You're eager to know what Doctor Aditi's part is in all of this?'

'Yes.'

'I approached him a few days ago because I needed to find a way to erase memories.'

'Why?'

'In the likelihood of this outcome. You'll try and use the quantum computer to extract information from my mind. However, the doctor showed me how to erase information.'

'Such as?'

'The location of the final terrorist, my hideout and other things.' Fielding chuckled. 'For you, I am effectively useless.'

'And what was the reason for murdering the doctor?'

'As I suspected, he also extracted information, hence why he could reveal Leveller's name. In a vain attempt, I wanted to kill him to cover my tracks.'

'Using drones isn't very subtle.'

'I knew he would ask for your protection. And I had to conceal my identity if he left the apartment. You must have suspected something when you received the intelligence?'

'I did.' The director frowned. 'What is Leveller—a terrorist group?

'I guess that is what you can call it.'

'What do you mean?'

'Well, there is a group, but of variants of myself, in multiple dimensions.'

'How?'

'Once I had traversed into them, I simply left damning information about the organisation. Once I left, they learnt the truth and joined the cause.'

'Why did you bomb only certain parts of London?'

'They were the heart of the establishment. Here below the South-bank, you had a front-row seat to watch.' Fielding smirked.

'Did you source the nano-bomb from another reality?'

'Yes.'

'You went to *all this* effort—the quantum migrator, enlisting variants, a nano-bombing killing millions of people, a plot to destroy the rest of the world, a contingency plan—*all because of what?*'

'There are many things we both know you are responsible for. Killing you would be too simple. It is time that you take accountability. I will humiliate you and bring down this corrupt organisation.' He noticed a trickle of sweat seeping down the director's forehead—this gave him great satisfaction.

'But why would you be willing to destroy a world you care so much about?'

'I could ask you the same question.' Fielding smirked. 'The end justifies the means.'

The director's jaw clenched. 'Was your variant always going to threaten to release the nano-bomb whether or not we caught you?'

'Correct—I had to make sure you couldn't find him. There is no point in unplugging or destroying your quantum migrator—he will release the nano-bomb by other means.'

'Through other quantum computers?'

'Correct. And I don't think you can shut down the internet and all power worldwide.'

'How does the technology work?'

'Consciousness and communication are not the only things that can traverse the dimensions. All that is required is a simple upload into the migrator. The nano-coding, transferred through the quantum network, can merge with computer circuitry and organics before consuming everything.'

'I will stop the variant from releasing the nano-bomb.'

'You do realise that trying to find one individual, across an infinite number of dimensions, within twenty-four hours is…*immeasurable* in its impossibility.'

'I'm sure variants of myself are planning to do the same thing.'

'Hopefully, they are not as foolish as you are.'

'I guess we all must have something in common,' the director said sarcastically.

'I hope you all come to the same logical conclusion—accept defeat. Meet my demand. Announce to the world the organisation's existence.'

'*That is not going to happen*, Fielding!' The director turned to leave.

'Very well. You know I'm always here if you want to reminisce about old times.'

'Excuse my reluctance,' the director said through gritted teeth over his shoulder before walking back down the corridor towards the entrance.

All the while, Fielding sat with his eyes closed, a triumphant smile on his face.

When the director reached the door, it opened automatically. Inside the corridor, the task force had gone. Instead, there stood Okoro. Without an utterance, the director started pacing down the hall toward the lift.

'I want a full neuro-scan performed on Fielding to see if we can extract any information.'

'Yes, sir,' Okoro replied, catching up to walk by him.

'Did you manage to find the dimension in the quantum network?'

'No, sir.'

He huffed. 'We must find this variant and stop him. Our time is running out.'

'I am putting together the task force—Penrose and Carroll are on their way.'

'Excellent.'

'But what about Webb's replacement?' They stopped by the lift. She pushed the door switch and looked back at the director.

He was in deep thought.

'Call in Agent Blake.'

Part Two

Reputation

Twelve

I remember the day it happened—opening my eyes for the first time.

Standing there, I looked at news footage on the television screen: surreal images of the terrorist attack. It was unbearable to watch. To process and accept.

Who had committed such an inexcusable atrocity?

I couldn't help but think about Julia. Her work office was in Farringdon. She would have been there by the time the attack happened. Her phone had gone straight through to voicemail.

The crippling discomfort. Powerless.

Suddenly, I was startled by the abruptness of my phone's ringtone. It awakened me from this unravelling nightmare. I reached into my bed robe pocket, pulled out the phone, instantly answered, and put it to my ear.

'Agent Blake?' It was a woman I didn't recognise.

I tried to mask my disappointment. 'Speaking.'

'I'm sure you are aware of what has happened.'

'Nanotech?'

'Yes.'

I gazed out the window, across the river towards the flattened, grey mass, now seeing Mile End in the distance. 'Do you know who did this?'

'We do—one of the terrorists is currently being held captive at the headquarters. The director has asked me to call you in.'

I paused for a moment to digest everything. 'What for?'

'We cannot discuss this over the phone.'

'I will get ready.'

'We will send someone to pick you up.'

'Understood.'

The line went dead.

I placed the phone back into my pocket and stood there, transfixed by the unimaginable scenes unfolding on the screen.

Had Julia made it out alive? The thought made me nauseous.

I could feel my jaw tightening with withdrawal symptoms.

Twenty minutes later, once showered, dressed, armed, and self-medicated, I got into the car. Like yesterday evening, I remained silent.

It was eerily quiet as we drove westwards along Tooley Street towards the Southbank. Helicopters flew overhead. I looked to my right. Buildings blocked my view of the devastation on the opposite side of the river. The army was present. Tanks and large blockades were diverting traffic away from the bridges. News channel teams stood in long rows, filming. Armed police herded a few civilians away.

When we got to Waterloo, the area was empty, and the station was closed. I was dropped at a street nearby, taking an unassuming, graffiti-covered side door towards the underground headquarters.

Clearing the biometric scan, I passed the security guards (who looked noticeably on edge), walking into the inner sanctum. It was bustling with activity. There was a tension in the air I had never witnessed before.

Amongst the crowd was a tall woman. She marched towards me. I suspected this was who I'd spoken to on the phone. We stood before each other.

'Agent Blake.'

'I don't believe we have crossed paths before.' I extended a hand. We shook.

'Agent Okoro. If you don't mind, there is scarce time for pleasantries, and other pressing matters are at hand.'

'Of course.'

'Please, follow me.'

She led me down the main corridor toward the director's office. As I followed at her heel, we said nothing.

Once outside, she knocked. A few moments later, we had permission to enter. Agent Okoro ushered me inside.

The director sat behind a glass desk facing us. Behind was a cabinet. He was looking at two computer screens. Hearing me enter, he looked up.

'Agent Blake, please, take a seat.' He gestured to two leather armchairs.

'Sir.' I nodded firmly, accepting the request, noticing to the side a stone abstract sculpture on a plinth.

Okoro shut the door, joining us.

The director leaned forward. 'I presume you know the full severity of what happened this morning?'

'Sir, I saw television footage—' For a moment, I wanted to express my anguish. But instead, I let out a sorrowful sigh through my nostrils. Composing myself, I asked: 'Is there an estimate of fatalities?'

'It is too early to tell.'

'What of the government?'

'The prime minister and several cabinet members were air-lifted in time. The king is currently visiting Canada. Unfortunately, others weren't as fortunate,' he said bluntly.

'Agent Okoro informed me that you have caught the suspected terrorist?'

'Correct. I have already conducted an interrogation, and hopefully, soon, we will gather more intelligence.'

'What was the motive?'

'It is strictly confidential.' The director eyed me intensely. 'You have a choice right now, Blake—either you agree to assist us with this matter, and I proceed, or,'—he pointed towards the door—'you can leave, and there will be no further mention of this meeting.'

Hearing this, I was taken aback by how the director was willing to discuss matters with someone of my rank. Why me?

Curiosity often outweighed reasoning when it came to preserving my health and well-being. After all, it was part of what attracted me to this line of work in the first place.

Without further consideration, I leaned forward in the chair and said, 'Tell me more.'

'Follow me.'

The director stood, gesturing for us to follow him out of the room. He then led us southwards down the main tunnel. We stopped in front of a door. Okoro turned to ensure no one had followed us. I suspected there was something untoward about where we were going.

The door opened. The director asked me to enter. I walked into the room where they had received the video transmission less than an hour ago.

An assistant was sitting at the desk. He looked at me briefly before returning to his work. On the screen was a twenty-four-hour count-down. To the right, I noticed the Greek letter on the wall.

I followed the director down an adjacent corridor. We walked into another room. At the centre was a long wooden table. To either side were leather chairs. At the opposite end was a large, blank screen. In front of this stood a man I didn't recognise, who I suspected was a few years younger than me, wearing a white lab coat. He was talking to two unknown people who sat on either side of the table with their backs turned.

The man looked toward us. Everyone went silent. The two seated people turned in their chairs to welcome us. I tried to mask my surprise, realising it was the two agents from the extraction—Carroll and Penrose.

'You had best take a seat, Agent Blake,' the director said.

I obliged, sitting down next to Penrose. Meanwhile, the stranger took a seat. The director began pacing from one side of the room to the other, his face conveying his conflicting thoughts. But then he stopped, facing me with his hands clasped behind his back.

Clearing his throat, he said, 'Are you aware of the name George Fielding?'

'Yes, sir.'

'What do you know of him?'

'He was a highly celebrated agent within the organisation.' I saw Carroll looking at me intensely from the corner of my eye. 'He died in action. That's as much as I know of him.'

'It is true—Fielding was once my best agent. However, as it has recently transpired, he is alive.'

'Fielding is the terrorist?'

'Remember Leveller?'

'Yes.'

'It is a terrorist group. Fielding is the founder and leader. But many years ago, he was once part of this organisation's secretive, experimental branch. Before you are a select few people who know how it operates.'

I looked at Penrose and Carroll, trying to decipher what that entailed. They remained silent. 'Is this to do with those devices that I saw at the safe house?'

'Correct. Please follow me.'

He started walking towards another door. Everyone stood and followed him.

Thirteen

We walked into a large room. It was like the safe house: at the centre were three reclining chairs facing outwards, their headrests facing each other, with large, dome-shaped objects on top of them. Each had life support equipment and cables leading off to a computer. It had several suspended screens above it. To the side of the room was a closed, single door.

The director walked towards the computer. I stood, perplexed. The others came into the room, circling us.

Facing me, the director says, 'What you are looking at is the pinnacle of computer technology. The accumulation of effort from some of the greatest minds in the world.'

'What exactly am I looking at, sir?' I asked awkwardly.

'This is a quantum migrator.' Everyone looked to see my reaction. But I stayed neutral. 'When big tech announced its intentions to use quantum computation to propel advancements in calculation, cyber-security, forecasting, and many other fields, the military-industrial complex saw the potential, investing heavily in research and development, recruiting field-leading scientists.'

'Like Doctor Aditi?'

'Correct.'

'I presume they succeeded?' I said whimsically.

'Their results surpassed expectations.'

'This computer looks much smaller than I would have expected.'

'For mobile use, the scientists had to downscale the device. Usually, atoms need to be at absolute zero for the computer to function. And are cryogenically cooled. This computer contains a microprocessor, allowing it to run at room temperature, downsized.'

I walked forward, looking at the dome-shaped objects. 'Forgive my ignorance, but what does the migrator do?'

'It would be an appropriate time to introduce you to the branch's technician.' The director gestured to the stranger. 'This is Qubit.'

The man walked forward, shook my hand, and said, 'Hello, Agent Blake.'

'Hello. What's with the codename?'

'Just a prerequisite I stipulated before taking on the role,' he explained.

'Interesting choice.'

'Fitting!' he smirked. 'How much do you want to know?'

'I guess—everything.'

'Very well.' He walked around to the other side of the room, rubbing his chin. 'What do you know about quantum mechanics?'

'Not a great deal.'

'Go on.'

'Something about how particles work?'

He pointed out a finger in an excitable manner. 'Precisely! It is about the micro-level world. Everything that makes up you and me and the reality we coexist within. At present, the science defies logic.'

'In what way?'

'The forefathers of the field discovered that it is impossible to say a particle has a definite position and momentum simultaneously. Only when we observe the particle can the measurements become definite.'

'That seems…strange?'

'Very.'

'Without being observed, the particles could be doing anything?'

'Correct. Now, we describe particles in terms of things called wave functions. Until observed, all outcomes of the particles' position and momentum can exist at once. There would be many wave functions—this is called superposition. Are you following me?'

'Sort of,' I admitted, noticing the others looking at me dubiously.

'Okay, now imagine a pond.' Triggered—I saw Charlie's face. The technician saw my expression. 'Everything all right?'

Shaking away the thought, I smiled. 'Please, continue.'

'Imagine on the pond's surface there are many patterns of ripples. These are the different wave functions, or, in other words—different realities.'

'Realities?'

'Yes, they overlap on the surface but don't interact. Each exists alone. When you observe the pond, the ripples will intertwine so that only one pattern of ripples—or wave function—remains. It creates what is called quantum entanglement.'

'What is that?'

'A sharing of information between the particles and you, the observer. Essentially, the observer only perceives one set of ripples, wave function, or reality.'

'Like we do anyway?'

'Yes. Now, what would happen if there was no observer?'

'All of the patterns of ripples would still be on the pond?'

'Right. And?'

'All possible realities can exist at the same time?'

'Correct!' he announced jubilantly.

'But we can't perceive them?'

'Exactly. The life you inhabit is on one forward-moving line. And there are infinite others, branching off and running parallel. Or, shall we say—layered on each other, like on the pond's surface.'

'Okay, I'm just about grasping this. But what does it have to do with the quantum migrator?'

'Quantum computers work just like the pond analogy. But don't simply function using ones and zeros, instead using a qubit—hence my codename,'—the technician chuckled—'which is a basic unit of quantum information, allowing far more advanced computation.

'Now, we experimented using one of the quantum computer prototypes, scanning a brain. And guess what we discovered? A form of quantum computation occurs. It was miraculous!'

'Our brains work like a quantum computer?'

'In a similar way, yes. Our brains are made of different regions, composing a highly complex network of cells called neurons, with billions firing simultaneously. Their combined activity might generate consciousness or be the entry point if generated externally.'

'What do you mean by that?'

'The brain might not produce consciousness, but instead channel it from an external source.'

'From where?'

'Let's just say—the greater beyond. Now, back to the pond analogy. When you look at it, your mind will enter an entangled state. Different states relate to the different realities, while you only perceive one.' Qubit became excitable. 'We then did something that changed everything. By making a non-linear addition to the Schrodinger equation—'

'The what?' I asked.

'Save the heavy mathematics for another time,' the director interjected, looking at his watch.

Qubit nodded at him, continuing: 'Let's just say we inputted a complicated equation into the quantum computer and were able to transmit information across all the wave functions.'

I eyed him curiously. 'Transmit?'

'Yes. By transmitting the quantum state, consciousness also changed.'

'Changed? What happened?'

'It traversed into a different reality.'

I looked at the others, trying to process what the technician said. It was all far beyond anything I could expect.

I looked at the device. 'How does this happen?'

'When connecting to the quantum network, you can traverse into variants of yourself. Or, as I call them—vessels. You can only go into the body of someone accessing a quantum migrator, living in a dimension with the same fundamental constants.'

'What does that mean?'

'The same laws of physics, or nature.'

'What happens to my original body when connected to the migrator?'

'It remains connected to a life-support machine.'

'And I would then take on the other version's body?'

'Yes.'

'But still, remember who I am and where I came from?'

Qubit nodded. I was astounded. 'It would seem like you are following the same narrative of the self—one moment here, the next in an entirely new world. Imagine—now able to traverse other dimensions, we can have more purpose in what we do and control which reality to reside within.'

That word hit me—control.

Qubit continued: 'And the learning potential is exponential—when first experimenting with consciousness migration, we traversed into more technologically advanced realities. They taught us how to improve our quantum computers.'

'This is incredible!' I expelled.

Qubit smiled. 'It changes everything.'

'Could life still be predetermined, following one path? Or do we now have true free will?'

'That might remain an unresolved mystery about existence. But, importantly, we can now make decisions and enact them in many different realities.'

'But what if everything outside of my mind does not exist? And the external realities are just a construct of my mind. Or a simulation.'

'The conscious mind does not create the universe, or universes, but is an emergent phenomenon. There is an objective reality outside that which we both currently observe. What we humans perceive is an agreed, controlled hallucination, just as other animals have their own subjective experiences. Levels of intelligence and self-awareness correlate with larger, more complex networks of neurons in the brain.'

'Are we all part of a universal consciousness?'

'That is another theory that may remain an unresolved mystery. Meditative teachings would agree with the notion. They say that the self is an illusion, beyond which is unconditioned consciousness.'

'Have you used the quantum migrator?'

'Yes.'

'What happened?'

'I traversed into a vessel, experiencing their reality, and as my consciousness interacted with the new brain and body, I noticed subtle differences in how I thought and felt.'

'What differences?'

'Stamina, strength, resistance to pain. That sort of thing. The gut bacterium inside each vessel is unique. And if the vessel has incurred brain damage, that can also affect how you perceive their reality.'

'How did you feel when you came back?'

'It was transcendental. I had a permanent change of perception and grander awareness. Unforgettable.'

'Are there any negative side effects?'

'Minimal. But some test subjects have been known to have mental breakdowns,' Qubit said casually.

'What?!'

'I don't mean whilst traversing. Instead, when they returned to their original reality.' Qubit smiled.

I frowned. 'That still doesn't give me much reassurance.'

The director stepped forward. 'The quantum network keeps a log of the different quantum entanglements, or, as we call them—configurations. We have them all saved on this computer. It means that when you use the device, you can select specific realities and vessels to traverse if they connect simultaneously. It is the next generation of espionage.'

I stood there processing everything they had said to me. I hadn't noticed that the Statera was flowing through my bloodstream. The euphoria heightened this conversation.

The director continued: 'Unfortunately, the technology wasn't kept under wraps and got into the wrong hands—they sold it on the black market. Could you imagine the detrimental impact it has when misused? It jeopardises the fragile balance this organisation maintains across all dimensions.'

'I was never aware of any of this,' I said, shaking my head.

'Barely anyone was. At first, only myself and other national directors were made aware. I put together this secret branch and enacted the Convergence Protocol.'

'What is that?'

'It is the intention to maintain the status quo across the dimensions. I enlisted agents like Fielding who traversed other realities to stop our enemies.'

'How is this all linked to his motive with the nano-bombing?'

'We disagreed over accountability for what happened in the other realities.'

'And because of this?'

'Because of this and his unruly methods, I stripped him of his position. He retaliated, nearly compromising our efforts. I ordered his assassination. And was under the impression that he was dead for three years until this morning.'

'Why did he go to all the trouble of releasing the nano-bomb?'

I stood there, listening as the director explained, detailing everything from his conversation with Fielding an hour ago. Once he had finished, I took a few moments to digest the sheer magnitude of the situation—inter-dimensional catastrophe. Unimaginable.

Finally, I said, 'I guess you've called me in because you need my help to track down this remaining variant?'

'Correct.'

I looked around at everyone gathered. 'Okay, how're we going to do it?'

Fourteen

'You are aware of agents Penrose and Carroll,' the director said as everyone took seats at the large table.

'Yes,' I replied, nodding at them. But they both reciprocated half-heartedly, as though being greeted by a stranger, which I found peculiar.

'I should have explained,' the director said, 'these are not *exactly* the people you met two nights ago.'

'What do you mean?' I looked at them sceptically.

'You met variants which were using our vessels,' Penrose explained. 'They wanted to question the doctor for information. We agreed to aid them but underestimated what happened. As you're aware, they were too late. Compromising one of our team members in the process.'

'I'm sorry about Webb,' I said.

'We heard you helped him,' Carroll replied. 'Thanks for trying.'

I nodded mournfully before looking up at the director. 'How was this mission coordinated?'

'We can communicate across the quantum network. But, as we discovered this morning, our methods are somewhat primitive compared to the advanced capabilities of other dimensions.'

'Like transferring heavily encrypted files?' I asked.

'Correct,' he said awkwardly.

I looked at Qubit. 'Just a few more questions: What happens to the consciousness of the variant you traverse?'

'It migrates into your brain, either using your vessel or is unconscious. The latter keeps your vessel alive.'

'I don't understand.'

'The subconscious mind regulates bodily functions like breathing, digestion, heart rate and blood flow. The variant would operate for you whilst you're using their vessel.'

'I see. Because our Webb's vessel died here, what happened to his consciousness in the other dimension?'

'He now exists in their dimension.'

'Trapped?'

'For lack of a better word—yes.'

'*Right*. Why would you put yourselves at such risk, allowing variants to use your bodies?'

The director interjected: 'Because, Blake, all the layered dimensions now interconnect through the various quantum migrators. We have a *shared responsibility*.'

'Have you ever tried uploading consciousness onto the quantum network?' I asked.

'At present—no,' Qubit replied. 'Although, I'm sure other realities have achieved this.'

'Anyway, back to the task,' the director said.

'Sir, could Fielding still prove useful?' Carroll asked.

The director explained, 'During the interrogation, he told me that Doctor Aditi had erased important information from his brain.'

'How did he do that?' Penrose asked.

'There are quite a few things the quantum computer can achieve,' Qubit replied.

'Like removing memories?' I asked.

'Correct.'

'Do you know how to do this?'

'No.'

That's a shame—I remembered the memory of the park pond.

The director continued: 'Fielding told me he doesn't know where his device is nor where the remaining terrorist is. I will dispatch a task force to investigate our variant's background. There might be clues there.'

'Sir.' Carroll leaned forward. 'Could we traverse into another reality and interrogate one of the captured terrorist variants?'

'They probably wiped their memories as well, leaving no bread-crumbs. As we speak, my counterparts in other realities are most likely facing the same dilemma.'

'We could use the captured terrorists to barter with the final variant?'

'Leveller intends to destroy multiple realities. Its members are willing to sacrifice themselves for the cause. Bartering would be pointless.'

'Sir, I know this sounds…unprofessional,' Penrose interjected be-fore leaning back, looking disconcerted. 'But the likelihood of what we must achieve is…impossible. We would allow other realities to snuff it, but couldn't we destroy all possible entry points and stop the nano-bomb from reaching us?'

'How? Since setting up this branch, we have tried to close down all other migrators. We cannot find every quantum computer worldwide in less than twenty-four hours!'

Penrose continued: 'Or, we could traverse another reality where the terrorist group never existed? We would be safe there.'

The director was appalled. 'It is imperative, a *moral duty* to ensure Leveller fails in releasing the nano-bombs across the dimensions! Penrose, if you are *not* going to be part of this operation—I suggest you leave.'

'No, sir, I am staying.'

'Good. Instead, we must gather more intelligence about the final terrorist's location.'

'How would we do that, sir?' I asked.

'Whilst I thought Fielding was dead, we have been monitoring sev-eral of his variants across the quantum network,' he explained.

'And as we speak,' Okoro spoke, 'data is arriving through the quantum network, detailing which variants were part of Leveller and have been caught or killed.'

The director continued: 'Because of this, we can begin to narrow down the list of possible realities where the remaining terrorist is.'

Disconcerted about this mission, I didn't dare ask how many realities they had recorded.

The director stood and walked toward the screen. He turned it on—a screenshot from the video transmission appeared. It was the first time I had seen one of the terrorists. This variant looked healthy and affluent, assured in his posture, with intelligent eyes.

'This variant is called Rufus Miller,' the director explained.

'The variants don't have the same name?!' I interjected.

'No,' the director replied.

'Well, that makes things easier,' I said dryly, under my breath.

'That looks like a house, sir?' Carroll asked. 'A dining room?'

'Some variants share similar histories, have communicated with each other, and might be able to identify where this video originated.'

'That is…a long shot.' Penrose sighed pensively.

'Sir, I didn't ask before,' I interjected. 'Are the other realities like ours?'

'The majority of them are. As you can imagine, they would have reached our level of technology to have developed the quantum migrator as well. But there are some subtle differences.'

'Sir, which variant are we going to approach?' Penrose asked.

'There is one we have been closely monitoring who goes by the name of Daniel Tate. He is a political candidate currently running for office,' the director explained.

'Just as idealistic as his counterpart,' Penrose scoffed.

'His reality was untouched by the attacks,' Okoro added. 'This afternoon, he will be hosting a campaign event.'

'We are going along to show our support?' I asked sarcastically.

'No, to question him,' the director replied sternly, unwilling to indulge my humour. 'You will traverse into variants which are also agents for the organisation. They are on standby. Blake, your variant is called Chris Styles.' I nodded. 'Bear in mind that your time is limited in their dimension.'

'Why is that?' I asked.

'Because of time dilation,' Qubit replied. He saw the baffled look on my face. 'Time is relative and runs differently across the dimensions—some at the same speed as ours, others slower, others faster. Every hour in Tate's world equates to two-and-a-half hours in our reality.'

'The twenty-four-hour countdown is different in other realities?'

'Correct.'

'Leveller must have a lot of clocks,' I muttered.

'We now have twenty-two-and-a-half hours,' the director said, checking his wristwatch.

'Did the remaining terrorist explain how he will know if we decide to meet his demand?' I asked.

'He did not. There might be others here working for him.'

'And they could transfer the news through the quantum network?'

'That could be the case. Hence, I must send out a task force to investigate how Leveller operates in our world.' He addressed Okoro. 'See if you can somehow decrypt that video file.' She nodded firmly. He stood and addressed everyone: 'I will notify the other dimension. You have a ten-minute break before we begin the operation.'

Everyone nodded, standing. Excusing myself, I walked out of the branch until I walked into the main corridor of the west wing. As the door closed behind me, I stood there, digesting everything.

Looking further down the tunnel, I saw colleagues, oblivious to what was happening. It seemed surreal knowing that whatever happened behind this door would decide the fate of the world (or, the many realities). I would spend the next day here physically whilst my mind went elsewhere.

Accepting that I could lose my life on this mission, I needed to reconcile things with Julia—if she was still alive after the terrorist attack.

I walked down the corridor until I reached the toilet. Stepping inside, I checked that no one else was present before locking the main door and withdrawing my phone.

I had a full signal. Still no response. Seeing this caused my stomach to churn.

I went into the recent call list and tried to ring her. Putting the phone to my ear, I started pacing anxiously around the room. And with every chime of the ringtone, my heart missed a beat, and my hopes dwindled. But there was still a possibility she might have lost her phone whilst escaping from the bombing.

It went to voicemail. I cleared my throat, composed myself, and when the tone sounded, I said, 'Julia, it's me. I hope you're okay and wasn't at the office when the bomb went off. Well, obliviously, if you're hearing this. Look, I don't have much time. I must do something right now, but I can't explain what it is. And I don't know whether I will make it out alive. I want you to know that I love you. I love you *so much*. I know I fucked up badly. I failed you and Charlie. There is not much I can do right now other than to apologise. I hope you eventually hear this message. We can meet up. Work things out. Bye.'

I cancelled the call, put the phone on the sink, and looked at my reflection in the mirror. Alone in this bathroom, away from the unbearable events unfolding outside, I was looking at my true self without the social mask to conceal my inner turmoil.

I wasn't a hardened agent. Instead—vulnerable. Pathetic.

I reached into my jacket pocket, withdrawing a bottle of Statera. Was there much point in self-medicating if I was about to separate from my body? However, the act of taking the drugs had a placebo effect. It helped to alleviate the stubborn itch.

Aware of the locked toilet door, I quickly opened the bottle and poured a few pills into my mouth, feeling the rubbery texture against my tongue and inner cheeks. I put the bottle into my pocket. Running the tap, I cupped my hands underneath it, collected some water, and then used it to lubricate my throat, swallowing the pills.

Refilling my hands, I splashed the cold liquid against my face to shake me from this unbalanced state. I turned off the tap, placed both hands on either side of the sink, and looked into my eyes, water dribbling down my cheeks.

I had the realisation—the quantum migrator.

Was there a possibility of finding a variant of Charlie in other realities?!

Suddenly, I was overwhelmed by an unfamiliar sensation: joy—a glimmer of hope.

A memory of reading him a bedtime story. His fascination with dinosaurs. That innocent ice cream-smothered smile with baby teeth.

I stood straight, took a paper towel to dry my face, and looked into my darkened eyes.

When I returned to the experimental branch, the director, technician, assistants, and agents were gathered in the main room with the quantum migrator. Without another word, I walked forward and sat on one of the chairs. I adjusted my posture, putting my head underneath the brain scanner. Carroll and Penrose took their respective positions.

I sat there patiently. Qubit approached me.

Fifteen

The scanner blocked my view. Looking down, I trailed my fingertips curiously across a touchpad on the right-hand armrest, asking: 'What does this do?'

'I'll explain shortly,' Qubit replied, adjusting the height of the brain scanner. He stood back, evaluated this, and nodded to himself. 'Are you comfortable?'

'Yes.'

'Good.' He produced a wire concealed behind the scanner. At its end were three ECG electrode pads. 'If you don't mind.' He pulled up my top and stuck it onto my bare chest. 'This is to monitor your heart rate and rhythm.'

'Will Styles be able to use my body whilst I am away?'

'Don't worry—the computer will restrict brain activity, putting Styles in an induced coma. And when you commence the migration, I will perform the intubation.'

"You will what now?"

'I will attach an endotracheal tube—to help with breathing when you are traversing. It connects to a ventilator behind your seat.' Once finished, he pulled down my top, standing back. 'If you stay in the other reality longer, we insert intravenous fluids, nutrition, and catheters.' He saw my apprehension. 'Are you comfortable with me performing these procedures, Blake?'

'Yes,' I said reluctantly.

'Good. Now, all you need to do is sit back and close your eyes. I will do the rest.' He pointed at the quantum computer.

'What does that entail?'

'The migrator will take a complex neuro-scan of your brain. I then select the destined quantum entanglement for each of you.'

'How do you have one for me already?'

'We have the configuration for Chris Styles and the other agent's variants. The computer will activate, changing the configuration of you, Carroll and Penrose, sending you all into the same alternative reality.'

'Seems simple enough,' I laughed. 'So, what does this touchpad do?'

He leaned forward, pointing at the individual buttons on the display. 'Basically, the top one is to move forward, the middle one to go back, and the bottom one is to send a distress signal.'

'I can't change the reality on this touchpad?'

'No, that must be done using the main computer. And it won't be required. It is a similar setup in the other reality. Once done, all you need to do is sit back down and press the middle button.'

'Got it.'

The director approached. 'Is everyone ready?'

'Yes, sir.' We all said in unison.

'I wish you the best of luck. The fate of the many realities is riding upon you.'

No pressure, I thought, leaning back, trying to relax.

In the distance, I could hear Qubit say, 'I am about to switch on the scanners. Blake, please close your eyes.' I followed his order, rubbing the palms of my hands into the leather upholstery of the chair's arms.

And then, I could hear humming inside the scanner. Nothing seemed to happen for a few minutes. I presumed the technician was conducting the neuro-scan, preparing the crossing.

Finally, I heard him announce: 'All set. See you on the other side!'

I was expecting something dramatic, a whirlwind experience. Eventually, I felt new sensations in and around my body. It wasn't the Statera, but a subtle difference in how I sat. There was a change in the room temperature. Voices were nearby.

I was cautious not to open my—or *his*—eyes without being instructed. Around me, I could sense movement. Carroll and Penrose were standing up from their chairs. Someone walked forward, leaning over me.

'Styles, it is okay. You have arrived,' the person said in an unfamiliar, reassuring voice. It took me a moment to process that they were talking to me.

Slowly, I opened my eyes. They focused on the underside of the brain scanner. I looked down. The chair was black. I was wearing different clothes, seeing a wire disappearing up my top. I assumed they had to monitor Styles as I took over his body.

I had a feeling I wasn't in my reality anymore.

The stranger's hand reached forward to detach the electrode pads. Impulsively, I reached up to swat them away.

'Please,' they said calmly, 'I understand this is your first time.'

'It's okay—I can do it myself,' I said.

The voice projected from the vocal cords was similar. But different.

'Of course.' The person stood back.

Reaching under the top, the hand brushing against my torso. It seemed more muscular and defined. This guy had been taking care of himself. Detaching the pads and withdrawing the wire, the person leaned forward again to take it from me.

I brought the hands closer to inspect. Although they appeared similar, I could see subtle differences in skin tone, new blemishes, and missing scars. I placed the hands onto the armrests, lowered the body, and leaned outwards from under the scanner.

Seeing the sight before me, I gasped in amazement.

There was a warmly lit room—the white walls looked metallic and pristine. The quantum computer was more compact. Standing before me was a young woman. I suspected the technician in this reality. Carroll and Penrose were to my left. But now she had long hair, whilst his appearance didn't look as different.

The director was standing further away. He now had a beard, wearing a grey suit with a scoop neck collar.

'Welcome,' he said nobly, walking towards me. I leaned forward, resting my crossed arms on my thighs, taking a few moments to digest my new surroundings. 'How are you feeling?'

I looked up at him. 'Fine, I think.'

The technician brought a glass of water. I accepted it. Drinking the contents, I returned the glass, thanked her, and attempted to stand up. As I did this, the technician came forward to assist me, but I didn't need the help, instead drawing to full height.

Carroll and Penrose turned towards me.

'You're looking good, Styles!' she joked.

'I feel great!' I smiled.

Honestly? I felt like shit.

Penrose handed me a small mirror. I looked at my reflection. It was the same person. But he looked healthier. The darkened circles were gone. His short stubble was immaculate. I started touching his face, feeling the smoothness of his—or my—new skin.

It made me feel mixed feelings.

I lowered the mirror.

'Please, come this way,' the director said, gesturing for me to follow him to a door. Handing Penrose back the mirror, I followed the leader out of the room and into a corridor.

To my right, there was a large window along the whole wall. And when I peered outwards, I stopped, taken aback, and had to put a hand to the mouth to muffle the expelling sound.

There was a vast landscape of cloud-breaching skyscrapers upon a gleaming horizon. Meandering around these gigantic structures were lines of flying vehicles.

'How, how is this possible?' I managed to utter, looking at the director.

'Our world took a different path to yours', the director replied, standing by my side, hands clasped behind his back, looking out proudly at the magnificent city. 'I have been to your world, understanding what happened: after the Second World War and the collapse of the Soviet Union in the early nineteen-fifties—'

'It collapsed that early?'

'Correct. There was no space or nuclear arms race.'

'What happened instead?'

'The United States saved tens of trillions of dollars. It flourished—democracy and unregulated, free-market capitalism spread without opposition—a focus on global unification. There has been the gradual universalisation of culture, values, currency, and prosperity.'

'Then why does the agency exist here?'

'Because it is integral that we uphold the world order. Some will always oppose, especially as we intend to colonise other planets and implement the same system off-world.' He turned to me. 'And you are overseeing this operation.'

'Sorry?'

'Blake, in this world—Styles is much higher up in the world organisation.'

I looked out of the window. 'Does Styles have a life outside?'

'No, he is career driven, avoids all distractions.'

'Are agents here allowed to marry and have children?'

'Yes. But Styles does not have a family.'

It was disheartening to hear this. But I maintained a neutral expression.

Carroll and Penrose joined us.

'Isn't it wonderful?' she asked.

'Yes,' I said pensively.

The director gestured for us to follow him, leading into another room with a circular granite table and low-hanging lighting. He walked up to a touchpad on the surface and typed a few commands.

A large holographic image appeared in the centre of the room. It was Fielding. The variant had similar clothing to the director.

'This is Daniel Tate,' the director said. 'I understand the severity of the situation and felt compelled to help with this investigation.'

'Does Leveller exist in this world?' Carroll asked.

'Not that I'm aware of.'

'And you haven't been threatened?' Penrose asked.

'No. In our world, the population is very aware of our existence.' I exchanged dubious expressions with the other two. 'Tate is hosting a campaign luncheon. I have sourced your invites. You will be attending as entrepreneurs working in the construction industry.'

'Is there still room for corruption in this world?' Penrose asked.

'I don't know how things work in your reality, but corruption is an infrequent occurrence here,' the director rebuked. He gestured to another door. 'Please, follow. Tailored outfits await.'

We followed him into another room where three garment bags were hanging on a rail. He explained which belonged to each of us. Walking forward, I took mine and unzipped the bag, revealing a black suit.

The director addressed us: 'You have five minutes to get ready. Transportation is waiting.'

We took individual corners in the room, undressed, and changed. The suit fitted immaculately.

Moments later, the director came in, ushering us out into the main corridor of the agency. Like the previous rooms, the walls were white and metallic. We saw various people walking by.

The director led us further into the building until we reached another door. He opened this. We followed him through.

There were steps leading down to a car hovering over a vast drop.

Sixteen

'Are we going to drive that?' I asked, admiring the wheelless mechanism and sleek design.

'No.' The director walked down the steps. 'A chauffeur is waiting.'

We followed him. Reaching the bottom, I looked over the side towards the surface below.

As the director approached, the back door automatically opened. He stood aside, allowing us to step in. As this happened, the vehicle gyrated. There was a glass partition. The driver nodded at us in the rear mirror. Carroll sat adjacent with her back to the driver. I sat next to Penrose.

The director leaned in. 'You are all connected to the mindlink. We are with you every step of the way. Best of luck.'

The doors closed.

I looked at the other two. 'What is the director referring to?'

'In this world, all agents have a thought-reading implant to communicate in the field,' Carroll explained.

'Telepathy?' I asked.

'Correct.' Penrose unbuttoned his blazer, reclining.

The car launched forward. I was surprised by the smooth propulsion.

'Can it read everything I am thinking?'

'No,' Carroll explained, 'the connection happens when your internal monologue purposely tries to engage with the subject.'

'Probably just as well,' I laughed.

'Try it,' Carroll said. 'Focus on me and think of something.' I did as she instructed. 'You just said hello to me.'

'Nice.'

'And hello to you, too!' Her voice suddenly announced inside my head. The sound was clear, as though she had spoken into both ears simultaneously.

'Impressive!' I exclaimed.

'It is as simple as that,' I heard inside.

We sat silently for a while as I looked at the scenery. There were countless skyscrapers, amongst familiar landmarks, and floating markers organising traffic. Every so often, there were billboards projecting holographic advertisements. Amongst these, I saw one announcing a new book release. On the front cover, I saw a young woman I recognised—Elina Wells, the investigative journalist.

I looked back at the other two excitedly. 'Did you see that?!'

'What?' Carroll replied.

'I recognise that person!'

'It happens,' she said casually.

I guess this was the norm for them.

'I haven't had a chance to speak to you both properly, considering what we have all agreed to do.'

'What are you expecting?' Penrose asked in a cold tone.

'Come on, Michael!' Carroll interjected.

'What?'

She eyed him judgmentally. 'No need to play the distant type all the time.'

'You guys refer to each other by your first names?' I asked.

'Yes.' Carroll smiled. 'If you want, you can call me Samantha.'

'Jackson,' I replied, exchanging awkward looks with Penrose.

'Take no notice of him. He doesn't like associating with people other than on a superficial, work basis.'

'It keeps everything in check. The less you know, the better,' Penrose said, staring out the window.

'A self-defence mechanism?' I asked.

He looked at me. 'What?'

'You don't like to form bonds with people. I get it.' I nodded, looking out of the window pensively. 'I've developed the same thick skin over the years. I find it hard to get on with people, in general.'

I questioned whether I had overshared but was relieved when Carroll said: 'Yeah, I find it hard to date. Things get to a certain point, and then I finish things with them. It is difficult trying to have a normal life in this line of work.'

'Nothing to do with you giving them such a hard time?' Penrose smirked.

'Shut up.' Carroll shook her head mockingly.

'I know what you mean,'—I looked at her—'I used to have a family.'

'Past tense?' she replied.

'It's a long story.'

Penrose wagged his index finger at me while looking in the opposite direction. 'And that is why I don't go out of my way to get to know people.'

'You're happy living with your cat?' Carroll asked.

Penrose shrugged. 'There's a mutual understanding.'

'I hope you left her enough food while you're away?'

'Either she is dead or alive by the time I return.'

'That sounds heartless.'

'She works in her own ways.'

'Right.'

Penrose changed the conversation: 'How are you getting on with the book you've been reading?'

'I'm enjoying the scale and ideas,' Carroll replied.

'What's it about?' I asked.

'It's a far-future epic adventure,' she explained.

'Oh, right,' I said. Uninterested, I changed the conversation: 'How come the variants I met the other night had the same names as you?'

'Because they chose to use our names,' Carroll explained.

'What are your vessels called?'

'I am Lorna Bell,'—Carroll pointed towards Penrose—'and he is Paul Wheeler.'

'But there is a serious reason why we use our original names in alternative realities,' Penrose said.

'Why is that? I asked.

'Just so we can keep a grip on who we truly are,' Carroll explained. 'When traversing all of these different realities, you can sometimes lose track of things.'

'The self is a combination of inherited characteristics, environmental conditioning, and memory,' Penrose explained. 'When continuously traversing into other vessels, you share the same DNA, but there are differences because of their world, which has sculpted them, and you must blend into them. Memories are vital to maintaining a sense of self. Using our original names helps to keep a grip.'

Keep a grip—got it.

'Qubit mentioned that some people have lost their minds after using the quantum migrator?' I asked.

'Yes, there have been cases of psychotic episodes. If someone had the predisposition, using the device was the push to send them over the edge.'

'Good to know,' I said dryly.

'When we return to our reality, Qubit will perform a mental health assessment,' Carroll said.

I wasn't looking forward to that.

'Did you both meet Fielding?' I asked.

'We used to work with him,' Penrose replied.

'From the beginning?' I asked.

'Yes,' Carroll said bluntly. 'When the director established the branch, he recruited all three of us.'

'And when they had their disagreement, Webb replaced him?'

'Correct,' she replied, pausing before saying: 'The director ordered us to carry out the assassination.'

'You can understand why I am reluctant to become pally,' Penrose said.

'I was adamant that we killed him.' Carroll looked out of the window.

'Did you see his body?' I asked.

'Well, yes—'

'Perhaps he staged the death?'

'He is a master of deception,' Penrose replied. 'Look at what happened after the nano-bombing—we caught Fielding. But that was irrelevant. All part of a bigger plan.'

'Because we didn't do our job properly,' Carroll interjected, 'this whole shit-show has unfolded ever since.'

'I guess this mission is personal for you both?' I asked, reading their expressions.

Penrose sniggered. 'You could say that.'

'Did he deserve to be called the best agent in the organisation?'

'Let's put it this way,' Penrose replied, 'it takes someone of high aptitude and strong abilities to bring variants across multiple dimensions to his cause.'

'And undetected,' Carroll added. 'How he has orchestrated everything is, how shall I say—remarkable. Borderline genius.'

'It's time we finished off the job,' Penrose said.

They nodded at each other.

'I'd feel more comfortable going to this luncheon with a weapon,' I said.

'This is a far more civilised world, Jackson,' Carroll replied. 'The objective is to corner Tate, gather intelligence, and leave.'

'Without a trace of suspicion,' Penrose added.

Carroll turned around and tapped on the window. The driver opened a small hatch.

'How long is it until we reach the location?'

'We'll be arriving momentarily.'

'Thank you.' She turned back. 'Now, we all remember the cover?'

'Three entrepreneurs working in the construction industry,' I said. Penrose nodded. 'It will be fine for us to use our vessel's names?'

'There is less cause for concern in this world,' Carroll replied.

I looked outside. 'I think I prefer it here.'

'It's not perfect, Jackson,' Penrose said. 'There is no such thing as utopia.'

'Like our world, there is rampant wealth inequality, and they're edging faster towards climate catastrophe,' Carroll added.

Moments later, the car came to a halt. Looking out the passenger window, I saw a walkway leading up to a large, lavish building. Other guests were also arriving, dressed in formalwear.

I stepped out onto the walkway and stood to the side. Taking a deep breath, I looked out at the bustling city. As the other agents climbed out of the car, I turned towards the entrance where other guests stood. Penrose thanked the driver and closed the door.

'Follow my lead,' Carroll said to both of us, adjusting her suit blazer before walking forward. We flanked her, surveying the building and joined a queue. Drawing to the front, Carroll presented her phone. The door attendant scanned the QR codes on the electronic invites and stood aside, allowing us in.

Seventeen

Carroll said over the mindlink: 'Sir, we have gained entry.'

'Very good,' the director replied. I heard his voice, walking past a cloakroom where people were queuing. 'Send me an update once you have engaged Tate.'

'Roger that,' she replied.

Large doors opened into the main area. We walked inside and stood surveying the event. It was in a grand, circular room with walkways on the upper floors. Above was a skylight, radiating sunlight down onto the gathering of campaign assistants, civil servants, business associates, media representatives, and socialites. To the right was a generous buffet. Adjacent was a stage and podium with a campaign banner hanging proudly behind it. And somewhere, a string quartet was playing Vivaldi.

Fancy, but nothing special—I'm sick of these places.

'Take both flanks. Report how many guards are present,' Carroll said over the mindlink.

'Roger that,' Penrose replied.

'And what about you?' I asked.

She turned to me, smirked, and said without opening her lips: 'I'm going to mingle.'

And with that, she started walking down the stairs. Meanwhile, we followed orders, taking opposite directions.

'Is she always this forthright?' I asked Penrose.

'I heard that!' Carroll suddenly replied.

Embarrassed, I looked down at her. 'You weren't meant to hear that!'

'I gathered, Jackson,' she said mockingly. Penrose laughed at us. 'I hope you're not vocalising that, Michael?' Carroll asked. 'It might give us away.'

'Or make you look insane,' I added.

'Don't worry.' It sounded like he was catching his breath. 'I was only laughing on the inside.'

'Okay,' Carroll said.

Penrose addressed me: 'Jackson, remember—do what she wants, and nobody gets hurt. I learned that a long time ago.'

'Got it.' I stood by a pillar, casually looking around. Amongst the guests were the hired muscle, wearing earpieces. I couldn't tell whether they were armed. 'I clock seven.'

'Same,' Penrose replied.

'Well, one thing is for certain,' Carroll spoke, walking by the buffet. 'These politicians don't skimp on costs when putting on a good spread.'

'Have some for me,' I replied. 'I'm trying to watch my figure.'

'Very good,' she said dryly.

'Six o'clock,' Penrose interjected.

Instantly, although subtly, we turned towards the doorway where Fielding, or Tate, appeared. He walked into the room confidently. There was loud applause and cheering of his name. The campaign anthem blasted from speakers. With effortless charisma, Tate started to meet, greet, and shake hands.

'D'you two recognise anyone here?' I asked, walking down the steps to join everyone. The crowd parted in the centre, allowing Tate to walk through.

'There are a few dodgy donors and lobbyists that we have monitored,' Penrose said, standing by my side.

'We'll fit right in,' I said dryly.

The politician walked past. We both joined in with the clapping.

'Does Tate have a significant other?' I asked.

'Once divorced, recently re-married,' Carroll replied, standing opposite us.

'Is the partner here?' I asked.

'She didn't enter with him.'

'What was his background before politics?'

'Real estate,' Penrose replied.

Tate jumped onto the stage and turned to face the ecstatic audience. He looked upwards at people standing on the upper walkways, waving at them before walking to the edge of the stage and clapping towards his loyal supporters down on the floor.

Carroll said: 'He is *loving* every moment of this.'

Finally, Tate stood back to admire the view, evidently astounded, before walking behind the podium, placing his hands down on it, and looking down at the congregation.

'Thank you, everyone,' he spoke into the microphone. The sound echoed into the room. The applause subsided. Small drones circled overhead, videoing him. 'I appreciate the warm welcome this afternoon. I didn't expect such a large turnout!' His eyes scanned the room. 'There are some old faces and some new, which is very reassuring. Firstly,'—he gestured to a few people standing to the side—'I would like to say a *massive* thank you to my team for helping to organise this luncheon, for supporting me along this campaign trail.' He turned to them, clapping. The audience joined him. There was an exchange of inaudible words of goodwill. Tate faced the audience. 'This is my first time running for office. There have been many lessons along the way. And the response has been overwhelming. Invaluable advice. Immeasurable wisdom. People are investing in me, confident I can win this election!' There was another rapturous applause. They were hanging on to his every word. 'Despite how well this global federation has thrived, some nations have not seen a fair deal joining it. *At all*. We compromised too much without reward. Therefore, I intend to recommence talks and renegotiate trade deals. I will ensure that we have a bigger say at the table, shaping the future of this sovereign nation! We will not be left behind!' The audience cheered. The atmosphere was infectious. 'Having worked all my life in real estate, I understand what it takes to build. Close a deal. I will transfer these skills and mindset as your *new leader*!'

Tate stood forward from the podium, clapping as his audience praised him.

I looked at Carroll. She had a sceptical look. 'Usual, empty rhetoric,' she said via the mindlink.

'Well, he gets my vote,' Penrose said dryly.

The quartet recommenced playing.

'What now?' I asked.

'Once he has finished doing pleasantries, we must approach him,' Carroll replied.

'But that could take hours?' I replied.

'I guess we'll have to find a way to catch his attention,' Penrose said.

Suddenly, a woman standing to my right, who had capitalised on the complimentary champagne, dropped her flute. The glass smashed against the floor, showering surrounding people. I looked off to the side where one of the security personnel was standing.

The sound of the breaking glass caused him to react, momentarily reaching inside his blazer. Seeing the noise source, he returned to standing firm with his hands clasped by his abdomen.

The drunken woman woozily apologised to those showered individuals standing nearby before staggering away accompanied by her embarrassed partner.

Moments later, Tate started walking through the crowd, talking to his supporters. Conscious of our limited time, I started edging toward him.

'What are you planning to do, Jackson?' Penrose asked via the mindlink.

'Getting us that private meeting,' I replied, walking up to where Tate stood with a small group. He was telling an anecdote. And at the right moment, I joined the gathering as they all laughed. I asked a man to step aside.

Tate turned to me with a curious look and said: 'I don't believe we have met?'

'No, I don't think we have.' I put out my hand to shake. He accepted the gesture with a firm grip. 'Chris Styles.'

'A pleasure to meet you.'

'Forgive me for speaking abruptly. But I'm pushed for time this afternoon and can't stay long. I was just wondering if you could give me a few minutes of your time in private?'

Tate smiled awkwardly. 'Whatever for?'

'Just to talk to you about infrastructure investments.'

'Why might that be?'

'I work in construction.'

His eyebrow rose. 'Is that so? I worked in real estate for over twenty years and didn't recognise your name.'

'Be careful, Jackson,' Carroll said, standing nearby.

'I'm new to the industry.' I leaned in closer and spoke quietly: 'And think it would be in your...*interest* to have me on board as a supporter for your campaign.'

I stood back. Tate laughed awkwardly. 'Very well. I need to do the rounds. I will ask my assistant to collect you. We can have a quick conversation in my private office upstairs.'

'Excellent.' I nodded.

'Now, if you don't mind, I have a few important people to speak to.' He stood back, nodded, and walked away, followed by his aid.

'That was very confident of you,' Carroll said.

'You can always appeal to their heartstrings or...the lining of their wallets,' I said before looking over my shoulders. 'When I go into that meeting, you two should stay here to keep an eye on these security guards. Depending on how he responds to my questioning, things might get intense.'

'Okay, but don't be too invasive. Remember, we need to maintain a low profile.'

'Understood.' I eyed one of the guards. 'I'm going to have a drink beforehand.'

'We'll keep ourselves entertained,' Penrose replied.

I walked to a waiter. He stood holding a tray of filled champagne flutes. Taking one and thanking him, I held it up to my lips whilst searching avidly through the crowds for Tate. By now, he was standing on the opposite side of the room. Refraining from drinking, I started walking around, waiting.

Several minutes later, I saw the target say something to his aid before walking away from the crowds and down a corridor—this was my cue.

I walked up the stairs by the stage, heading towards a guard standing at the top. As I approached him, I looked back, pretending to be preoccupied, and intentionally barged straight into him. As we collided, the contents of the flute spilt all over his face and torso. He reacted by raising his hands upwards, blocking his view, and causing the fabric of his blazer to open outwards. And in that split second, I reached with my left hand and extracted the harnessed handgun. As he staggered backwards, I theatrically vocalised my shock. Ensuring to cover him with every drop of the champagne, I simultaneously stuffed the weapon into the back waistband of my trousers. The handgun was lightweight. Hopefully, it would take a while for him to notice it had disappeared. He stood back, brushing off the liquid, giving me a stern look.

'I'm very sorry!' I exclaimed, wide-eyed. 'Please, let me get you a napkin.'

He put his hands out defensively as champagne dribbled down his cheeks. 'No, it is fine.'

'I misplaced my foot on that last step,' I said, looking down at the staircase.

'What are you playing at, Blake?' Penrose said over the mindlink.

'Don't worry,' I replied.

The guard shook his head dismissively, walking toward the toilets. With that, I placed the empty glass onto the side, pacing around the platform, circling the room, keeping my eyes trained on the aid. She was looking into the crowd for me. Ensuring no one was watching, I quickly withdrew the handgun, checking it was loaded, and put it back, concealed behind my blazer.

'I'm about to engage the target,' I said over the mindlink.

I heard Carroll informing the director.

Walking towards the aid, I said in a friendly tone, 'Were you looking for me?'

She turned to face me. 'Ah, yes!'—and gestured to the corridor—'please, follow me.'

'Certainly.' I nodded.

Eighteen

We walked down the hall to a set of spiralling steps that took us into a large office. To my left was a window looking down upon the luncheon. On my right were bookcases and a seating area with a bar. Adjacent was a large desk that Tate was sitting behind, awaiting me.

'Thank you once again for allowing me a few minutes of your time,' I said, leaning over the desk.

We shook hands. I heard the aid leave.

'Please, take a seat.' He gestured to one seat by my side. 'Can I offer you a drink?'

'No, thank you. I accidentally spilt champagne over one of the security guards. It is best that I avoid drinking,' I said whimsically, sitting down and keeping my back straight, away from the cushion.

'Oh, right!' He cackled, leaned forward, clasped his hands on the desk, and looked at me curiously. 'What exactly was the necessity for this private meeting?'

'We are finalising a big development and want to ensure you will support it.'

His eyebrow rose. 'You mean I won't get in the way?'

I laughed. 'I suppose that is the way of wording it. We believe you will win this election. Because of your ties, I hope your new government won't enforce tight regulations or heavy taxes on the industry?'

From the corner of my eye, I saw the same security guard—he was now roaming around the room. I suspected he was looking for me.

'And what is the incentive?' he said with irony.

I returned my gaze to the politician. 'I'm sure you can imagine.'

Tate smirked. 'And you didn't come here this afternoon to ask for something else?'

That question took me off guard. 'What are you referring to?'

'Someone in my position might have access to classified information.'

'I'm sure you do.'

'And it only took a phone call to find out your name is unknown within the industry.'

'As mentioned previously, I'm only a first-time entrepreneur.'

He leaned back in his chair, hands clasped. 'I suspect you didn't come here just to discuss business matters. But instead, something else entirely different.'

What did he know? Could I angle this in my favour? I needed to learn more about his background—possible connections to the dining room in the video transmission.

There was limited time before the security guard found out where I was. I addressed Carroll and Penrose via the mindlink: 'Can you stall that security guard? I need more time with Tate.'

'Roger that,' they both said in unison.

'Would it be possible to arrange another meeting? So that we could talk about your firsthand experiences within the industry. I would appreciate hearing your knowledge.'

'You want to pick my brains?' He leaned forward. Suddenly, his friendly demeanour subsided. 'Let's not stand on ceremony here.'

'Sorry?' My facial expression remained neutral.

There was a protracted silence.

'It was a nice effort you made.'

I placed my right hand down on the armrest. 'If you are suspicious because of not recognising my name—'

'Oh, I know your name, all right.'

I forced a smile. 'I can imagine you need to return to your guests.'

'You probably think every businessman like me, aspiring to become a politician, is easily corruptible?'

'Not at all.'

'And gullible.'

'I'm sorry if I have been at all disrespectful.'

'Disrespectful? You only know the half-truth.' He stared at me intensely and said: 'An admirable effort, I must say, Mr Blake.'

A cold shiver seeped down my spine. 'Excuse me?'

'Jackson Blake. That is your real name?'

'There must be a misunderstanding. My name is Chris Styles.'

'That is the vessel you are using.'

I took a deep breath through the nostrils in a vain attempt to calm the vessel. Its heart was beating frantically—fingernails digging into the leather upholstery.

Tate smirked. 'It just so happens I was given quite a few details about who could be coming here today.' He looked out of the window towards the audience. 'Are they here with you?' I remained silent. 'My variants made me aware that your director would send a task force here to track down the remaining member of Leveller.' He said mockingly: 'And I know all about you, Blake. What a tragic, pathetic existence you lead. A failed marriage. Dead son—'

At that moment, knowing we had failed—and admittedly provoked by the mention of Charlie—I swiftly reached around under my waistband for the handgun. Withdrawing it, I aimed for his forehead.

Tate registered what was happening, eyes widening.

Without another consideration, I pulled the trigger.

His head violently jerked backwards with the force of the bullet ripping through his head—the wall behind splattered with brains and blood. His corpse slumped down in the chair.

What had I done?

Suddenly, I could hear the gathering below reacting to the gunshot sound. There were hysterical screams and movement.

'Blake, what happened?!' Carroll asked over the mindlink.

'We are compromised,' I said, standing.

'What?!'

I saw the security guards look upward towards the office. 'We need to get out of here, *now*.'

Walking away from the desk, I approached the spiral staircase. And below, I could hear two of the hired muscles heading towards me.

I had to get out of there.

Nineteen

Without hesitation, I started descending the spiral staircase with the handgun firmly in my grasp. As the two guards ascended, they saw me approaching, snarled, withdrew their weapons, and prepared for engagement. I hurtled towards them, kicking out with my right foot. It connected with the first guard's chest. The full force sent him flying backwards and taking out the other.

They both tumbled down the staircase, crying in agony, landing on the ground floor. I jumped over them and turned back to kick them both in the face. They fell unconscious.

Turning towards the corridor, I sprinted forward, expecting other guards. As I appeared into the main room, all five, including the soaked one, launched toward me. At that moment, Carroll and Penrose came forward, intercepting the guards.

I drew my gun forward, swivelled it in my grasp, and used the handle as a beating implement. I went for a guard nearby, blocked a punch, and smashed the gun into his cheek. The force sent him falling to the floor. Meanwhile, the other two attacked the remaining guards.

'Get to the entrance before they pull out their weapons,' I said over the mindlink.

Feverishly, Carroll and Penrose drew away from the fight, following me out of the main room and into the lobby. All the while, the guards tailed us, firing in our direction.

Guests were trying to escape from the commotion. A large gathering was slowly filtering through the main entrance. The guards saw this and stopped firing. As the guests heard us nearing, many started to shout and push. I aimed the handgun at the ceiling, releasing a few rounds, and the echoing sound jolted them.

'Move!' I exclaimed.

It had the desired effect—the crowd parted in the centre, allowing us three to negotiate through. With my eyes trained on a row of hovering cars parked outside, I waded through the people, holding the gun high in case I needed to use it.

Forcing myself through, I walked onto the top steps. Instinctively checking my periphery for other hostiles—convinced that the coast was clear—I sprinted forward. Overhead, storms were amassing, and a light rain started to fall. There was the distant murmur of thunder.

'Get into one of those cars,' I ordered.

The other two followed at my heels.

As they ran forward, I stopped and turned towards the main entrance. Holding up the gun, I aimed at the guards breaching the crowd. I didn't want to cause civilian casualties, maintaining this position whilst Carroll and Penrose hijacked one of the vehicles. The guards saw me and refrained from advancing.

Moments later, I heard Penrose calling my name. I turned and ran for the car. As this happened, I heard gunfire. The pinging of bullets ricocheted against nearby vehicles. The back door was wide open. I dived into the backseat, rolled onto my back, and aimed at the guards. They drew towards us. The car took off. I fired a few rounds and leaned forward to close the door.

Sitting upright, Penrose was driving. Carroll was sitting in the passenger seat. She turned towards me, expelling: 'What the *fuck* was that, Blake?'

'He knew it was us,' I explained, catching my breath.

'Tate didn't buy the cover?'

'Not just these vessels.'

'What do you mean?' Penrose asked, looking at me in the rear mirror.

'Tate knew that it was me—Blake. Fielding must have known the director would send us out to find information from his variants.'

'How is that possible?' Carroll asked.

'I guess he was one step ahead of us.'

'Tate was part of Leveller?'

'Or was just assisting them.'

'But why did you have to shoot him?' Penrose asked.

'Because he was too dangerous to be kept alive. Tate could have notified Leveller, making them aware we are hunting for the remaining terrorist.'

Carroll sat back to process what I had said.

Suddenly, bullets started hitting the car—the back window exploded. Glass dispersed everywhere. Reacting, I turned around, aiming the handgun outwards. Two other vehicles were tailing us.

'The security guards, by any chance?' Penrose asked.

'Correct,' I said before releasing a few rounds.

Suddenly, Penrose made an abrasive move, turning the steering wheel right, adjusting upwards, sending the car banking down through countless rows of traffic. Colossal skyscrapers framed our view.

'Hold on!' he shouted, turning on the windscreen wipers to accommodate the rainfall.

He started manoeuvring the hover car through the dense congestion, narrowly missing a few. The guards continued to follow us. I held on. The vehicle gyrated. There were loud, howling winds circulating from the back. But I could still hear a loud explosion as one pursuing car collided with traffic.

The remaining attacking car had avoided the congestion, flying overhead. And as we eventually reached the other side of the traffic, it curved downwards until coming parallel alongside us.

'They seem very loyal for hired guns,' I said. 'I guess Tate must have paid well.'

'You did just kill their saviour,' Carroll replied sarcastically.

I undid my side window, revealing the handgun—firing at them. Conscious of limited ammunition, I asked Penrose: 'Are we close to the headquarters?'

'Not too far.'

The attacking car suddenly swerved erratically, hamming into the side of our vehicle, causing their back door to swing wide open. Penrose momentarily lost control of the steering. A guard in the backseat started firing at us. Instinctively, Carroll and I ducked, shielding our heads.

Looking back, I saw the guard had emptied his clip, reaching for a replacement in his breast harness.

The door was now attached loosely at the hinges.

I directed at Penrose: 'Get closer to the car.'

'What?'

'Just do it!'

Reluctantly, Penrose obliged, swerving the car towards the attackers. As this happened, I opened my car door, took a moment to evaluate the distance, and pushed myself outwards.

I flew forward, weightless, an endless drop below, rain cascading down upon me, the wind blowing against my face, the muffled sound of distant car horns nearby, as I focused on the car opposite. At that moment, considering the possibility that I had miscalculated the jump, I watched as the guard, loading his weapon, looked up, registering me hurtling towards him.

I impacted, my muscular frame engulfing his. I rolled over, crumbling against the opposite door. Barely able to process the pain and world from this angle, I reached for his wrist, pushing it towards the rear window. He reacted, firing a few bullets. The sound was deafening in this enclosed space. With my handgun, I repeatedly smashed it against his head until he stopped firing and recoiled in agony, blood dripping everywhere. As he did this, I grabbed his weapon, manoeuvring myself into a sitting position with the guns aimed at him and the driver.

Expecting them to submit, I was outraged when the driver produced a gun, turned back, and started firing. Instinctively, I leant down to cover myself. He peppered the other guard.

The driver had lost control of the steering wheel. I felt the car turning. He returned his focus. I chanced upon the opportunity, leaning upward and smashing him in the side of the head with one of the handguns. He fell unconscious. Frantically, I leaned over, grabbed the steering wheel, and tried stabilising the vehicle.

I looked back at Carroll. She gestured ahead. I followed her eye line. In the short distance stood the towering, white agency headquarters. Looking downwards, I could see we were now close to street level. I adjusted the steering wheel, forcing the car downwards.

It started hurtling towards the ground.

I waited painstakingly for the right moment.

Just before impact, I let go of the wheel, leaned back, pushed aside the dead guard, and launched myself out of the back door.

I flipped forward, colliding with the ground. Because I was facing in a different direction from the vehicle's momentum, I suddenly flipped leftwards onto my side. I tossed over repeatedly until I came to a stop, lying on my back. The hover car smashed against the ground, skidding until finally grinding to a halt, missing oncoming pedestrians.

I lay there in excruciating pain, looking upwards at the hostile, grey skies. Had I broken any bones? I refrained from moving the vessel and focused on taking deep breaths. Adrenaline pulsated through his bloodstream.

Suspecting that the vessel had a concussion, I couldn't judge how long it took for Penrose and Carroll to land and reach me. But they eventually knelt next to me with grave expressions on their faces.

'Jackson! Are you okay?' Carroll asked.

'I've been better.'

'Talk about making a scene.' Penrose laughed anxiously.

I looked around at civilians gathered nearby, looking equally shocked and curious.

Penrose looked at my body. 'Can you move?'

'I guess there is only one way to find out.' Again, I became aware that I was using someone else's vessel. Ignoring specific signals firing in the brain, I first assessed the fingers and toes, which worked, and once confident, I forced the body to sit upright. Gradually, it responded. I was able to lean upwards.

I could feel a searing pain erupt down the body. Carroll and Penrose put an arm around the back for support. I took a few moments, allowing the body to adapt, before pushing both hands down onto the wet floor for support and standing to full height. I felt a tense pressure in the head from the concussion.

They ushered me towards the headquarters.

An assistant showed us into the room with the circular granite table. The director was sitting at it, preoccupied with a tablet computer. Hearing us enter, he looked up, noticing the disconcerted expressions on our faces.

'I didn't hear from you after Styles engaged the target?'

'Yes, sir, things got a little out of hand,' Carroll said awkwardly.

We stood before him.

The director placed the tablet down and stood up. 'What do you mean?' I walked forward and explained the situation. As this happened, the variant, like the one I knew, looked at me with that constant sceptical glare, digesting the news. Once I had finished, he looked away, clearly restraining himself, before looking at me. 'I don't care how you operate in your world. But we *do not* have instances like this *here!*'

'I hold myself fully accountable, sir,' I said, raising my chin.

'You said that drones were filming the luncheon?' he asked.

'Yes, sir.'

'We will have to remove you three from the footage.'

'Despite that effort,' Carroll interjected, 'there might have been informants in the crowd who could notify Leveller?'

'That might be the case.' He eyed us all. 'But quite frankly, I approved this mission for your world's interests, not mine. Subsequently, you have assassinated a public figure and caused collateral damage.'

'Sir,' I said, 'with all due respect, although the terrorists have not directly targeted your world, they are still operating here. Without our input, you would have been none the wiser.'

The director tensed his jaw, looking me fiercely in the eyes. 'The *real* Styles wouldn't have made such a misjudgement.' Despite how much those words cut into me, I maintained a neutral expression. Would another variant have done better in my situation? 'I think it's time you returned to your world.'

'Yes, sir,' we all said in unison.

The director gestured us towards the room containing the quantum migrator. The same technician was waiting. She asked for us to take our original seats.

Following her command, I sat on the recliner, eased the battered body, and submerged the head inside the brain scanner. There was an uncomfortable silence. I could sense the director standing nearby, waiting for his variants to return.

I allowed the technician to attach the three ECG electrode pads to the chest. As she did this, I looked at the vessel for the final time, experiencing an unpleasant feeling.

Now, I knew what it was like to experience a different life. A different outcome. Better prospects.

Was it wrong to feel reluctant to leave?

Moments later, the technician announced everything was ready to traverse into our original dimension. My finger hovered over the button. Looking down at the touchpad, I was hesitant to press it.

But I remembered the mission. Closing my eyes, I took a deep breath, activating the migrator.

Twenty

'What *the hell* were you thinking?!' The director slammed his hands down on the long table. 'A *complete lack* of emotional intelligence. You have undermined our relations with that reality and potentially ruined this mission.'

'Sir, I—'

'In Blake's defence, sir,' Penrose interjected. We exchanged glances across the table. 'Before we even walked into the place, Tate already knew we were coming.'

'How is that possible?'

'Sir,' I said firmly. 'We now know that civilian variants of Fielding are aware of our organisation and plan, which, despite making things harder for us, is invaluable intelligence. We were effectively walking into a trap. Those guards weren't just average security but had some military background. Recruited for Tate's protection, not just to herd the chauvinistic cattle. Unless I took action, Tate could have contacted the remaining terrorist and made him aware that we were doing what he expected us to do.'

'It's better to appear one step behind instead of being two, sir,' Carroll added.

'But you could have brought Tate in for questioning?' the director said.

'Yes,' I replied, 'but I had to decide. There were too many guards and civilians in the way.'

The director looked at all three of us individually, evidently concocting a throwback. But instead, he stood upright, breathing through his nose.

'How was Fielding able to contact Tate? Did the variant mention anything about a quantum migrator?'

'No, sir. Fielding might have people working for him in Tate's world.'

'Let's just hope no one else contacted the remaining member of Leveller on Tate's behalf. It would appear highly suspicious that the variant dies during this twenty-four-hour countdown.'

'Politics,' I muttered.

The director heard this, frowning. 'You will each receive an assessment from Qubit. Once done, we can discuss the best course of action.'

And with that, he stormed out of the room.

'Well, considering, I thought he took that pretty well,' Carroll said, sitting back in her chair. She saw Qubit looking at her and pointed at herself.

'Yes, you're first up.' Carroll followed him through.

'I have to admit.' Penrose turned to face me. 'Your methods are unorthodox. But it took courage to make that call. You're not the first person to trail-blaze through other dimensions. Ironically, Fielding was just the same when we worked together.'

'The director is right, though—Tate caught me off guard and knew which nerves to hit.'

'How so?'

'He talked about my family.'

'Why didn't you mention this?'

I sat there trying to make an excuse but decided to be honest: 'It was my ego.'

'How did he know about your family?'

'Perhaps Fielding gave Tate information in the likelihood that I would join the task force and approach him.'

'That makes sense.' Penrose stood. 'I will inform the director.'

'He will probably rip my head off for not mentioning that before—'

Penrose smiled, putting out a hand to stop me. 'Look, this has more to do with Fielding outwitting the director. That will be his biggest priority.'

'Good point.'

'Take a breather. I will go in next for an assessment to give you extra time.'

'It's appreciated.' I nodded. 'In that case, I will follow you out.'

And with that, I stood, and we walked into the control room where the director was in deep discussion with Okoro and Alejo. I hurriedly walked past, opened the door, and emerged into the main corridor.

Once this happened, I reconnected with the ordinary world, taking a deep breath. Suddenly, I felt an unexpected sensation. Because of the heated debriefing, confined within that room, I hadn't paid attention to the disorientation I felt.

Was it a side effect of being in a variant's vessel? Or, because my body had just been linked up to the quantum migrator whilst high on drugs?

I didn't expect to feel so out of balance. The nausea was overwhelming.

It struck me—the memory of Tate's face.

There was so much at stake. I couldn't make reckless decisions. Was I going to derail the mission? Would I be accountable for the deaths of billions, perhaps trillions of lives?

I knew the sensible thing would be to wait until my assessment with Qubit. But I was irritable—a craving for the Statera.

I walked down the corridor to the toilets, went inside, checked nobody else was present, locked the door, and topped up the dosage.

Minutes later, I felt slightly relieved. My hands were no longer quivering.

I thought about Julia. Withdrawing my phone, I turned on the screen and couldn't see any notifications from her. I felt nauseous.

What had happened to her?

Riddled with fear, I paced back towards the experimental branch. Noticing that Penrose was no longer in the control room, I walked straight through. Carroll passed me, smiling. I stood aside, allowing her to go past.

'I hope that wasn't too painful?'

'What can I say? Qubit seems to think my sanity is just about intact.'

'Is it an in-depth assessment?'

'He just asks questions to ensure you are completely certain of your reality.' She looked towards the doorway. 'Nature calls. See you shortly.'

I walked into the main room where the quantum migrator was based. To the side was the single door. Behind this, I could hear the muffled, indistinct conversation between Penrose and Qubit.

Deciding to wait, I walked over to the computer and array of suspended screens, displaying data and graphs I couldn't decipher. One screen showed the primary interface for the quantum network.

Easing forward—I looked over my shoulder to check no one was looking—and inspected the screen. Upon it were separate tables for each task force member. They homed long lists of ten-digit numbers. I presumed these were the different configurations.

I looked at my table, amazed by how many were listed. Using the down button on the keyboard, I started clicking through the list, looking at the collection of configurations, pondering what realities these would reveal.

As I stood there looking on, thoughts circulated in my head.

Suddenly, a voice was calling out to me. Looking towards its source, I saw Qubit standing nearby.

'Blake?' he repeated.

'Yes, sorry,' I said, looking towards him.

Behind, Penrose was making his way towards the conference room.

'Ready for your assessment?'

'Just through there?' I pointed to the side door.

'Correct.' Qubit read my expression. He knew there was something untoward.

'I was just, um,' I waffled, looking back at the screen. 'I was admiring the migrator.'

'Ah, yes.' He stepped forward. 'Isn't it an amazing experience?'

'It has changed my life.'

'Then let's ensure you're all present and correct, shall we?' He gestured towards the side door.

'Of course.'

And with that, I followed him.

Twenty-One

He was awoken abruptly by the ringing phone. At first, it was like a hypnotic, repetitive noise, muffled in the background of a dream, before coming to the forefront of his attention.

Once acutely aware that it was real, Sebastian opened his eyes, trying to register the noise source. He was lying in bed, his naked frame entangled with the young woman. Her groans of protest forced him to search for the phone. It was on a bedside table, rattling.

Sebastian leaned over, picked it up, and answered the call.

'Yes?' he croaked, rubbing one eye with the palm of his hand.

'Mr Howler, I hope I haven't caught you at the wrong time?'

He didn't recognise her voice. 'I just…No, it's fine. Who is calling?'

'This is Mr Miller's P.A, Emilia. You can call me Em.' She giggled. 'I just wanted to check in and ensure we are all set for this evening.'

Sebastian became wide-eyed. 'What is happening?'

'You are coming on Rufus's show.'

'Ah, yes! Sorry, I lost track of the days.'

'We are excited to have you on as a guest. I have listened to the new album and *love it*.'

He leaned back, smiling. 'Oh, really?'

The young woman stirred, looked up, and asked who was calling. Sebastian put his hand to the receiver, mouthing the answer.

Meanwhile, the P. A continued: 'If I may say so, Mr Howler, it is your best effort yet.'

'Thank you.'

'Most arrangements are in place for your performance. We are still trying to source dry ice and a few items for your rider. Out of interest, have you decided which song you'll play off the new record?'

'Most probably 'One Man Army'.'

'Oh, great! I love that song. We will need you in the studio at four o'clock for the sound check.'

'No problem,'—Sebastian looked at his wristwatch. He still had a few hours—'You should speak to my manager about the backing band and equipment.'

'Yes, I have been on the phone with Marvin. I just wanted to speak to you personally.'

'Then I shall see you later?'

'Yes, thank you, Mr Howler.'

'You can call me Sebastian, by the way.'

'Okay.' She giggled.

'Well, I look forward to meeting you later, Em.'

'Bye for now.'

'Ciao.' He ended the call, threw the phone onto the bed, and lay back.

'Do you have time before heading off?' the woman asked, hugging his bare chest.

'Yeah. But I need to get into the right mindset.' He uncurled, stood up, and walked over to the closed curtains.

Reaching forward, he drew them open. Sunlight radiated into the room. The woman protested with a groan, burying her face in a pillow.

Sebastian stood fully naked, stretching, looking out at the world. Above, blue skies were breaking through the clouds. Below, various people were walking around. On either side of the road, large billboards offered underwater package holidays, cosmetic surgery deals for children, and virtual reality dating.

Howler looked at a billboard with his face brandished across it— one of many around the city. Part of the marketing campaign for the new album. He looked at himself, critiquing the photo they had used, not pleased with how it looked. They made him look fat. He rubbed his jaw, sighing.

'I wouldn't stand there for too long if I were you,' the woman said, rolling onto her back. 'Paparazzi will be waiting downstairs. And you don't want to scare them with that small thing hanging out!'

Sebastian closed the curtains, turned to face her, and sulked, 'At least that would give me *some* publicity.'

'Oh, come on!' She sat upright. 'You can't be that desperate. Just because album sales haven't skyrocketed.'

'Clara, things could be a lot better. I'm just hoping tonight helps.' He sat down on the edge of the bed.

She leaned forward, throwing her arms around his neck.

'Miller has the highest viewing ratings. Anyone who goes on his show always gets good exposure. Just show everybody the *real* Sebastian Howler.'

'Instead of what?'

'Instead of this arsehole persona you always put on.' Clara whispered in his ear: 'I know the real sensitive, poetic soul.'

'Well, I better do something right; otherwise, I will lose that endorsement. I need the cash. This lifestyle won't pay for itself.'

'Which endorsement?

'For the appetite-suppression tablets?'

'Oh, yeah. Look, Miller is renowned for asking provocative questions. He always gets the answers out of people. That is why he is the best talk show host. Just go on there tonight and be honest.'

'Yeah, you're right.' Sebastian turned, looking her in the eye, smiling.

Clara pulled him backwards. They fell onto the bed.

Twenty-Two

After my assessment, which was stress-free, we joined everyone in the conference room. I took a seat next to Qubit. The other two sat adjacent. Meanwhile, the director was standing at the head of the table.

I was waiting for the drugs to kick in.

'You were in Tate's reality for three of his hours. We currently have twelve left of our own,' the director spoke.

'Has anything materialised from questioning Fielding? I asked.

'Nothing,' the director said bluntly. 'We have tried every single method in the book. But Fielding isn't giving any information. He was telling the truth—Doctor Aditi wiped memories from his brain.'

'What about the task force?' Penrose asked.

'Again, nothing.' The director huffed. 'Every trace of Fielding's operations was lost in the nano-bombing.'

I exchanged disconcerted glances with the other two.

'Have they had better luck in other realities interrogating the terrorists there?' Penrose asked.

'Negative,' the director replied. 'The only good news is that agents in other dimensions are also on the case. But, I think we can unanimously agree that we can no longer rely upon the resources of agent variants to help with this search.'

'What is the alternative?' I asked.

'On a few occasions, we have traversed into civilian variants,' Carroll suggested.

'How do they have access to quantum migrators?' I asked.

'There are some realities where devices have been developed purely for commercial or scientific means,' the director explained. 'We have kept a log of these realities where there are civilian variants of you all.'

'Sir, how about we each go in separate directions?' Penrose asked.

'What do you mean?' I asked.

'We don't go into the same shared reality,' he explained. 'Both Carroll and I have done that before.'

The director nodded. 'We could cover more ground that way. Unless you need to discuss anything else, let's proceed.'

He gestured towards the door. And with that, we all stood, following him through. I retook my seat at the device. Meanwhile, the director and Qubit went over to the central console.

I looked over, watching them interact with the interface. Thankfully, they didn't notice I had tampered with it. Instead, they searched for a new reality to send me to.

Minutes later, Qubit came to me and said, 'There is one civilian variant currently plugged into their device. It is the ideal opportunity for you to traverse.'

'Who is he?'

'His name is Thom Sayer. He is a freelance photographer taking part in a scientific experiment. The agency doesn't exist in his reality. Fielding's variant is a business tycoon. His name is Wallace Braithwaite.'

'How do I gain access to Braithwaite?'

'You will just have to use your training, Blake.' He smiled.

'Don't I need a full debriefing before traversing?'

'We don't know much else. I'm sure you can adapt.' That wasn't standard procedure. 'Just remember that you will be using Sayer's vessel without permission.'

'Okay,' I said reluctantly. 'Is that ethical?'

'"Desperate times...", Blake. You know the rest.'

I lowered myself underneath the brain scanner. 'How did you find Sayer in the first place?'

'When we first discovered their computer in the network, we added his configuration to our database. And then I established a continuous connection with their computer.'

'How does that work?'

'I sent through an unnoticeable patch that is essentially a bridge between realities.'

'What is that for?'

'Basically, it enables the sending and receiving of information.'

'Will they know it is on their computer?'

'Highly unlikely.'

'Is my consciousness the only thing you can send using the patch?'

'We can use the patch to communicate across dimensions.'

'How can I access this?'

'The patch will install a small program that adapts to the design of their computer's interface. In this case, it will appear on the hard-drive utility application as an additional tab called 'QN'.

'Quantum network?'

'Correct. Through this, you can traverse dimensions and communicate.' He brought forward the cable.

'What is the time difference in his dimension?'

'Four of our hours equates to one of their days. Now listen carefully—When you step away from the computer, you disconnect from the quantum network. Once you re-engage, you will traverse.'

'Once I reconnect to their computer, will Sayer's consciousness return to the vessel?'

'Correct.' Qubit attached the ECG electrode pads.

I closed my eyes. A few minutes later, I could hear humming from inside the scanner. I reached for the touchpad, hovering my fingers above the button.

I had to do better this time.

The director authorised the activation.

And with that, my consciousness traversed the new reality.

Twenty-Three

I opened my eyes. There was a clinically lit glass cubicle. Beyond were several other areas. In front of me were three people dressed in laboratory coats. They had their backs turned, preoccupied with their quantum computer, similar in shape to my reality, with several cables sprouting off and overhanging screens relaying data.

Usually, when undercover impersonating someone, you would have prior knowledge of their behaviour through observations and heavily detailed descriptions. But I had walked into this blind. Although I was using Sayer's vessel, I had to be careful not to convey my personality and body language—the less unwarranted attention, the better.

In my reality, I had an abundance of resources at my fingertips. Infiltrating the inner circle of a target was relatively straightforward. But here, as a civilian—and not understanding this reality—I had limited chances of gaining access to Braithwaite.

I looked down at the vessel. Like in my reality, this variant required an endotracheal tube to help breathe whilst sedated. It was protruding from the mouth. Sayer had a thinner frame, less muscular. For a moment, I sat there observing sensations within the body. Despite not having my physique, he felt healthier. Not as mentally congested.

I returned my gaze to the three scientists—an older man with grey hair, a goatee and glasses. And two younger colleagues. One was a young woman with tied-back ginger hair. The other was a tall man with a shaved head.

They saw that my observations had caused a change of activity in the vessel—there was an image of a brain on the screen, now pulsating. The older scientist turned around. Seeing me sitting there with my eyes open, he appeared shocked, walking forward.

He was wearing a lanyard with an identity card attached. On this, it read UCL Knowledge Lab. Underneath was a photo and his name: Professor Maxwell Everett.

'Mr Sayer?' He leaned over, looking into my eyes. 'Can you hear me?'

I nodded.

'Are you fully awake?'

I nodded again.

'Let me remove this.' He reached up, unfastening tape on either cheek, and slowly withdrew the tube from my trachea. A small trail of saliva dripped onto the torso. Placing the tube aside, he looked back at me.

I tried to convey confusion: 'Do you know what happened?'

The vessel's voice sounded gentler—I suspected Sayer didn't lead the same high-risk, self-destructive lifestyle.

'We were taking scans, examining your brain activity in an unconscious state.' He looked down at the intravenous cannula attached to the vessel's left arm. Around the other was wrapped a heart monitoring pad. 'This is most strange!'

'Everything okay?' the woman called.

'Mr Sayer *is* awake,' he announced.

They drew forward, looking over his shoulders at me.

'Can you move your body?' the other man asked.

I moved the limbs, feeling tension in the right leg.

'Can you remember how you got here?' she asked.

Good question.

'I came here,'—at the corner of my eye, I saw the professor's watch—'this morning. You've been conducting experiments using the quantum computer.'

'Very well.' The professor stood upwards, rubbing his goatee. He turned away to exchange comments with his colleagues. A few moments later, he turned to me: 'Mr Sayer, I don't want to cause you

138

alarm but should make you aware that what has happened is…unexpected.'

'What do you mean?'

'You were in an induced coma. The anaesthetic I administered was a high dosage to ensure you remained unconscious during the procedure. Admittedly, there have been cases when subjects have woken up.'

'Will this cause any brain damage?' I asked.

He was hesitant to respond. 'I can't imagine that would be the case. We have tested various scenarios using simulations.'

'No animal testing?'

All three of them looked at me, puzzled. 'Of course not, Mr Sayer! Why on Earth would you suggest such a thing?' I was beginning to distinguish dimension dissimilarities. I laughed in a manner to suggest I was being sarcastic. The professor acknowledged this, shaking his head mockingly. 'Hilarious, Mr Sayer. I think it best that we stop tests for today. Are you available at the same time next week?'

'I'm sure that won't be a problem.'

'Very good. Now, let me help you with those. Please stay still.' The professor withdrew the cable, applied a plaster to alleviate the bleeding, and unwrapped the pad. I eased the vessel from under the small brain scanner and stood up. Meanwhile, his colleagues went back to analyse the data on the screen. 'What with scarce funding, we appreciate you freely offering yourself in the name of scientific discovery.'

'Just mention me in your Nobel Prize speech.'

'The what?'

Another dissimilarity.

'It doesn't matter. Why can't you source more funding?'

'The university believes that consciousness transference is not their highest priority and would rather invest in other initiatives.' His eyebrow rose. 'I have explained this to you before.'

'Sorry, I can be forgetful.'

He smiled. 'That is quite all right. Are you okay to see yourself out?'

'Not a problem,' I said, looking towards the door. 'See you next week.'

'Once again—thank you, Mr Sayer. We appreciate your help.'

'Bye, for now.'

I walked towards the entrance, exchanging smiles with the other scientists, before stepping out into the main area, which consisted of walkways interlinking the various glassed research areas. Briefly, I looked over my shoulder, seeing the professor looking in my direction—he was concerned about my change in temperament.

A few people walked past. I followed them, unclear how I could get out of the facility. They led me down a corridor to changing rooms. I walked inside. Before me were rows of lockers and benches. Other people were preoccupied with undressing and talking amongst themselves.

I rummaged inside the trouser pockets and found a key with a numbered tag. Finding the locker, I opened it. Inside, there was a black rucksack and jacket. I withdrew them from the locker, put on the jacket, and slung one of the rucksack straps over a shoulder before leaving the changing rooms. Scaling the stairs, I reached the ground floor and found the white-framed glass entrance.

Stepping out onto metal stairs leading to the street, I looked at the buildings in front of me made from brick—possibly factory conversion offices. This reality didn't appear as physically dissimilar compared to my last experience. Knowing where the University College London campus stood, I suspected I was somewhere nearby in the city centre.

I took a right, walking down a long, cobbled street until I emerged onto a busy road. On the left corner was a pub. I sat on a wooden bench outside, drawing forward the rucksack to inspect it.

In the front pocket was a wallet containing a credit card from an unrecognisable bank, keys and a phone. The latter had a cracked screen and scuffed case. The battery was dead. I opened the main compartment, looking for a phone charger, but Sayer hadn't packed one.

Instead, inside was a laptop, a large black case—I suspected to accommodate a digital SLR camera—and a passport. Inside the latter were Sayer's personal information and several stamps. He was well-travelled. In a paper bag was a half-eaten croissant. There was also an empty metal water bottle and another phone.

I withdrew it, turning on the screen. The locking function recognised the variant's face, opening onto the main screen. The background was a generic photo of a lake surrounded by snow-capped mountains. I opened a web browser application and typed in the name of Fielding's variant in this reality—Wallace Braithwaite.

The search result presented links to recent news articles about the tycoon. I opened the latest. It showed a photo of Braithwaite. He was tanned, wearing expensive clothing, posing with an equally smug multi-billionaire. They appeared to be standing aboard a yacht in blazing sunshine.

The article detailed Braithwaite's latest venture, landing him a higher position on the world's richest list. I skimmed through, reading that he had just amassed a large fortune from significant tech investments.

These variants struck well in life.

I remembered the memory of the park pond.

Reading further articles, I couldn't find his current location. How was I going to reach him?

I opened the email application and scrolled through the inbox. There were messages from various business partners and commission invoices. Amongst these was one name that kept cropping up—Amara Lennox.

I read some of their conversations, seeing she was a freelance journalist. Sayer had collaborated with her on several occasions. What drew my attention was the mention of articles about high-profile people.

Could she have written a piece about Braithwaite?

I used the search function, typing in his name. It proved unforthcoming.

But if I spoke to her, could she offer me information?

I opened the contacts application and searched for her name. A bartender came outside, collecting empty glasses nearby, asking if I wanted anything. Politely declining, I pressed the call button, placing the phone to my ear. Looking at the passing traffic, I waited patiently as the phone rang. It continued for a minute. Cancelling the call, I put the phone aside and inspected the camera.

Suddenly, the phone started ringing. I picked up the device—Lennox was returning the call. Accepting it, I placed the phone to my ear.

'Hi, Thom!' She sounded younger. There was a sharpness in her voice.

'Hi, Amara.'

'I was literally walking back into my office and missed your call. How are you?'

'Yeah, I'm okay! I just thought I'd check in with you. See how things are.'

'I'm good. Work has been pretty dry at the moment. Considering taking on some mindless-rags work to help pay the rent.'

'What do you mean by that?'

'You know—do some pieces for glamour and high-end magazines. It's beneath me but might open doors to a new audience.'

'True.'

'How about you?'

'Oh, you know—the same old. I was calling to see whether you might have any work on and need assistance?'

'I'm meeting an editor in the afternoon to discuss potential work. They might pay for an external photographer.'

'Perhaps we could meet beforehand?'

'I'm available now.'

'Great. Where at?'

'I'll send you the location. It's a coffee shop on Dalston Square I love going to. Wait a sec.' Moments later, a notification came through. I clicked on the link. The phone opened a map application, showing directions to the meeting point. 'How long will it take for you to get there?'

'About forty minutes.'

'Sounds good to me.'

'See you shortly.'

'Bye.'

'Bye.' I cancelled the call.

Fastening the bag, I slung on both straps, stood, and followed the provided route. My estimation was correct—I was in the Holborn area. The travel itinerary on the application showed that the tube system was the same as in my reality. I would head for the nearest station.

All the while, I was aware of a tension in the right leg.

Walking further, I saw nuances in the city design—hydroponics covered most buildings. Around me, the streets were pristine, bustling with civilians.

Thankfully, the credit card in his wallet was contactless for me to use for public transport. But by using it, I couldn't fully cover my tracks—he would eventually receive a bill detailing my transactions. There was an element of guilt in using his vessel and money without permission. But it was necessary for the mission.

I took the Piccadilly Line from Holborn to King's Cross, the Victoria Line to Highbury & Islington, and the Overground to Dalston Kingsland. All the while, I contemplated how I would engage Lennox.

Exiting the station, I headed southward on Kingsland High Street, crossed the road, took a left onto Dalston Lane, and a right onto Dalston Square. To either side were large apartment buildings. Trees framed the open area. To the left stood the coffee shop. In most situations, I would survey the surrounding area before entering but had to remind myself that I was not an agent in this reality.

Approaching the coffee shop, I closed the application, turned off the screen, pocketed the phone, and walked inside. To the right was the service area, where a few baristas stood making drinks. I looked around and could see one table available. I walked over to it, removed the rucksack, placed it underneath, and sat down. In quiet contemplation, I thought about the time difference in this reality.

Suddenly, I felt the presence of someone standing over me. As I looked upwards, a casually dressed woman sat down.

'Hi, Thom!' she said, placing a shoulder bag aside. She looked at the awkward expression on my face. 'Are you…okay?'

Self-conscious, I sat up straight, smiling. 'Sorry, Amara. I was a million miles away.'

'What would you like?' she asked.

It took me a few moments to process her question, focusing on her appearance. I recognised her. In my reality, she was the woman trying to expose the extraction—the same woman on the billboard in Tate's world: Elina Wells.

Twenty-Four

'A flat white would be great,' I finally replied.

'Sure.' She stood.

'Thanks.'

As she walked off, I took a few moments to compose myself, realising that I wasn't playing the part of Sayer or whatever that was supposed to be. His voice was softer. He was a photographer. Perhaps he was more of a silent type.

I hoped their relationship was strictly professional and she wouldn't ask personal questions. Otherwise, I would blow my cover. Overly conscious of the vessel's posture, I sat upright but relaxed.

Moments later, I heard Lennox returning.

'There you go.' She placed the coffees down before retaking her seat.

'Thanks.'

'No worries.' She rustled in her seat to get comfortable. 'So, how's life been treating you?'

I knew that was coming. 'It's been… all right.'

Seriously?

She laughed. 'You're always nondescript.'

Just as well.

'How about you?'

'Yeah, I just moved into a new flat with my partner. It's *so* nice having our own space instead of flat-sharing with random people. I've set up an office where I can write.'

'Sounds nice.'

'How is the dark room coming along?'

I took a sip of the coffee. 'The what?'

'Last time we worked together, you told me you were building a darkroom to develop your photos?'

'Oh, yeah—it is nearly done.'

'Even though we live in the digital age, I can see the appeal of using film.'

'I appreciate the aesthetic and development process.'

'Yeah, I hear you. Like, I enjoy the convenience of having a voice recording app but prefer a good old pad and pen.'

'Definitely.' I decided to move forward from the small talk: 'Has work been quiet recently?'

'Yeah.' She sighed pensively. 'I do the odd piece for lifestyle blogs. They can pay good money. Everything is good nowadays. I don't have much to sink my teeth into.'

Based upon her variant's interests, I asked: 'Like more social issues, do you mean?'

'Exactly! I mean, I can't complain—we live in a great society. Everyone has equal opportunities and treatment. The economy is healthy and sustaining. We are avoiding the threat of ecological collapse. And have a government that stands for the people.

'For someone like me, there needs to be something *real* to investigate, you know? But, I have been side-lined to writing boring pieces. I guess I need to be a little more,'—she presented bending, opposing double fingers to represent abbreviation—'positively minded. Embrace how well things are. And just be grateful for how I am making a living from my passion.'

'Definitely.' It was time to shift the conversation: 'I don't suppose you read the news this morning? I saw an article about Wallace Braithwaite.'

'Yeah, I heard about him becoming even more exceedingly rich. Comes across as a bit of a prick, from what I have seen.'

'Have you considered doing a piece about him? I'm sure he would be an interesting person to interview.'

'I mean, the guy is probably very busy and wouldn't agree to be interviewed by someone like me.' She took a large sip of her drink. 'But now you mention it, I've considered doing something. More a break away from the norm, shall we say.'

'What do you mean?' I took another sip, wiping away the crème moustache.

'I have researched his empire and would like to do further digging.'

I sat forward. 'You think there is something suspicious going on?'

'That might be the case. But it's difficult gaining access to people like him.'

'Do you know of Leveller?'

She shook her head. 'No, I've never heard of that before. What is it?'

'Never mind. Who are you meeting this afternoon?'

'Eva Courtney. Editor-in-chief for Fortuna magazine.'

'What is that?'

She found this comical. 'A glossy magazine that showcases the super-rich.'

'Why have you decided to write for them?'

'She contacted me. I can't turn down a meeting.'

'Fair enough.'

Lennox picked up her phone, turning on the screen. 'I have a meeting with her in thirty-two minutes. Best to book a taxi. If the meeting goes well, shall I ask her if there is any work for you?'

'Please.'

'No worries.'

'What is it you suspect about Braithwaite?'

'Possible illegal dealings.'

'What like?'

Operating the phone, she looked up at me. 'I suspect Braithwaite is trying to play outside the regulations and tax system.'

'Isn't that always the case?'

Lennox put down the phone. 'Not at all. International legislation prohibits it.' Another dissimilarity. 'He has amassed wealth from mineral mining, big tech and energy investment. I suspect he is also money laundering and tax-evading.'

I placed the empty mug down, sitting back. 'You seem pretty sure of this?'

'It is common knowledge for those who do their research. But he works so discreetly, meandering through the loopholes. It goes unnoticed.'

'You want to expose him?'

Amara looked fiercely into my eyes. 'You bet.' She looked at her phone. 'The taxi is nearly here. Let's see what happens. I can call you afterwards?'

'Perfect. Thanks for the coffee.'

Lennox stood, collecting her shoulder bag. I joined her at eye level. 'You know, there seems to be something about you today, Thom.'

'What do you mean?'

'I don't know. You seem less reserved?'

'Aren't I always?'

She laughed, putting a hand on my wrist. 'Speak later.'

With that, she walked away. Moments later, the entrance closed behind her.

The meeting was a dead lead. I needed to consider other ways to gain access to the variant.

The other phone in the rucksack—perhaps that could provide some ideas?

Twenty-Five

Leaving the coffee shop, I walked out into the square. Sunlight radiated down upon me. Sayer's wristwatch showed it was eleven hundred hours and seven minutes. I walked back onto Kingsland High Street, passing hipsters, elderly shoppers and young families. Car horns sounded. Music was blaring from a distant speaker.

Aware of tension in the right leg, I ignored it.

In the distance, I saw an electronic shop advertising the refurbishing and unlocking of phones. Entering, an assistant stood behind the counter.

'My friend, how are you?' he asked in an overly friendly manner.

'I am good, thanks. Do you have chargers for this type of phone?'

Inspecting it, he brought one forward. Making the payment—and asking for a receipt in case Sayer eventually wanted a refund—I saw a plug socket nearby.

'Do you mind if I charge my phone over there?' I asked.

'Of course,' the assistant replied, handing me the receipt before serving another customer.

I walked over to the wall, removed one strap from the rucksack, swung it around, opened the front compartment, withdrew the phone, and plugged in both ends before setting aside the phone to charge. Knowing I had to wait, I removed the camera case from the bag. Unzipping it, I pulled out the device. There was a large lens attached. Replacing the case into the rucksack, I turned on the camera. The LED screen came to life.

I activated the photo library. Nothing appeared. The SD card inside the camera was the only one I could find. Despite it having one-hundred-and-twenty-eight gigabits of memory, he hadn't left anything on there.

Replacing the camera into the rucksack, I pulled out the laptop and opened it. The screen instantly came to life. The background was, I suspected, one of Sayer's photos: a black-and-white street scene. Possibly in Paris. Excellent proportions and use of shadow. Along the bottom of the screen, there was a photo editing application. I opened folders, looking for anything, but just like the camera, the laptop also appeared empty.

Replacing the laptop into the bag, I picked up the charging phone. Pressing the power button, I expected to see a symbol on the screen appear telling me that the phone was charging. But nothing happened. I then lay the phone aside and waited several minutes until trying again. But still the same issue.

I walked over to the assistant. 'This phone charger doesn't seem to work. Can I try another one?'

He presented another option.

'Umar?' someone called from the back of the shop.

The assistant responded, walking to speak with them.

I tried the same thing again. But this also proved unforthcoming.

'No luck?' the assistant returned, peering over my shoulder.

'I think there must be something wrong with the phone.' I withdrew the charger cable.

'Probably the battery.'

'Do you sell replacements?'

'We are currently out of stock for that model.'

'Thanks, anyway.' I opened the rucksack, throwing the phone and charger inside.

'I can direct you to another shop nearby that might sell them?'

I faced him. 'I would appreciate that.'

I withdrew the working phone, opened the map application, and gave it to him. He typed in the address of the other store—it was in Hackney Central.

'There you go.'

'Thanks for this.'

'I'm sorry we don't have the battery in stock.'

'No problem.' I looked at him. 'This gives me a chance to stretch my legs.'

'Now that you mentioned it, Thom—I was going to say something.'

I refrained from vocalising or looking surprised, instead smiling. 'What do you mean, Umar?'

'Your leg? Have you lost the limp?'

I felt a surge of blood rush to Sayer's cheeks. That would explain the tension I'd felt in my right leg.

'Oh, yeah.' I laughed awkwardly. 'It doesn't seem to give me as much stick these days.'

'Well, that is good to hear.' He patted me on the shoulder. 'I wasn't sure how you would recover.'

'Some days are worse than others.'

'Perhaps it isn't a long-term effect?'

'From what?'

He looked at me curiously. '…The stroke?'

'Yeah, of course.' Again, I laughed awkwardly, then said self-deprecatingly: 'It has impaired my memory.'

He laughed. 'Well, it's good to see you back on form, Thom.'

'Thanks, Umar.'

'How is the dark room coming along?'

'Nearly done.' I was conscious of the time. 'I will drop by again next week.'

'Good to hear.'

He walked towards the entrance, opening the door for me. I accepted his gesture, slung the rucksack over my shoulder, and walked outside.

Turning back, I could see him looking at me.

'You take it easy now, Thom.'

'I will do. Thanks, Umar.'

I would have to take an eastward direction towards the other shop. But I could feel the tension in my right leg increase. Unaware of its weakness, I had subjected it to strain from trying to walk unassisted.

Eventually, walking down Ridley Road past market stalls, I felt an immense, spasming pain erupting. It was as though someone had twisted a knife into the nerves in my upper thigh.

Sayer had a lesser threshold. The pain was unbearable. Dealing with a disability was something I had never experienced before.

I staggered to a bench and sat down, pocketing the phone. Taking a moment to catch my breath, I rubbed the throbbing muscles.

Two thoughts dawned upon me: What else did I not know about Sayer that could compromise the mission? And having this experience, why would I subject my vessel to so much torment by taking an excessive amount of drugs?

I stretched out my leg, hoping this would ease the strain, sitting there surveying the market, hoping people-watching would distract me. I lost track of time, trying to ignore the pain.

Suddenly, the phone started to ring. I withdrew it. Lennox was calling.

Was there a point in answering the call?

I took a moment to compose myself before accepting.

'Hi, Amara.'

'Thom, long time no speak.'

'How did the meeting go?'

'It went well. Eva used to be a freelance journalist and understands the hustle. Anyway, she liked the piece you helped me with about Miriam Olivia—the actor. D'you remember we did it last year?'

'Yes.'

'Well, Eva has offered me to come on board and do some commissions. Because she liked your work, she also agreed to take you on to help me.'

'That's great to hear! Thanks for asking.'

'No worries.'

I considered ending the conversation.

'Eva has an interesting proposition.'

I sat up straight—forgetting about the leg—winching with pain. 'What is it?'

'One of her in-house writers has called in and had to cancel work last-minute because of a family grievance.'

'What was the offer?'

'To review Hotel Tramonto Sull'Oceano. It has just opened.'

'Travel journalism. Okay. And where is that?'

'On the Amalfi Coast in Italy. She told me that Braithwaite is currently holidaying there.'

'That *is* an interesting proposition.'

'Are you thinking what I'm thinking?'

I was beginning to like this woman. 'You bet.'

'But there is one catch.'

'Go on.'

'The writer is meant to fly out this afternoon at five-forty-five from Stansted Airport. It would be for two nights. Are you available?'

'Definitely,' I tried saying casually.

'Okay, great! I'm still at the restaurant and will confirm with Eva. They will need to amend the flight booking. I still have your passport number from last time. Once done here, I will swing past my flat to collect some bits. Is it okay to meet you at the airport?'

'Yes. I have my camera, laptop and passport here with me. I can buy some spare clothes when we get out there.'

'Nice one. Okay, speak shortly.'

'Bye.' I cancelled the call, amazed.

The dead phone battery would have to wait. But I would buy a walking stick.

Fielding's variant was on the Amalfi Coast. I would soon be there. Getting to him was finally tangible.

Twenty-Six

Once I arrived at Stansted Airport, with a stick to aid, I walked towards the departure times board. I scoured the list for flights at the time Lennox mentioned. One of these was for Naples International Airport.

I pulled out the phone and texted Lennox, saying I was waiting near the terminal entrance. Moments later, she replied, letting me know she was nearby.

I still felt aftershocks of pain in my right leg. Walking to an unoccupied seat, I placed the walking stick aside and sat down. I looked at the sea of tourists and business people going about their day.

Overhead, there were screens showing airline advertisements. The aeroplanes had nuclear fusion engines and were more sophisticated in design. There were slogans stating the companies were carbon neutral. Everything seemed advanced, but not at an unsustainable, accelerated rate like in Tate's reality. It seemed better than my reality.

Several minutes later, I received another text from Lennox—she had arrived and was looking for me. I suggested we meet under the departure times board. Walking towards it, I could see her approach from a distance. She had changed into light, comfortable clothing, carrying a backpack.

Smiling as she approached, Lennox said: 'Hey. Ready to go?'

'I sure am. Our departure gate is number seven.'

'Great. I emailed over your boarding pass.'

We proceeded to security. Thankfully, experiencing no issues, we walked through, collected our belongings and headed to the departure lounge. At a shop, I found a pair of sunglasses, a charger for the work phone, and an international plug adapter. Lennox offered to put them on her credit card—Fortuna Magazine would pay for travel expenses.

We then sat, waiting to board.

'What word count is Eva expecting?' I asked.

'Two-thousand. Straightforward stuff.'

'How much is the commission?'

'Twelve hundred for me. One thousand for you.'

I presumed that was a good amount. 'Nice. When is the deadline for the piece?'

'Monday. With a Tuesday release. We fly back Sunday evening, giving us enough time to see what Braithwaite is doing. I wish I could brush up on my Italian before getting there.'

'I'm fluent.'

She looked at me with surprise. 'I never knew that, Thom?'

It was a requirement for an agent operating for a clandestine global organisation. I just hoped there were no linguistic differences in this dimension.

Twenty minutes later, we boarded the flight, placed our bags in the overhead compartment, took our seats, and waited for the flight to take off.

'Do you want one of these?' Lennox leaned over, presenting a bag of sweets. 'I know you get earache whilst flying.'

'Sure, thanks.' I accepted the offering, unravelling the wrapper.

'If you don't mind, I will listen to music.'

'Sure.'

She put on a pair of headphones, sat back, and closed her eyes. It suited me.

Thankfully, there was enough legroom for the flight. I had become accustomed to the limp. I looked out the window, watching the plane reverse, contemplating how to gain access to Braithwaite.

* * *

It only took two hours for our flight to Naples International Airport. Once through passport control, we walked outside and caught a taxi.

The journey took over eighty minutes, circling the city, heading south along the coastline past Vesuvius National Park—via the historical Pompeii ruins—before heading southwards along the peninsula, heading inland, turning westwards, and descending towards the stunning Amalfi Coast, heading for the village called Positano.

Renowned for its multi-coloured buildings perched on the cliffside, surrounded by vibrant greenery. And the pebble beachfront below, where sailing boats and yachts filled the turquoise waters. The view basked in the mellowed glow of evening sunshine.

Julia and Charlie would have loved a place like this. I remembered he was obsessed with the seaside, running along the waterfront, and us building sandcastles.

The taxi drove down through narrow, winding streets lined with boutiques and cafes, passing a bustling scene of tourists and merchants. We eventually ascended an incline towards our destination. The Hotel Tramonto Sull'Oceano was large, traditionally designed, and white-washed, with countless terrace suites overlooking an infinity pool and ocean beyond.

I exchanged impressed looks with Lennox. Our taxi drew over the cusp onto the driveway. It was circular, with an ostentatious water-sprouting angel fountain in the centre. A door attendant stood by the marble entrance, flanked by large, antiquity-inspired pillars.

'I feel underdressed,' I joked, peering out of the car window.

'We can go shopping once we have checked in,' Lennox replied.

The car drew to a halt. She leaned forward to pay the driver. It took a few moments of broken communication to establish a mutual understanding about the fare. Lennox paid using her credit card, asking for a receipt.

There was a warm breeze and smell of the sea air as we left the car. Lennox gestured for us to enter. I followed at her heels. The door attendant greeted us, opening the glass doors.

Like the exterior, the lobby was predictably ostentatious. White marble covered every surface. There was a large crystal chandelier overhead. Pre-recorded wooden chimes played in the distance. In front of us was the main desk where the clerk stood, smugly tapping away at a computer. I suggested speaking to him. Lennox followed my lead.

Several minutes later, once given the keys, I sat inside my hotel room. It had a double bed, a side table, a large flat-screen TV, a wardrobe, a chest of drawers, an en-suite with all amenities, and a small balcony. From here, I looked out across a lawn. At the bottom was a sheer cliff drop. Beyond, I could see an array of yachts.

We would soon meet the hotel manager. First, I put the camera battery on charge before taking a shower. But I had to put on the same sweaty clothes.

I sat down at the laptop, looking at online tutorials to grasp how to use the camera. After this, I played around with the device. Once moderately convinced, I took the photography equipment and headed to the ground floor.

Here were guests of varying ages and nationalities walking around. My gaze drifted to a seating area near the front desk. Lennox was sitting with her pad and pen, scribbling notes.

'Settling in, okay?' I asked, taking a seat adjacent.

'The room is *gorgeous*.' She smiled. 'It's nice to see how the other half live.'

I looked around. 'I know.'

'Ready to take some photos?'

'Yeah,' I said confidently, pulling forward the case and withdrawing the device.

After throwing the strap around my neck, I turned on the camera, pointed it at the chandelier, put my eye on the viewfinder, adjusted the lens and took a photo. It was too dark. I changed the mode dial to put the camera into auto mode and made a better attempt.

Over my shoulder, I smelt a waft of expensive fragrance. I sensed someone approaching. Putting the camera down, I looked upwards.

Standing there was a man in his early forties. I assumed he was local, with attentively sculpted short hair, dressed in a fitted black suit, with a navy silk tie and matching pocket square. There was a small stain on his lapel. His tanned loafers had specks of the same substance. Either he was a clumsy waiter or had rushed to eat his dinner whilst standing up.

'Good evening. My name is Marco. I am the hotel manager. I believe you are the journalists who will be staying with us?' He asked, perfectly enunciated in English.

Lennox stood to address him. They shook hands. There was a small faded tattoo on the outer side of his index finger. I tried to make a possible crime connection. But in my reality, the Italian mafia avoided tattoos, instead preferring to blend into society. Perhaps not the same here?

'I am Amara Lennox,'—I stood to join them—'and this is my colleague, Thom Sayer.'

I shook his hand.

He continued: 'Welcome to our hotel. It is a pleasure to have you here as guests. I hope that the rooms are to your satisfaction?'

'Absolutely!' Lennox expelled.

I nodded encouragingly.

'Would you like a tour of the grounds?'

'We would appreciate that,' she said.

'Please,'—he gestured—'follow me this way.'

With that, we followed the hotel manager. He took us away from the lobby towards the main dining area, where there was a Micheline star restaurant.

I stood back, surveying the room whilst Lennox spoke to him. Servers manoeuvred around the room, presenting dishes with the finest locally sourced produce to guests sitting at circular tables with white covers and silverware. There was a wall-spanning tank housing various exotic fish. A cellist was sitting in the corner playing one of Rossini's string sonatas.

The hotel manager showed us the bar area, traditionally furnished with mahogany panelling, a long marble-topped bar, leather stalls, and a spacious reclining room. All bathed in soft lighting.

Whilst the hotel manager continued to give his sales pitch, I started taking photos of the room, trying my best to attempt something that looked professional. Thankfully, the camera was high quality; its capabilities salvaged my efforts.

He showed us through to an atrium courtyard. There was a walkway surrounding a lawn with a fountain at its centre. After this, he showed us the spa area, tennis courts, and infinity pool. They turned on the lights under the surfaces as the sunset.

I adjusted the camera's lens aperture, continuing to take photos as Marco guided us onto the lawn below my room. We could see the brilliant crimson sun falling towards the horizon. Light streaked the few pink clouds above. There was the distant sound of lapping waves.

'Isn't it a magnificent view?' he said, standing outwards.

We joined him. I took several photos of the sunset.

'Look at all those yachts down there!' Lennox observed, pointing down to the water's surface.

I looked at the collection of large vessels floating on the calm waters.

'Yes, many affluent people come here from spring through autumn.'
He pointed to his left, where a single yacht sat in the water. Lights
onboard illuminated its sleek, white body. It looked to be eighty feet
in length and had multiple layers. There was a helicopter stationed at
the bow. A pool deck at the stern. 'Do you see that one?'

'It is hard to miss,' I laughed.

'It is owned by the businessman Wallace Braithwaite.'

'Oh, right,' I said, exchanging glances with Lennox before photo-
graphing the superyacht. 'Have you ever met him?'

'Yes—a few times. Signor Braithwaite is a good friend of the hotel's
owner, Signor Esposito.'

Interesting.

'I would like to interview Signor Esposito. Is he here?' Lennox
asked.

She took the words right out of my mouth.

'He arrives tomorrow morning, Signorina Lennox.'

Very interesting.

Twenty-Seven

Once the hotel manager had finished giving us a tour around the grounds, we enjoyed a dinner of seafood spaghetti. Unsurprisingly, it tasted incredible. He then gave us directions into town where I could buy fresh clothes.

We walked down the driveway into the streets past busy restaurants and bars. I found the recommended shop, which was still open late. I bought two shirts, a pair of shorts, and underwear. These were mismatched to replicate Sayer's uncoordinated style. Lennox insisted that I put these on our expenses.

Cautious about the conversation divulging into personal matters, I declined her offer to go to a bar. And my right leg was hurting. Instead, we walked back to the hotel. Once there, I had another shower before putting on complimentary pyjamas and standing on the hotel room balcony.

By now, the bay was shrouded in darkness, illuminated by the blue glow of the moon. I looked towards Braithwaite's yacht, contemplating how we would meet him.

The following morning, I went to the breakfast hall and met Lennox. She was pleased with the photos I had taken the previous evening.

Unsure about the formalities of travel journalism and how much downtime was allowed, I followed her lead with the day's schedule. We decided to take another walk around the grounds, observing and taking more photos. Once she was satisfied, we walked into the lobby. I took a seat.

Meanwhile, Lennox spotted the hotel manager at the front desk. She walked over to speak to him. I watched their exchange, unable to decipher what he was saying. She came back, looking jubilant.

'What is it?' I asked.

She sat down in front of me. 'Signor Esposito arrived an hour ago. Marco has already asked about the interview—he was more than happy.'

'Nice. Did Marco say when?'

'Apparently, in ten minutes. Signor Esposito is just dealing with a few things.'

In other circumstances, I would lead by asking the right questions. Because Lennox was the journalist, and I was playing the part of her subordinate photographer, I hoped her investigative skills were competent.

We sat silent for a while. Lennox wrote notes and answered emails. Then, we heard a commotion from the far side of the lobby.

Looking towards the source, I saw a middle-aged man stepping forward, surrounded by assistants. He was tanned, had red-framed glasses with tinted lenses, slicked-back grey hair, wore a vertically pin-striped shirt tucked into chinos, concealing his protruding spread, with an open collar revealing the top of his bushy hairy chest. On his wrist was a silver watch. Approaching us, he brandished a veneer-teeth smile. By my immediate deductions, there was already something about him that I didn't like.

We both stood to address Esposito. He came forwards with his hands held out wide.

'Buongiorno!' We reciprocated. 'Welcome, welcome.' He went to shake our hands over-zealously, the palm facing downwards, before standing boastfully with hands on hips. We introduced ourselves. 'I hope that your stay has been pleasant so far?' He had a thick Italian accent—I couldn't distinguish which region. We complimented him. 'I understand you would like to ask me a few questions?'

'Yes, just so I can add a few quotes into the review,' Lennox explained.

'By all means. Come, we can sit out on my private veranda.' He gestured for us to follow him.

Lennox took the lead, walking by Esposito's side while I stood back, eavesdropping on their pleasantries. He guided us down a corridor away from the guests. Subtly, I checked our surroundings, wondering whether Brathwaite's friend had tight security measures. I only surveyed a few standard cameras.

We eventually came to a pair of French doors opening onto the veranda. Before us, there were brown wooden-framed seats with white furnishings surrounding a long table covered in a blue-patterned throw. Above were large wooden beams wrapped in dense foliage, below a mosaic design framed by sandstone tiles. To our left was a view across a sloping lawn towards the cliff and ocean.

'Please, take a seat,' Esposito gestured towards the table. We obliged, sitting on the left, facing the seat at the head of the table where the owner reclined. 'Would you both like caffè? Espresso?'

'That would be nice,' Lennox replied.

I nodded.

Without a word, the waiter walked back into the building.

Esposito inspected us for a moment, whimsically (it seemed), and then looked out at the ocean. 'We have the best sights here, wouldn't you agree?'

'It is stunning,' Lennox said.

'Have you gone down into the village?'

'Last night we went for a walk. I would like to see more before the end of our visit.'

'You have come just at the right time with the spring blossom and cool temperature.' He leaned forward, cupped his hands on the table, smiling. 'Now tell me—what would you like to know about Hotel Tramonto Sull'Oceano?'

Whether this is a money-laundering scheme?

Lennox produced her pad, opened it, and withdrew a pen. 'Why did you decide to build the hotel here?'

'The village has great sentimental value to me. My grandfather used to be a fisherman in these waters. As a child, I would holiday here with my family. I have great memories of this place. And wanted to bring that sense of joy to my clientele.'

'That is a nice angle I can work with,' Lennox said, making notes. She then skimmed through earlier pages and found research she had written down. 'I understand, Signor Esposito—'

'Please,' he interjected. 'Call me Alberto.'

Lennox smiled. 'Okay, Alberto, you have opened a chain of internationally renowned luxurious hotels across Italy. Why did you only decide to build one here now?'

'Mainly because this is such a lucrative destination. Local families have owned the land for generations and, understandably, are reluctant to sell to outside investment.'

'How did you go about that?' I asked, gazing at Lennox momentarily to see whether she was bothered by her photographer asking questions. But she seemed unfazed.

'As all good businessmen do, Mr Sayer,' he eyed me, 'I simply made them an offer they couldn't turn down.' He smiled. 'Everyone has a price.'

The waiter returned with the three drinks. We all accepted them, smelt the aroma of the coffee, and took a small sip before placing the cups down onto the saucers.

'Isn't it delicious?' Esposito asked excitedly.

'Eccellente,' I exclaimed.

'Lei parla italiano?'

'Sì.'

He nodded, impressed.

'And what would you say makes this hotel stand out compared to any other in the village?' Lennox asked.

'We offer the finest experience. Everyone knows the reputation of my hotels!' He put his hands out, saying matter-of-factly: 'It is as simple as that.'

Lennox looked out towards the ocean. 'You said your grandfather was a fisherman. Do you enjoy doing it as a sport?'

'Oh, yes! Since childhood.' he said, taking another sip. 'Have you tried any of the seafood dishes on the menu?'

'Yes, we had the seafood spaghetti last night.'

'Freshly caught from the bay.'

'You catch them yourself?' Lennox joked.

He laughed. 'If I weren't preoccupied with managing a multi-million dollar franchise, that would be nice!'

She closed the pad. 'Do you own a sailing boat here?'

I could see where she was leading this.

'Yes, I do.'

She looked out towards the bay. 'And you stay at the hotel instead of on one of them?'

'Yes, of course.'

'Do you associate with any other people who moor here?'

'Yes, I have friends who visit regularly. Now that the hotel has opened, I can see them more often.'

She pointed towards the superyacht. 'Your hotel manager Marco told me that Wallace Braithwaite owns that one?'

'Ah, yes! He is a dear friend of mine. I haven't seen him for a long time. We plan to dine together this afternoon.'

A fleeting glance with Lennox.

'Alberto,' she leaned forward. 'We appreciate you giving us some of your time this morning. I have one final thing to ask.'

He smiled. 'And what might that be?'

'Could we go with you to meet Signor Braithwaite? I am a massive fan and would love to write a piece about him.'

It was not the most subtle way of going about things.

He eyed us both. 'You would like to join us for lunch?'

'If possible?'

'You know,' he sat back, 'I admire your passion and straight-talking attitude. A woman who is not afraid to ask for what she wants. You remind me of my mother!'

'You have to be like this as a journalist.'

'Very good!' He put a hand in his pocket. Instantly, my mind thought of the worst-case scenario. But I didn't remember seeing the indentation of a weapon. Thankfully, he revealed a phone. 'I will call him now and see if you can join us.'

Esposito turned on the screen and started to prod it with his index finger (clearly not confident at using the device) before placing it to his ear. Meanwhile, I exchanged another glance with Lennox. We both kept neutral expressions.

'Ah, Wallace, il mio caro amico!' Esposito suddenly erupted. We looked towards him. I could feel the heart rate increase. 'How are you?' There was a pause. 'That is wonderful to hear. Yes, what?' Another pause. I could vaguely hear Fielding's variant speaking. 'Oh, I arrived this morning. Yes, I will be coming on board for lunch. That was why I called. I have journalists from Fortuna Magazine staying here at the hotel. They are doing a review.' He listened. 'Yes, yes. Look, could they come with me to meet you?' There was another pause. He looked off into the distance, nodding. 'Their names?' He looked towards us. 'Amara Lennox and Thom Sayer.' I considered whether Fielding's variant knew about what I was doing. 'That is fine with you? Great! I presume Diego will be waiting at the same spot to collect us?' Another pause. 'Then, we shall see you there at one o'clock. I look forward to it, my friend. Ciao, ciao!' Esposito cancelled the call, placing the phone down on the table. He looked up at us, smiling. 'There we are. I am sure you heard the plan?'

'We did,' Lennox replied.

Esposito stood to leave. 'In that case, we can meet at the hotel entrance at twelve-forty-five.' He put out one finger. 'But just one thing.'

'Yes?' she asked; I sensed concealing her nerves.

'Please make sure to be punctual.'

Lennox smiled. 'Of course!'

'Very good!' he said jubilantly, clapping his hands together. 'Now, if you don't mind, I must deal with matters. I shall see you both later.'

And with that, Esposito walked through the French doors, away from the veranda. All the while, we sat there, digesting everything, astounded by our fortunes.

It was time to meet Fielding's variant.

Twenty-Eight

Later, we were chauffeured down the cliffside to the bay. Here, a jetty stretched outwards across the water. Overhead, there were clear blue skies. We could see parasailers and speedboats hurtling around. There was the sound of swaying water lashing against the shore.

I followed behind Lennox and Esposito, walking along the wooden decking, listening to their superficial conversation whilst looking southwards towards Braithwaite's moored superyacht—a white spearhead upon the horizon. I took a few photos.

A young man drew towards us with a faded haircut and face-spanning sunglasses. He wore a white polo shirt, beige chino shorts and brown leather boat shoes—custom attire for yacht employees. I suspected this was Diego.

He drew towards Esposito. There were a few loud exchanges. They shook hands. He introduced Lennox. I came forward. He did the same. Diego ushered us to follow him further down the jetty until we reached an off-branch where a luxury speedboat waited. It was long, sleek, covered in polished, wooden panelling, and had white leather upholstery, with a sunbathing area at the rear.

Diego asked us to board. We climbed over the side. The boat rocked gently beneath us. I joined Lennox by taking the back seat whilst Esposito stood at the front, resting his hands upon the windscreen. Diego untied all the ropes, threw them on board, got on, and handled the steering wheel.

A few moments later, the engine ignited. Diego ensured we were sitting comfortably before pressing down on the throttle lever. The speedboat launched forward, barely making a sound, skimming smoothly upon the water's surface.

We curled around the end of the jetty, changing course for the superyacht. It loomed closer. The speedboat pounded against the waves.

Lennox stared towards the shoreline. Thinking back to my encounter with Tate's accomplices, I surveyed the cabin. There were no visible signs of weapons on board.

It only took less than a minute for the speedboat to arrive. As we approached, the large vessel consumed us within its shadow. Seeing the superyacht in such proximity was an impressive, foreboding sight.

Diego guided the speedboat to the centre of the port side. There was a small jetty for the boat to moor. As we drew nearer, a few of his colleagues appeared. We aligned with the ship. They threw ropes aboard.

Esposito gestured for us to go first. I thanked him, climbing over. The shipmates greeted us in English, ushering us up a set of stairs and taking us onto the front deck. It wasn't easy because of the weak leg.

When we climbed to the top, there was a seating area, a bar under a canopy, a shipmate casually chopping fruit, and lounge music playing over speakers. We stopped and allowed Esposito to pass. There were no guards.

And that is when I saw the silhouette of someone approaching from a corridor at the rear. I caught Lennox's attention, eying the direction of the person.

We both looked.

It was Fielding's variant.

Twenty-Nine

Suddenly, I had a flashback of shooting Tate—a reminder of my past mistakes.

Braithwaite walked forward, tanned, and oozing self-assurance, dressed in a partially opened white linen shirt, marl grey trousers, and brown sandals. Approaching Esposito, he smiled. They embraced in a firm hug.

All the while, we stood there looking out of place.

The friends turned towards us, walking forward, talking feverishly like reunited school friends. Braithwaite looked in our direction.

Although I ensured Sayer appeared relaxed, I analysed the variant's features. He acknowledged us. I couldn't deduce any visual indications that he recognised Sayer. From observing his speech and mannerisms, Braithwaite appeared more interested in his friend. He might have received training from Leveller.

After shaking Lennox's hand, he turned to me.

'And you must be…Thom?' His tone of voice and eye squinting suggested he wasn't sure. It would be an Oscar-winning performance if he were putting it on.

'That is right,' I said, forcing a timid tone. I shook Braithwaite's hand, intentionally making it a soft embrace. 'Thank you for allowing us to come today.'

'Welcome on board.' Braithwaite gestured to the seating area. 'Please, take a seat.' We joined Esposito, sitting down whilst Braithwaite waltzed towards the bar. 'What can I get you all to drink?'

Esposito leaned back, threw both arms onto the backrest, and stretched out his legs, pushing out his crotch. 'I will have my usual. Thanks, Wallace.'

Braithwaite leaned against the bar, picked up a cocktail stick, and pointed it at Lennox. She said: 'Oh, I'll have sparkling water.'

'Are you sure?' he said, twiddling the cocktail stick around his mouth.

'Yes, thank you. I like to keep a clear head whilst working.'

'And how about you, Thom?'

'I'll have the same.'

'Okay!' Braithwaite turned to the barman, acknowledged the order with a nod, came back and reclined next to Esposito.

Suddenly, another person appeared from the rear corridor. I could tell by their proportions that it was a woman. When she entered the sunlight, everyone averted their attention toward her. She had striking, supermodel looks, was tall, slim, and wearing a light, flowing dress with a neck strap. She had a disinterested grimace.

'Ah, here she is!' Braithwaite expelled, extending a hand towards the woman. She stopped before us. 'I would like to introduce you to my wife, Tamara.'

She nodded politely toward Lennox and me before kissing Esposito on both cheeks.

'Alberto,' she said, 'it is a pleasure to see you again.'

The same posh English accent.

'And it is wonderful to see you too, as always!' he exclaimed, blushing.

She took a seat next to Braithwaite. I could tell by their body language that there was an underlying tension between them.

A few moments later, the barman came forward holding a tray of drinks. Our sparkling waters came in tall crystal glasses, whilst Fielding's variant and Esposito received tumble glasses containing cocktails. Tamara ordered a glass of champagne.

The two businessmen became reacquainted for a few minutes, talking incessantly. Tamara walked over to the bar to wait for her drink. Meanwhile, we sat there admiring the aesthetic. I wasn't sure about the protocol in these situations, resisting taking photos without permission.

'So, tell me.' Braithwaite directed at us. Tamara retook her seat with a filled champagne flute. 'Has Alberto done a good job?' He patted the hotel owner playfully on the shoulder. 'Or are you planning to give a scathing review?'

Lennox forced a laugh. 'Unfortunately, I can't share anything until the review is published.'

'You won't accept a bribe?' Braithwaite joked.

Tamara rolled her eyes.

'Not for all the money in the world,' Lennox said dryly.

It was a bit blunt. But the two businessmen found this comical.

A waiter approached, announcing the serving of lunch. Braithwaite excitedly got to his feet, gesturing for us to follow. We proceeded from the lounge area, passing the bar, and down the corridor until we reached another canopy-covered area with a long table for lunch.

Braithwaite took a seat at the head of the table, naturally. Esposito and Tamara took seats on either side. I sat next to Lennox, placing the camera and walking stick underneath and reclining.

Around us, servers approached, holding Bruschetta starters. There was the pouring of white wine. Braithwaite signalled for us to begin eating.

'I just wanted to thank you for allowing us to join you for lunch,' Lennox said.

'That is quite all right,' Braithwaite replied, taking a large sip of wine.

'We heard about the new business acquisition and your higher place on the Fortuna list.'

'It is flattering to be recognised. But my increased wealth is all based upon shares, which can fluctuate at any time.'

'Big tech investment seems to be the way forward,' Esposito said, dabbing his mouth with a napkin.

Lennox continued: 'If I may, can I ask why you invested in those companies? Was it genuine interest or because you saw the financial gain?'

'I have an interest, sure. But I'm an opportunist. I like to have my fingers in many pies. The world is my playground. Isn't that right, Alberto?' He slapped his friend on the shoulder. They both laughed.

I looked at Tamara—she seemed repulsed.

'Are you happy about how the markets function?' Lennox asked.

'In what respect?'

'There are many regulations to ensure the economy doesn't balloon and crash. Do you think that stunts opportunities for enterprise?'

'Of course—it affects technological development.' He placed his cutlery onto the empty plate.

'Do you not like the way the global system works?'

Braithwaite took a large sip of wine, exchanging dubious glances with Esposito. 'I guess I would prefer more…leeway.'

'He can't stand the tax man constantly knocking at his door. Isn't that right?' Esposito laughed. By now, his face and neck had turned red. Most likely a reaction to the alcohol.

'You seem very interested in my opinion about these things, Miss Lennox?' Braithwaite asked.

She had struck a nerve.

'I'm just fascinated by how you've been able to amass such wealth so quickly. And I want to understand your opinion about how everything works.' She forced a smile. 'It is very inspiring!'

'Well, thank you!' He cupped his hands on the table.

Servers drew forward to take our empty plates. Braithwaite accepted another helping of wine.

There was an uncomfortable atmosphere.

I needed to intervene.

'Mr Braithwaite, could you tell us about your big tech investments?'

'By all means,' he said jubilantly, evidently relieved. He sat back, holding the wine glass. 'Much of it revolves around artificial intelligence, advanced computation, and space exploration. I'm far from a pioneer in those fields, but I'm willing to invest to ensure they have the funding to take humanity to the next stage.'

'You mentioned advanced computation. Does that involve quantum computers?'

'Yes, do you know much about them?'

'A bit. I'm currently volunteering at a university for a consciousness experiment. I believe they are using quantum technology to do this.'

'Oh, really?!' Braithwaite sat back. The beef cheek main arrived. Again, he did not acknowledge the waiter. He directed at me: 'What does that entail?'

'They take scans of my brain using the computer.'

'I see. Extraordinary! Perhaps I need to get in contact with these people.'

'Are you not familiar with such technology? The idea that our brains perform similarly to quantum computers?'

Everyone looked at me, evidently baffled that a humbled photographer would know such a thing.

'No, I was not aware,' he said, taking another sip of wine. 'Can you explain the science?'

'Not really. The professor was vague.'

'I will have to look into it.'

'Apparently, there is even the possibility of consciousness migration.'

'What does that mean?' Tamara suddenly asked, looking at me curiously.

I addressed her: 'To traverse alternative realities.'

I analysed Braithwaite's face, trying to deduce a reaction. But his expression conveyed intrigue and openness. Frustratingly, there was no indication that he knew what I was doing.

'Now, that is a subject I am completely oblivious to,' Braithwaite laughed.

'This is a very intense conversation for lunchtime!' Esposito enunciated, gobbling a mouthful of beef.

Braithwaite continued: 'But to give more explanation to your initial question, Thom, the advanced computation I am investing in is cybersecurity.'

'I see,' I said, cutting into the meat on my plate. 'Is hacking a problem?'

'Yes. On several occasions, I've been victim to email hacking and financial records theft.' I saw Lennox from the corner of my eye. 'These criminals are always one step ahead of the curve. I have taken it upon myself to see that the technology advances.'

Could these documents hold any clues as to whether he affiliated with Leveller?

'How does that involve quantum computers?'

'To be honest, I don't understand the exact science. Complex equations and algorithms. But the software can heavily encrypt data files.'

He seemed more interested in the outcome instead of the means.

Suddenly, I remembered the video transmission file.

'You say about encrypting data files. Does that include the ability to remove or scramble metadata?'

'Yes, I believe so. Why do you ask?'

'I'm always concerned about people stealing my photos. As a failsafe, I imagine encrypting the files would be a way to protect them?'

'Precisely!' He sat back, satisfied from the half-eaten meal, throwing his napkin onto the table. 'In fact, I have a prototype for a piece of software.'

'Oh, really?'

'Yes, I use it to protect my files.'

I picked up the camera from under the table. 'I don't suppose you could show me how that works? We could use my camera's SD card.'

'I don't see why not.'

'Is this software on sale?'

'No, it is still being developed. I can show it to you after lunch?'

I tried to conceal my eagerness. 'That would be good.'

'Very well.' Braithwaite smiled.

The conversation moved toward Esposito's hotel, the Amalfi Coast, and Braithwaite's hiking interest. There was a serving of Lemon syllabub dessert. Lennox started to talk to Tamara. Meanwhile, I sat there contemplating whether the cybersecurity software could be helpful in the mission.

Braithwaite threw his spoon onto the plate. I listened.

'It has been a long time since I have partied, Alberto.'

'Come on; it will be fun!' Esposito chuckled, guzzling the last drips of wine from his glass.

'What is he saying?' Tamara interjected, leaning over.

Braithwaite addressed her: 'He said a new private member's club just opened. We can get access.'

'I am telling you, Wallace—it would be fun!'

'Why don't you go?' Tamara suggested, for once seeming enthusiastic about something.

Braithwaite looked at Esposito. He was nodding, trying to arouse approval. Braithwaite snuffed through his nostrils and said: 'Yes, okay!'

'Buono a sapersi!' Esposito expelled.

'Tamara, would you mind showing our guests through to the bar? I am going to show Thom the prototype software.'

'Of course,' she said.

Braithwaite stood, gesturing for me to follow him down a set of steps on the opposite side of the dining area.

Thirty

I took the walking stick, pulled the camera from underneath the table, stood, and walked toward the stairs, exchanging smiles with the variant. Again, I couldn't deduce any sign of concealment in Braithwaite's features. However, I was reluctant to walk down the stairs first. But I knew it would be suspicious and impolite to refuse his offer.

Down I went, taking my time. The right leg reacted with every step. Meanwhile, Braithwaite walked behind me, muttering something about being too old for private member's clubs.

At the bottom was a corridor where several assistants were walking around. I couldn't sense any form of hostility. Braithwaite proceeded past me, signalling towards a door further down the hall. We walked towards it. On the way, I saw another door. There was a security sticker on it. No cameras were visible in the corridor.

I considered the possibility of being led into a trap. Lennox was vulnerable in the company of Braithwaite's wife and the intoxicated hotel owner.

Once we approached the door, I saw a lock with a fingerprint scanner. Braithwaite activated this with his right thumb. The door opened. He gestured for me to walk through first. I accepted the offer.

There was a white, circular room. Adjacent, large windows looked out across the superyacht's bow, helicopter pad and surrounding waters. To the right, there was a conference table. Behind it was a mini-bar. Above, a single security camera faced the opposite side of the room, where a semi-circular desk with an accompanying chair stood. Upon this, there was a sleek computer with a large, thin screen. A piece of contemporary art was hanging on the wall.

Braithwaite walked towards the desk and sat down. He turned on the screen and quickly typed in the password before I could see it.

I looked subtly at the vessel's watch. It read fourteen-hundred hours, fifteen minutes and ten seconds.

Walking around to his side, I looked at the computer screen. The wallpaper showed Braithwaite and Tamara looking excited, wearing skydiving equipment, and standing by a small plane.

He looked up at me. 'The photo was taken a few years ago. We had such a great day. Have you ever done it?'

'No, not yet.'

'You should!'

'The only problem is my leg.'

He looked at the walking stick. 'Oh, I see. What happened?'

'I had a stroke.'

'I'm sorry to hear that.'

Braithwaite leaned back, put a hand into his pocket, and pulled out a small, rectangular object: a USB stick. He leaned forward, plugging it into the back of the computer screen.

I presume he kept the software separate from his files in case anyone got onto his computer. Smart move.

A small icon appeared on the screen. Braithwaite opened this, revealing a contents folder for the drive. It contained the software, appearing as an unsuspecting black box.

'D'you want to hand me the SD card?'

'Sure.' I drew forward the camera case, opened it and took out the digital SLR before opening the side hatch housing the SD card. I presented it to Braithwaite. 'Here you go.'

The variant removed the SD card, held it pinched between his thumb and index finger and leaned forward to insert it into the back of the computer. Moments later, he opened the SD card's folder, storing all my amateur creations categorised in reverse chronological order. The most recent were shots of the superyacht I had taken aboard the speedboat. Braithwaite opened one, revealing a large photo on the screen.

'What a great shot!' he exclaimed. 'It looks magnificent. Do you mind if I keep a copy of this?'

'By all means,' I smiled.

Braithwaite pasted a copy of the photo from the desktop into a separate folder before removing the SD card. I asked him to place it inside a plastic case this time, which he did. I put it away safely.

'Now, this is the interesting part.' Braithwaite opened the prototype software. All that appeared was a window with multiple lines of coding on a black backdrop. 'It still doesn't have an accessible user interface. As you are already aware, the picture file works. But…'—he dragged the file, dropping it onto the software window—'look what happens when processed through the algorithm.' Instantaneously, a new file appeared on the desktop. Braithwaite rested the mouse over it. 'Notice that it has the same name as the original picture?'

'Yes.'

'Now watch.' He clicked on the new file. A box appeared, saying it was a corrupted file. 'The computer cannot open the file. It's encrypted heavily with multiple layers of quantum protection.'

'And how do you decrypt it?'

'You simply do the reverse.' He dragged the file onto the window. Moments later, a file appeared on the desktop, resembling the original picture. 'It is as simple as that.'

'And you have done the same for all your data?'

'Correct. Everything has to pass through the software before I can access it.'

'I'm impressed.'

Braithwaite turned around, nodding smugly.

Suddenly, there was a knock at the door.

I moved aside. The variant stood to answer it. All the while, I looked at the computer and considered the possibility of stealing the USB stick. But, I knew I needed more time to access and download his sensitive data.

Braithwaite opened the door. There stood Esposito. By now, he appeared more inebriated—wobbling in the doorway, a big, cocktail-splattered smile upon his red face.

'I hope you're both finished. Come upstairs! Tamara wants to see the hotel. I can give you a grand tour.' He chuckled, throwing an arm around Braithwaite's shoulder.

'How many cocktails have you had, Alberto?!'

'Enough to get our night *started early*!'

I started moving towards the door, following them out, ensuring Braithwaite would be distracted. Noticing me coming behind, this instigated the variant to walk out into the corridor with his friend. I joined them, pulling the door shut behind me. The mechanism sounded.

'…But I need to get dressed before we go, Alberto.'

'You look *fine*!' Esposito slurred. 'Doesn't he, Thom?'

'Oh, yes,' I said confidently.

'Okay,' Braithwaite sniggered before following his friend down the corridor towards the stairs.

Before I followed them, I turned back, looking at the door.

Whilst Braithwaite was out that evening, I would have to get back on board.

Thirty-One

Diego ushered everyone from the lounge area down the stairs to-wards the moored speedboat. All the while, I trailed at the back with Lennox.

'Impressed by the software?' she asked, looking over her shoulder and descending the stairs.

'Yeah, I was. What have you been up to?'

'I wandered around admiring the scenery whilst Tamara and Alberto became reacquainted.'

We reached the bottom. Before us, Braithwaite offered his wife a hand to help her on board whilst Esposito stumbled forward, telling an anecdote.

'Amara,'—she stopped to look at me—'when we get back to the mainland, would you mind if I have some downtime?'

'What were you thinking?'

'Buy a few gifts.'

'Sounds good. I need to start work on the review. Do you think you have enough photos?'

'Yes. Shall I drop by your hotel room later to give you the edited results?'

'Perfect.'

Diego ushered for us to get on board. We climbed on deck, taking seats alongside the variant, his wife, and the intoxicated hotel owner.

The speedboat took off. Esposito continued with another anecdote. I looked towards the coastline, deliberating how I would gain access to the software and data. Because I was operating in an alternative reality, there was the impulse to do whatever I needed, knowing I had limited time. Still, I didn't want a repeat of what happened with Tate. I couldn't leave a trace in case Braithwaite had connections to Level-ler.

We reached the jetty. Diego moored the boat. Everyone disembarked. It took me a few minutes to talk my way out of accepting Braithwaite's proposal to join them for drinks at the hotel. I politely excused myself. They drove away.

The first thing I needed was equipment. I knew resources would be limited because this was a holiday village. I walked from the jetty inland, scouring the streets for any shops that didn't just sell local produce or tourist souvenirs.

Firstly, I went into a shop selling scuba diving and snorkelling equipment. An assistant greeted me, offering help, which I declined. I chose a long-length wetsuit, a microfibre towel and a waterproof bag. After paying, I placed all of the goods inside the new bag. Sealing the top flap, I slung a strap over one shoulder and the camera case strap over the other.

I would have to get past the scanner to access Braithwaite's office. The first idea that came to mind was to fake a fingerprint using the print left on the SD card by Braithwaite. I had the camera, laptop, and a photo-editing application at my disposal to take a high-resolution image of the fingerprint on the SD card and could create a computer-generated mould. But I had to consider how I would produce this. I highly doubted anyone nearby had a 3D printer. Plus, it was debatable whether the fingerprint scanner took thermo-readings.

I walked past a hardware store. The thought struck me: could I use a magnet to deactivate the fingerprint scanner? Placing one of these in the correct location of the reader could force the electromagnetic relay inside to trip.

I walked inside, said hello to the owner and began my search. I came across a small collection of switchable magnets. One of these would enable me to turn it on and off, which meant I wouldn't have contact with the scanner, minimising the risk of leaving forensic evidence.

I bought the magnet and headed up the hillside towards the hotel, looking across the water towards Braithwaite's superyacht. From my estimation, it was only a short distance from the jetty. But I was concerned about Sayer. Hopefully, the vessel had muscle memory to swim, and the leg wouldn't prove too much of a hindrance.

Conscious of arousing suspicion, I found some thick bushes by the roadside at the bottom of the driveway. I hid the bag and took a short rest.

After a strenuous hike up the driveway, I walked towards the entrance. The door attendant welcomed me inside. I went through the lobby, took a lift to my floor, and went straight to my hotel room.

Once inside, I took a bottle of chilled water from the fridge, sitting for a few moments to rehydrate and give the vessel's leg time to rest. I grabbed the backpack, took the laptop and placed it on the coffee table. Turning it on, I withdrew the small case from my pocket, took out the SD card, and inserted it into the laptop.

I went through the SD card library, choosing suitable photos, before copying the selection onto the desktop. Opening the internet browser, I searched for videos explaining how to use the laptop's photo-editing application.

Once moderately educated, I proceeded to edit the photos, doing my best to adjust their exposure, tone and saturation. Not a true professional's work, but enough to show I hadn't made a half-hearted effort.

I felt guilty for putting Sayer's reputation on the line. This mission was taking advantage of his life for something completely irrelevant. I ignored these conflicting thoughts and stored the edited photos in a new folder on the SD card before heading toward Lennox's room.

Upon arrival, I knocked on the door. Moments later, Lennox opened it, inviting me inside.

'Did you get anything nice?'

'Yes, I did. Oh, thanks.' I accepted the offer to sit at the table. 'I've decided to go for a long walk along the coastline this evening.'

She sat down adjacent. 'Really? You're going to be okay with the leg?'

I patted it. 'I'm not going to let that hold me back.'

'You've come out of your shell since we last worked together, Thom.'

'I guess I will take that as a compliment.' I deviated: 'Did you accept the offer to drink with the others?'

'I went for a bit but didn't have anything alcoholic. Not going to lie —I can only stand a short amount of time around people like that.'

'Yeah, I get you.'

I revealed the SD card, handing it to her.

'Thanks.' She inserted it into her laptop. A few moments later, I directed her to the edited photos folder. She opened it, scrolling through it before looking up at me.

'Are you okay with the edits?'

'They seem fine to me.'

'How are you getting on with the review?'

'I've done one draft and will do another before we catch our flight tomorrow morning.'

'What time is that?' I asked, taking hold of the laptop and pasting the photos folder onto the desktop.

'Nine.'

'Okay.' I withdrew the blank SD card, placed it inside the case, and put it back into my pocket. 'I'm heading off for my coastal walk.'

'Just take it easy, yeah?' she said, looking up at me with concern.

'I will.'

And with that, I left, eventually reaching the lobby and outside. Ensuring not to exhaust the vessel, I strolled down the driveway, hoping I wouldn't see Braithwaite's variant. Thankfully, I was okay and reached the bushes. Here, I found the concealed waterproof bag.

The jetty was too open for me to swim. I hailed a taxi and asked the driver to take me further around the bay towards the moored superyacht. We set off. I stayed focused on the present moment, not contemplating worst-case scenarios once I got on Braithwaite's superyacht.

We drove from the village and down a narrow road hugging the beach line. It meandered towards where the bay circled to a small cove where young people enjoyed the last light of the day. I had plenty of time to prepare myself and would use the cover of the night to my advantage. I asked the driver to pull over. He obliged. I paid and got out to be met by spring evening's warm air.

The sun was steadily moving towards the horizon, painting the landscape. In the foreground, I could see the superyacht, like a thorn protruding from the water. I walked down a set of sand-covered stairs until I reached a rock outcrop that met the ocean's edge.

I looked around to ensure no one was watching me before withdrawing the SD card from my pocket and placing it aside, along with the walking stick. I undressed and put on the wetsuit. Then, I neatly folded the clothes, disassembled the walking stick, and placed all into the bag. After this, I laid the SD card and switchable magnet on top of everything for ease of access before sealing the flap.

Once ready, I sat on the rock, waiting until the sunset. During this time, I looked out across the water, clearing my mind of thoughts.

Not too long later, the sun disappeared. I was the only person remaining. Standing up, I put on both straps of the waterproof bag and walked down the outcrop until I reached the water.

I lowered, precariously putting out the left foot to find support, feeling the cool temperature, before gradually easing the vessel further into the shallow water. Keeping the head above the surface, I waded in, assessing the vessel by pushing the arms outwards in a breaststroke. Confident that this worked, I submerged until I could no longer find footing, proceeding to tread water and test the legs.

Assured the vessel could swim, I launched away from the cove toward the superyacht. To avoid over-exerting—and ensuring the hair remained dry to minimise drippage on board—I continued with the breaststroke. Salty water lapped against my sealed lips.

As expected, there was discomfort in the right leg. It took me approximately five minutes to reach the superyacht. The skies had darkened. But the lights on board guided me. Drawing nearer, I couldn't see any activity, swimming cautiously towards the rear jetty.

Reaching the ladder, I looked upwards and didn't see or hear anyone in the minimal light. The hands and feet felt slightly numb, but I climbed up, feeling the strain in my right leg.

Once on board, I quickly moved towards the side, finding cover. Here, I took off the bag and withdrew the towel. I started drying off the vessel, ensuring I wouldn't leave a water trail. I placed the saturated towel back into the bag, closed it, and put on both straps. Feeling discomfort in the right leg, I gave the vessel a few moments to rest.

Taking a fleeting glance, I started walking across the decking crouched. Meandering outside the small swimming pool, I looked upwards at the higher levels.

Again, there were no signs of Braithwaite's assistants.

I drew to the back of the deck. Here, a door led inside. By now, I could feel Sayer's heart pumping fast. Adrenaline was surging through the vessel. His senses were on high alert.

Taking a big breath through my nostrils, I opened the cabin door, looked briefly inside, and walked into a dimly lit corridor. It seemed to span down the port side of the superyacht. From my recollection, further on was the stairway leading to the lounge area. And from my earlier observations, I knew this corridor did not have security cameras.

I started edging forward, listening intently for any disturbances in the silence. And as expected, I could hear talking and laughter in the distance. Braithwaite's crew must have taken the opportunity to enjoy themselves whilst their boss was partying on the mainland.

My priority was finding the security room, hopefully showing live feeds of the cameras. Hands raised, I was ready to engage if I needed to knock anyone unconscious.

I drew towards the speedboat jetty. Ensuring to stay hidden within the shadows, I looked up the stairs. Not sensing anyone present, I continued forward in the direction of Braithwaite's office. To the left, I saw the door with the security label.

Looking both ways, I held the handle, slowly pushing down, thankful it would open. I composed, expecting someone inside. But the room was clear.

On the opposite wall was a small collection of screens. In the foreground was a computer on a desk. Around this were piles of boxed goods. A thin layer of dust coated the room, showing they didn't check the security footage regularly.

I walked in, closing the door gently behind me. Inspecting the screens, I found the camera inside Braithwaite's office. It was empty. The CCTV footage was in black and white. It did not have a time or date signature.

I sat at the desk and moved the mouse, bringing the screen to life. It displayed the security software on which each camera had a separate window. I clicked on the one for the office. It opened a new screen showing the live feed and a timeline. I used the mouse to operate the timeline function, dragging back the footage to fourteen-hundred hours-and-fourteen-minutes. When this happened, it started playing the footage of us entering the room.

I typed in a command to enlarge the image. It zoomed in on the space just below the rear of the computer screen. I waited, seeing Braithwaite's hands typing on the keyboard. When it came to the moment when he wrote the password, I was unable to make it out and had to zoom in closer. Thankfully, the image quality wasn't pixelated and compromised because these were high-spec security cameras. This time, I leaned in closer, squinted, and saw Braithwaite type the password.

Commanding the computer to replay the footage on a loop, I looked at where his fingers hit the keyboard whilst painstakingly comparing this with the one in front of me. After a few minutes of rewatching the footage, it revealed the password: 'leveller'.

What did that mean to Braithwaite? Was he a terrorist?

I commanded the computer to return to the live footage. To be especially cautious, I made a one-minute video of the empty office using the recording function, put this on a loop, bypassed the screen's feed, and displayed this footage instead.

Replacing the chair under the desk, I walked towards the door and opened it slightly. Checking that the coast was clear, I eased out into the corridor. I waited for a few moments, listening intently, before closing the door behind me and making my way towards Braithwaite's office. Taking off one strap, I pulled the bag forward, undid the top flap, and withdrew the switchable magnet.

Once at the office door, I knelt and placed the magnet near the top of the fingerprint scanner. I rechecked the corridor and took a deep breath before enabling it.

Nothing happened.

Breathing out through the nostrils with restraint, I drew away the magnet. Looking along the scanner, I placed the device closer, gradually moving it downwards.

I heard the noise. It nearly caused me to tumble backwards.

The scanner sounded, confirming someone had opened the lock.

Resisting the urge to smile in celebration prematurely, I used my free hand to reach for the handle. Pressing down, I opened the door. I withdrew the magnet and switched it off. Standing, I stepped into the room before swinging around, checking the corridor, and closing the door.

As I heard the locking mechanism, I let out a sigh of relief. I drew the bag forward, replaced the magnet, and withdrew the SD card. Lights streamed into the room from the deck below. I edged towards the computer and saw Braithwaite's USB stick plugged into the back of the screen. I inserted the SD card and walked around to sit at the screen.

Touching the space button brought the screen to life. Looking out of the windows, I could imagine the light emitting from the screen would attract attention. I turned down the brightness on the keyboard. After this, I typed in the password, hit the enter button, and smiled when given access to the desktop.

By now, a small icon had appeared for the SD card. I proceeded to open the documents folder. Inside were folders containing encrypted files. I opened the SD card folder and copied these across. As this happened, I opened the USB stick folder and replicated the prototype software.

As the animated loading bars showed the progress of the data transfer, I sat back in the chair, waiting.

But suddenly, I heard something—it was the fingerprint scanner activating.

Instantly, I went to turn off the computer screen, about to hide under the desk. But I was not quick enough—the door opened.

I looked at the person standing at the entrance—Tamara Braithwaite. She was pointing a small pistol at me.

Thirty-Two

'I thought you seemed overly interested in my husband's affairs,' Tamara said, closing the door. She walked in front of the computer, noticing the USB stick and SD card inserted into the back of the screen. 'You went to great lengths to break in. Are you here to steal the prototype? Hoping to expose him for something?'

'You could say that,' I uttered, looking into the barrel. In the minimal light, I noticed something on Tamara's thumb—the curved surface of a silicon mould. I said sarcastically: 'I see you also have permission to access this office.'

Momentarily, her eyes flicked towards the thumb holding the pistol. She tightened her grip. 'What I do is none of your business.'

I reclined in the chair. 'What are we going to do about this?'

'You will return whatever you have stolen and leave immediately.'

'I cannot do that.'

Our eyes met intensely.

'Are you willing to put your life at risk just for the sake of a tabloid scoop?'

'I wouldn't jump to conclusions. It is much more than that.'

'How did you gain access to this office?'

'A magnet.' I leaned forward. 'Earlier today, I noticed your indifference towards him. Are you doing this out of spite?'

'I don't know what you mean.'

'Are you trying to get hold of your husband's information to ruin him?'

'Again, that is none of your business, Mr Sayer.'

'Do you know the computer's password?'

'Yes. I wouldn't be in here otherwise.'

I eyed her curiously. 'What does that mean to you?'

She averted her gaze. 'It is of no great significance.'

'Why would you emphasise that?'

'Pardon?' She looked at me once again.

'I was simply asking if you know what it means. But you felt compelled to downplay the importance of the password.'

'Mr Sayer—quit the mind games.'

Tamara leaned over the screen, pointing the pistol at my forehead.

I could see she was unnerved, perhaps cautious to reveal anything about the terrorist organisation to an unsuspecting photographer. But why would that matter in a reality not connected to the agency?

Unless.

'Do you know of George Fielding?' I asked.

She stood back, shocked. 'How do you know that name?'

'I could ask you the same question.'

'Are you the real Thom Sayer?'

'Are you the real Tamara Braithwaite?'

There was a moment of silence—she was contemplating a response.

Slowly, she loosened her posture, lowering the pistol. 'That explains how earlier you knew so much about consciousness migration.'

'Correct. I was trying to gauge a reaction from Braithwaite. I didn't consider how you responded.'

'How do you know about George Fielding?'

'In my dimension, he is a variant of your husband.'

'Are you working for the agency?'

'I presume you are as well?'

'My real name is Victoria Alexeyev. I have been here for several months monitoring Braithwaite,' she explained, holstering the weapon on the thigh under her dress.

'Jackson Blake. Are you from my dimension?'

'No. But my superiors informed me yesterday that Fielding is the leader of Leveller.'

'Why were you sent here to monitor Braithwaite?'

'Because of his business exploits.' She removed the thumb mould.

'How did you traverse into this dimension?'

'A while back, Braithwaite bought out a small start-up experimenting with quantum computers and consciousness analysis. During a demonstration, his wife offered to be the test subject. I migrated into her vessel.'

'Earlier today, Braithwaite said he didn't know about consciousness migration. Was he lying to me?'

'Of course. Braithwaite didn't want to draw attention and will probably do whatever he can to stop the university from rivalling his business.'

'Is Braithwaite linked to Leveller?'

'Not intentionally.'

'What do you mean?'

'Braithwaite has also been a test subject for the start-up. We suspect, without consent, Fielding used his vessel and has done whatever he needed to in this dimension.'

'You monitored Braithwaite whilst Fielding was possibly using his vessel?'

'I suspect so. There were subtle changes in behaviour.'

'And what did Fielding do whilst here?'

Alexeyev pointed at the USB stick.

'Braithwaite doesn't know what Leveller is?'

'I don't suspect it.'

'But how come Braithwaite uses the terrorist group's name as his computer password?'

'Variants often share likenesses from similar earlier experiences. The word could have a different meaning to Braithwaite.'

I looked up at the camera opposite. 'Did you look at the CCTV footage to figure out the password?'

'I did. And you?'

'Yes. Fielding possibly did the same, logged into the computer and found the prototype.'

'Why do you want it?'

'It might help us track down the final terrorist.'

'How?'

'The final member of Leveller possibly used this prototype to encrypt a video message sent to my dimension.'

'They sent the video to my agency as well. How are you going to send the prototype?'

'Hopefully, through the quantum computer at the university.'

'Are you going to copy it onto the SD card?'

'Correct. What is your intention?'

'I need to extract his data. It has taken a while for me to plan. Braithwaite has always kept the USB stick close, even when we slept together. It took a while to produce the fingerprint mould. Earlier this evening, I noticed he didn't have the USB stick.'

'How so?'

'I stroked his legs flirtatiously. Other than a phone, his pockets were empty.'

'He didn't mention anything about not having it?'

'No.'

'Good.'

'Whilst he is partying with Esposito, I thought it was the ideal opportunity.'

'But how were you planning to do this?'

'I was going to transfer the data onto the USB stick and get out of here.'

'No. We need to be more subtle than that.'

'Why?'

'Because Braithwaite cannot know of a theft. If the variant does, he could notify the remaining member of Leveller. They will then be aware that we have the prototype.'

'But, I told you—Braithwaite has been an unknowing puppet for Leveller.'

'Are you one hundred per cent certain he isn't involved with the terrorist group?'

'…No.'

'It is best that the USB stick stays here. Do you have anything else to transfer the data onto?'

'No. What shall I do?'

'You need to leave this to me.'

'But that means I am compromising my mission.'

'I will ask my superior to contact your dimension and explain the situation. We can transfer the data from our end.'

'Okay.'

'In that case, can you help me?'

'Yes, how?'

'I must go back down the corridor and escape via the pool deck. Can you distract the shipmates?'

'Okay.'

'Thank you, Alexeyev.'

She walked towards the door, opened it and looked at me. 'Best of luck, Blake.'

'We might see each other again in another life.'

'Perhaps.' She nodded, walked out into the corridor, and closed the door.

Thirty-Three

Sitting back for a few moments, I processed the unexpected exchange. I was frustrated that the director and Qubit hadn't fully debriefed me, making me aware that other agents were operating in this dimension.

I turned on the screen, re-entered the password, and opened the SD card folder where the prototype and personal data lay before ejecting the device. After this, I turned off the computer. Standing, I walked around, withdrew the SD card, and placed it into the plastic case before putting it into the waterproof bag.

Opening the door, I checked that both ends of the corridor were clear before continuing toward the security room. Easing inside, I sat down and turned on the screen.

I ended the video replay, deleted the file from the computer, and checked that the live camera footage was playing again before turning off the screen. Standing, I replaced the seat and walked back out into the corridor.

With haste, I started moving towards the stern, my hands raised, expecting one of the side doors to open. I walked underneath the stairs that led to the lounge area above. I stopped, hearing Alexeyev talking loudly and laughing, obviously putting on a drunken act.

It extinguished the possibility that she was a double agent.

Confident I would not face confrontation, I moved faster towards the end door. Opening this, I checked the pool area was clear before edging outwards. Above, I couldn't see any people or lights on the upper levels. I started edging towards the rear deck and ladder.

Standing, I allowed the vessel time to prepare for the swim back to the mainland. Rested, I climbed down the ladder and lowered into the water.

The return swim took longer because the vessel's right leg was aching. Eventually reaching the cove, I climbed up onto the same outcrop. I sat down, rubbed my right leg and regained my breath.

I unstrapped the waterproof bag, placed it down, took off the wetsuit, dried the vessel with the towel, dressed, and put the wetsuit, towel and magnet into the bag. Withdrawing the SD card case, I placed it into the pocket with the credit card and room key. I reassembled the walking stick, put on the sealed waterproof bag, and made my way inland.

From here, I headed northwards along the dusty track until I reached the main road. There were no street lamps to guide my way. I looked across the water at the superyacht, hoping my presence had been undetected.

I hailed a taxi. It took me up the cliffside and into the main village. I asked the driver to stop before getting to the hotel driveway.

After paying, I walked down one of the adjacent streets. I found an industrial-sized bin at the back of a restaurant filled with food waste bags. Removing the waterproof bag, I placed it inside and pulled layers of rubbish to conceal it. Checking that no one was watching, I started walking to the hotel.

Several minutes later, I arrived at the entrance. Greeting me, the door attendant opened the door. I walked towards the lift and went to the floor where my room was situated.

Moments later, I entered the room, closed the door, stood there and let out a sigh of relief. Other than the aching right leg, I suddenly felt a tension in the vessel disappear.

Turning on the light, I hobbled over to the table, sat down, placed the walking stick aside, and opened the laptop. Withdrawing the SD card, I inserted it into the side of the computer. Moments later, the folder appeared, housing the prototype file and Braithwaite's data.

Suddenly, I heard a sound nearby—it was a muffled rumble.

Looking for the source, I noticed Sayer's work phone lying on the side, facedown, charging. I stood up and walked over to it. Picking up the device, I turned it over.

The screen came to life. There were various missed call notifications from a person called Mimi. It was the first time I had heard of the name in this dimension.

It rang again.

Accepting the call, I placed the device to my ear. 'Hello?'

Thirty-Four

'Thom? Thank God! Are you okay?' I heard a woman speaking. It was a voice I didn't expect. '…Thom, are you there?'

'Yes, I'm here,' I eventually said.

It took a moment for me to accept who it was—a variant of my ex-wife, Julia.

'What the hell happened? I tried calling your normal phone. But it went straight to voicemail.'

'The battery is broken.'

'Why didn't you call me on this phone? Where are you?'

'The Amalfi Coast in Italy.'

'What?!'

'I'm here for work.'

'Who with?'

'Amara Lennox.'

'Then why the hell didn't you tell me?'

'I am sorry, Ju…Mimi.'

'Look, I know things have been tough. But you have been distant. Figuratively and literally. Please tell me these things. I was worried *sick*.' She had a similar temperament to Julia.

'I don't know what to say.'

'Were you intentionally ignoring my phone calls?'

'No, I…I left the phone in the hotel room.'

'I understand you are feeling down because of Ollie.'

'Ollie?'

'…Our son?'

'What do you mean?'

'…Are you okay?'

'Yes, I just…How is he?'

'Still the same—in a coma,' she said dryly.

Charlie—alive?

'Where is he?'

'Here at our home, of course.'

'Look, I'm sorry I didn't tell you where I was. My mind has been all over the place. We're flying back tomorrow morning. I will come straight home.'

'Okay…Just don't do this again!'

'I won't.'

She expelled a sigh filled with irritability and relief. 'How has work been?'

'We are doing a hotel review for Fortuna Magazine.'

'That sounds fancy.'

'Yeah, it's been nice.'

'We need a holiday together.'

'I know. We can discuss it when I get home.'

'Okay. Message tomorrow before you get on the flight?'

'I will.'

'I love you.'

'…I love you too.'

'Good night.'

'Good night.'

I cancelled the call. My arm involuntarily slumped down.

I was aware that my ex-wife and son could exist in another dimension. But witnessing it was hard to digest.

Another life. Another chance.

Was it wrong for me to visit them just this once?

But I shook my head, thinking about the real Thom Sayer, knowing I had to focus on the mission.

I placed the phone on the side, leaned over the laptop, removed the SD card, and put it on the bedside table. I then called room service, asking them to wash my main clothes. A few minutes later, an assistant arrived, taking them away, saying they would be ready in less than two hours.

I took a shower to wash away everything from the long day. I was grateful that the plan had worked.

But all of this was eclipsed by the memory of the last time I saw Charlie: the park pond. His disappearance. My inability to deal with things.

The crippling guilt.

Perceiving my thoughts spiralling, I switched the shower to cold. Feeling the sensation against my skin, I resisted pulling away, instead standing there—distracted.

Once clean of impure thoughts, I dried off, walking into the bedroom. I stood by the balcony, looking looking listlessly into the distance, until the assistant returned with my clean, ironed clothes.

Thanking him, I set them aside and checked the phone. Lennox had messaged, asking to meet at reception at zero-six-hundred-hours. Confirming this with a response, I threw the phone aside, lay on the bed, and switched off the light.

Even though the vessel was exhausted, I was overwhelmed, unable to shake the possibility of seeing my family again.

Oblivious to the fact I was smiling.

I managed to get a few hours of rest before dawn. When I had dressed and packed, I walked to reception and waited for Lennox. She soon arrived.

'I doubt Esposito will be up this early to say goodbye,' she said, handing in her room key to the desk clerk.

We waited by the entrance for the taxi to arrive.

'Did you finish the review?' I asked, sitting in the back seat and closing the door.

'It is nearly done. Once home, I will do another draft before submitting.'

'What did you think about Braithwaite?'

'Something is going on—he seemed defensive when I asked him questions. And to go to such an extent with protecting his data?'

'I agree.' I looked out of the window as we descended the driveway.

If only I could tell her the full extent of the truth. But divulging too much could compromise the mission.

I stayed quiet while travelling to Napoli International Airport, gazing out the window. My thoughts gravitated towards Mimi and Ollie. But I had to remind myself about my duties. The immediate obstacle was figuring out how I would gain access to the university's quantum computer to transfer the information and traverse back into my original dimension.

We arrived at the airport. I sent Mimi a text and took the return flight. And once we landed, another taxi took us to the city centre. We arrived at Dalston Square. Here, we got out and stood to the side.

'Thanks for helping me with this commission, Thom,' Lennox said.

'Any time.' I smiled.

'Once Eva has approved the work, we will be paid. I assume you have the same banking details?'

'It is the same.'

'And I have all your receipts to claim back for expenses?'

I would spare her the inconvenience of not knowing (for now) about the wetsuit and other gear.

'Yes.'

'Great!' She looked in the direction of her flat. 'Well, it has been fun.'

'Are you going to do some more investigating into Braithwaite?'

'I think so.'

'I wish you the best of luck with that.'

'Thanks. Hopefully, we can get some more work from Fortuna soon.'

'Sounds good.' Standing there looking awkward, I was unsure whether to go in for a hug. 'Bye for now.'

'Bye, Thom,' she giggled, walking off.

Time is precious. But I couldn't resist—I would buy a replacement battery for the personal phone.

On the other device, the map application still showed directions from Umar. I went right onto Dalston Lane, heading easterly towards Hackney Central.

Walking into the shop, I presented the device. The assistant searched through a rack on the wall behind her, finding the matching battery. Purchasing it, I walked back out in the street and placed the new, fully charged battery into the phone.

Turning it on, I saw the wallpaper: a photo of Mimi and Ollie standing in a garden. They looked happy. She had dyed her hair auburn. He was a few years older than when I had last seen Charlie.

It was a disorientating sight. I felt a shiver envelope the vessel.

Unsurprisingly, moments later missed calls and text notifications from Mimi flooded the screen. I skimmed through them all before opening the contacts application. There, I found Sayer's home address.

Calling a taxi, I gave directions. The flat was off Newington Green.

Driving there, I could feel nausea churning in my stomach. I took a few deep breaths to settle my nerves.

I would only go there for a short time. To experience how it felt to have my family all together again.

Several minutes later, the taxi drew towards the small park area, surrounded by a circular road, houses, shops and restaurants. Passing a zebra crossing, the driver indicated, pulling left onto a small layby. Paying the driver with contactless, I exited the car and walked back on myself.

To the right was Ferntower Road, entered by a small, open area. There were flowerbeds and seating. Two restaurants were to the right. The two-storey flat was above one of these.

Walking to the doorway, I set the stick aside before rummaging in the front pocket of the rucksack for a key. Inserting it, I took a moment to compose myself.

The hand was shaking. Remembering that I was inside Sayer's vessel, I had to show self-restraint.

I turned the key and opened the door. Instantly, the smell of sandalwood—Julia's favourite fragrance for our old home. It was as though I was stepping back in time. Before me was stairs. Walking inside, I listened intently, hearing someone moving around upstairs.

Scaling the stairs onto a landing, before me was a single door. I opened it, revealing a small living room—with windows looking out onto the road—adjoined by an archway to the kitchen at the back. In there, I could see Mimi. She had her back turned, washing the dishes. I closed the door behind me, watching as she acknowledged this, looking at me.

Our eyes met. I felt vulnerable. Mimi smiled at me. Julia hadn't done that for a long time. I couldn't muster any words.

Mimi launched forward, throwing her arms around my neck, and embraced me in a kiss. It was the first time in years that I had held her, feeling the soft tenderness of her lips. She didn't let go. I relaxed, closing my eyes. After throwing the camera bag and walking stick aside, I put my arms around her.

Mimi stood back. She could see the awkward expression on Sayer's face. 'How was the flight?'

'It was fine,' I managed to say.

There was a moment of silence. Mimi looked at me inquisitively. She could tell that something wasn't right. Julia always had a strong intuition.

'Do you want something to drink?'

'No, thanks.'

'Okay.' She squinted her eyes. 'Give me your backpack.' I obliged. 'You left your walking stick at Professor Everett's laboratory. How has your leg been?'

'I think I overdid it with all the walking.'

'What is the Amalfi Coast like?'

'Stunning.'

'Can you show me any photos?'

'I've already given them to Amara.'

'Okay.' She placed the bag down on the sofa.

There was another moment of silence.

'I just wanted to apologise again for not telling you where I was.'

'It's fine.' She smiled. I could see melancholia in her eyes, just like Julia. Always so accommodating.

'I should've replaced the phone battery straight away. But when I went to buy one, I got distracted by Amara. She called to offer me last-minute work. It's why I randomly went to Italy.'

Thom, please forgive me.

'I understand.'

'How have you been?'

'Not bad, I suppose. Work has been busy. I met Selena yesterday for a few drinks.'

'How is she?'

'Yeah, fine. Standard—dating drama.'

'Who was looking after Charlie?'

'Who?'

'Sorry—Ollie.'

Her eyebrow rose. 'The nurse came round for a few hours.'

'Oh, yeah, of course.'

'Thom,' she said in a stern tone. 'Are you okay?'

'What do you mean?'

'You just seem to be… acting strangely.'

'There is just a lot going on in my head now.'

'Do you want to talk about it?'

'Ever since Friday morning's session at the university, I have felt a bit…off.'

'What did they do to you?'

'They put me in an induced coma and performed brain scans.'

'Are they any closer to finding a way to bring Ollie back?'

'Not yet.'

'If you're not feeling too good, perhaps I should call Professor Everett?'

'That's a good idea. I might need to go back in to ensure I'm all right.'

'Let me call him.' Mimi picked up her phone from a table. 'When I couldn't get to you, I rang him. He told me you seemed a bit absent-minded.'

I rubbed the side of Sayer's face. 'I guess so.' I looked towards the door leading back onto the landing. 'I'm going to see Ollie.'

'Okay,' she mouthed, waiting as the phone rang.

Her saying that gave me confirmation that he was here. Alive.

A shiver enveloped Sayer's body—my body. It didn't matter.

I took the walking stick and went back onto the landing. After taking the next flight of steps, at the top, through the wooden bannisters, I could see three doors.

The first two were ajar, showing the bathroom and master bedroom. At the far end, there was one door that was closed.

Approaching it, I could feel Sayer's heart beating with excitement. The stomach-churning grew relentless. I took another large breath, trying to calm the vessel.

Our collective experience.

I opened the door and walked inside.

Thirty-Five

Ollie was lying there, looking peaceful, connected to a heart monitor, a tube protruding from his mouth, tucked into a single bed illuminated in the darkness by a free-standing lamp. I stood there for a moment digesting the view, unaware that tears were trickling down the vessel's face.

The soft, repetitive beeping of the heart monitor—a mechanical sign of life making this seem real despite my son lying there motionless.

I walked over to the bedside, drew a chair forward, and sat beside Ollie. Reaching out, I touched his forearm and felt his skin.

The sensation sent a shiver seeping down my spine.

My son was alive.

Wiping the tears from Sayer's cheeks, I looked at Ollie's face and stroked his fringe. How long had he been in a coma? How did this happen? What experiences had this child had with Sayer? I couldn't ask Mimi these questions because I didn't want to arouse further suspicion about Sayer's behaviour.

This child was my own, but at the same time wasn't.

Just being here for a short time would be enough. Despite Ollie's present condition, it gave some semblance of comfort knowing that my son was still alive in another dimension.

Hearing footsteps approaching, I turned to the doorway. Mimi stood, looking at us. We exchanged pensive smiles. This time, I wasn't putting on an act.

She walked behind me, placing a hand on my shoulder. I reached upwards and held it. With the other hand resting on Ollie's forearm, I closed my eyes, paying attention to the sensation of their skin.

'Thom, I spoke to Professor Everett,' Mimi said softly.

I opened my eyes. 'What did the professor say?'

'He seemed concerned and suggested you see him.'

'Okay.'

Mimi walked around to the other side of the bed, drew forward another chair, and sat opposite me. She held my free hand, taking Ollie's right hand—joined together, looking down at her unconscious son, chewing her lower lip.

There, we would remain for a while in silence.

A brief moment with a family I had never met before.

I desperately wanted to stay with them but knew I had to leave.

I stood, tears still trickling down Sayer's face. Reluctantly, I walked back down the stairs into the lounge, brushed away tears, and picked up the backpack. I withdrew the laptop, lay it on the dining table and sat down. Mimi entered the room.

'I just need to email Amara,' I explained, slotting the SD card into the laptop.

I opened a private window in the internet browser and turned on a virtual private network to disguise my activity and the laptop's IP address. I searched for a website where I could send large files. On this, I uploaded the prototype software and the folder containing Braithwaite's data. I inputted Lennox's email address before creating a fake email account to use as the sender. I then added a message explaining how Lennox needed to use the prototype to decrypt Braithwaite's files. It would appear to come from an anonymous sender.

I sent the transfer. Opening the new web account, I received an email letting me know that it had successfully delivered the documents to Lennox's email account. After this, I deleted the email and account, removing any trace of the transfer.

Less than an hour later, I walked into the university building where I had traversed into this dimension only a few days prior. Recollecting the layout of the building, I walked up the stairs, passing the locker room, and down a corridor until I entered the laboratories.

Walking inside, I scoured the large room for the glass-walled cubicle where Professor Everett worked. Passing a pair of conversing technicians, I reached the cubicle. Seeing me approach, the professor came forward to open the door.

'Thom, how are you?' he said warmly.

'I feel a bit unsteady, professor,' I replied.

'Please, come in.'

He gestured for me to enter. I accepted, ushered to a chair in front of the desk where the quantum computer stood. Professor Everett closed the door, sat down at a nearby chair and pushed toward me on the casters.

Now, a short distance away, he looked at me analytically. 'Mimi told me you haven't been yourself for the past few days?'

'That's right.'

'Perhaps we should scan your brain to see if that could shed some light on the matter.' He turned to the computer, typing commands into the keyboard.

As he was preoccupied, I reached into Sayer's pocket where the work phone was sitting, the screen left on, ready to be used.

Suddenly, the professor heard a ringtone resounding from inside his laboratory jacket. He withdrew the phone, seeing it was from a withheld number. Cancelling it, he placed the phone down on the side.

Remembering the phone's layout and functions, I tried the call again. This time, the professor leaned over to silence it. I allowed the call to ring out. The professor ignored it. I tried again. Huffing, the professor picked up the ringing phone and turned to face me.

'I had best take this, Thom,' he said, standing.

I smiled.

The professor walked out of the cubicle and exited the laboratory. As he did this, I pulled out the phone, placed it down, and took out the SD card. I quickly slotted this into an external reader. Moments later, a folder appeared on the computer's desktop.

I entered the computer's applications folder and found the hard-drive utility application. Opening it, I looked across the top tabs until I found one named 'QN'. When I clicked on this, it showed the list of quantum configurations, a conversation box, and an upload function.

Suddenly, I heard Everett answering the call: 'Hello?'

I picked up the phone, cushioned it between my neck and shoulder, and answered with a fake voice—default salesperson: 'Hello, am I speaking to Professor Maxwell Everett?'

'You are.'

I clicked on the upload function box. It opened a folder from which I could source the files. 'Is now the best time to talk?'

'Not really. Who is it I am speaking to?'

'I am conducting market research and need a few minutes of your time to ask some questions?' Clicking on the SD card folder, I selected the prototype file and data folder.

'Market research? What exactly is it for?'

An upload box appeared on the screen, showing the files uploading onto the quantum network.

I looked around, trying to source inspiration. '…Laboratory equipment.'

'Are you from the company we order from?'

'Yes.'

The upload function asked for a destination—I chose my configuration.

'Now is not the best time. Would you mind calling me back in an hour or so?'

'That should not be a problem, professor. I apologise if I have interrupted you.'

As the uploading ended, I shut the hard-drive utility application. 'That is quite all right.'

'In that case, I shall call you later.'

I went into the SD folder and deleted all the files.

'Bye for now.'

'Bye.'

The line went dead.

I went into the phone's call history, deleted the list, closed the application, and turned off the screen. I withdrew the SD card and pocketed both of them.

I knew that Sayer would have to deal with the repercussions of sleepwalking through the past few days. His next credit card bill would contain random purchases. Thankfully, he would receive a handsome reimbursement with the commission payment.

I just hoped what happened wouldn't impact his health, career and relationships.

In my periphery, the door closed behind the professor. He walked back into the laboratory. Sitting back casually in the chair, I looked around, pretending to look inconspicuous. Moments later, the professor walked into the cubicle.

'Sorry about that, Thom—it was a damn marketing call.'

'No problem.' I smiled.

Everett retook his chair in front of the screen. It looked untouched. 'Now, just bear with me.'

He started typing on the keyboard. A few minutes later, he gestured for me to walk to the seat where I had first entered the dimension. I sat down. He brought forward the small brain scanner attached to a metal frame.

'Please relax, Thom; this will only take a few moments.' He returned to the quantum computer. 'Okay, you can now close your eyes.'

I did as he asked, leaving his dimension.

Thirty-Six

I opened my eyes, seeing the familiar sight: the inside of the brain scanner. The endotracheal tube was protruding from my mouth. The heart monitor was attached to my chest. Intravenous lines were in my arms. I couldn't feel catheters inserted elsewhere.

Nearby, I could hear the quantum computer making noises.

Hearing this, Qubit rushed to my side, leaning forward to look into my eyes. 'Blake, are you okay?'

I nodded.

The technician proceeded to aid in removing all the equipment. Shuffling from underneath the scanner, I sat forward, rubbing my eyes. 'How long have I been away?'

'Ten hours.'

'And how long do we have left until the remaining member of Leveller releases the nano-bombs?'

'Two hours.'

The director walked forward, looking exhausted. 'I hope your time spent in Braithwaite's dimension was productive?'

I stood up to address him. 'Yes, sir.'

'Did you discover any information about the whereabouts of the remaining variant?'

'Sort of.' His eyebrow rose. 'You might want to check the quantum network—I attempted to send something through.'

Qubit went over to the computer, typing in commands. He clicked on a small box. It opened up a folder. Inside was the prototype and Braithwaite's data.

I joined him. From behind, Carroll and Penrose appeared. I nodded at them. They reciprocated the gesture.

'How did you both get on?' I asked.

'My lead went cold,' Carroll replied, frowning. 'And Penrose's Fielding variant couldn't provide intelligence about the video location.'

'What exactly are we looking at?' The director asked, walking over to inspect the screen.

I turned to address him. 'I managed to confront Braithwaite. What you are seeing is prototype software.'

'What does it do?' Carroll asked.

'It encrypts files using quantum technology.'

'And what are all these?' Qubit asked, sifting through hundreds of corrupted files in the folder.

'Braithwaite's documents. They are currently encrypted and must pass through the software to be accessed.'

'Do you think there is something amongst these documents that could lead us to Leveller?' the director asked.

'Actually, sir, I hope the prototype could do something else.' Everyone looked at me. 'The original video transmission—didn't you mention that the metadata is corrupt?'

'Correct,' the director replied.

'Do you think this software could fully decrypt the video and provide the location of Leveller?' Qubit interjected excitably.

I nodded.

'Qubit, ask Okoro to send through the video file,' the director ordered.

'Yes, sir.' The technician picked up a phone and called through to the control room. Moments later, the video file appeared on the screen. Putting down the phone, Qubit addressed me: 'What do I do now?'

'Open the prototype and simply drop the video file into it.'

He nodded, following my instructions. As he did this, everyone walked closer to the screen.

I could feel my heart rate increasing with anticipation. My body was feeling the effects of Statera withdrawal.

Suddenly, a new file appeared on the computer's desktop. Qubit right-clicked on it, bringing up the information box. Inside this was the metadata.

'Well?' the director asked impatiently. 'Does it have the location metadata?'

Qubit did not respond. Instead, he brought up the quantum network database before rifling through the list of configurations.

Eventually, he stopped, turning to face us.

'Blake was right—the prototype decrypted the file.'

I felt tension alleviate my body. Carroll and Penrose expelled sighs of relief, patting me on the shoulders.

'But?' the director asked sternly.

'The video's location was not on our database.'

My heart skipped a beat.

The director walked forward, analysing the screen. 'Does that mean it is fake?'

'It looks legitimate.'

'What then?'

'It could be that we haven't discovered this dimension before, or something else—'

'Could Fielding have removed it from the database?' I interrupted.

Qubit and the director turned to face me. The former nodded.

'As part of Leveller's contingency plan, Fielding removed the dimension from the database to ensure there is no trace of it on the quantum network?' Carroll asked.

'That is the most probable case,' Qubit replied.

'That's why we couldn't track down the dimension by comparing time differences,' the director explained. 'What does the database say about that dimension?'

'It recognises it—someone has traversed before.'

'Are there any profiles associated with it?'

'Profiles?' I asked.

The director turned to address me. 'If you have traversed into a vessel in that dimension, a profile is created on the database.'

'There is only one, sir,' Qubit replied.

'Who?'

'Fielding.'

'Does that mean we don't have variants in that dimension?' Carroll asked.

'That could be the case,' Qubit replied.

Penrose asked, 'Sir, we have made great efforts to find every dimension where the agency exists. Is there a possibility it doesn't exist in that dimension?'

'I wouldn't be surprised,' the director replied.

'It would make sense that the final member of Leveller resides in a dimension where neither the agency nor ourselves exist,' I said.

The director stood there, his arms crossed, stroking his chin in deep thought.

'How the hell are we going to get there?!' Carroll questioned.

'We will take a ten-minute break,' the director replied. 'Qubit, proceed with Blake's assessment.'

'Yes, sir.'

'Bear in mind our limited time.'

'Yes, sir.'

'And, Blake,' the director said, facing me.

'Yes, sir.'

'Excellent work.' He nodded firmly.

'Thank you, sir.'

Thirty-Seven

Qubit ushered me to the door leading into the assessment room. I followed through, taking a seat at the table. The technician closed the door and eased himself into the seat opposite.

'By now, you know the drill. Let's get this over with as quickly as possible,' Qubit said, opening a folder. He pulled out a questionnaire worksheet before taking a pen from his top pocket and clicking the cap.

'Sounds good to me,' I replied, noticing my hand shaking with withdrawal.

'Now, I am going to ask you a series of questions. Answer them with the first response that comes to mind. Understood?'

'Yes.'

'Okay. What is your name?'

'Jackson Blake.'

He started making notes on the worksheet. 'Your alias?'

'Ridley Hewitt.'

'What day is it?'

'Saturday.'

'What is the agency?'

'A clandestine global organisation.'

'How many years of service do you have with the organisation?'

'Ten.'

'What is the director's name?'

'I don't know.'

'Are you baseline?'

I could feel my leg twitching. 'Affirmative.'

'Where are we sitting?'

'In an assessment room within the secretive branch at the organisation's headquarters.'

'And where is that situated?'

'Underneath Jubilee Gardens on the Southbank of London.'

'Other than myself, can you hear other voices?

'Negative.'

'What is the objective of this mission?'

'To track down the remaining member of the terrorist group named Leveller.'

'Other than myself, can you see anyone else?'

'Negative.'

'Why is it important to stop the target?'

'Unless we meet his demands, the variant will release nano-bombs across multiple dimensions.'

'Are you baseline?

'Affirmative.'

'Why can't we meet the terrorists' demands?'

'Because he wants us to reveal the organisation's existence to the world.'

'And why is that non-negotiable?'

'Because it could lead to destabilisation.'

He looked me in the eye. 'Who is Ollie Sayer?

The name sounded like an ice pick slamming into my skull. My body was awash with anxiety. In that split moment, I fumbled my words: 'He, he is a variant of my deceased son.'

'How do you know this?'

'…Because he is Thom Sayer's son.'

'Whilst in Sayer's dimension, did you contact his family?'

'…Affirmative.'

'Are you baseline?

'…Affirmative.'

'Did you step away from the mission to spend time with Sayer's family?'

I looked downwards. '… Affirmative.'

'Are you baseline?'

I sat there for a moment, contemplating his question. Why was he asking me about Sayer's family? How did he know they existed? Were they aware that it was my weakness?

He spoke first: 'I can see we have a problem, Blake.'

'Sorry, I—'

Qubit scribbled a few more notes at the bottom of the sheet before signing and dating it. He looked up at me, smiling. 'Well, you passed the assessment.'

My posture loosened. 'Oh, right.'

'Blake, we are aware that you have a trigger. The director knows that Tate used this against you. We will deal with it after the mission's completion.'

'I understand.' I nodded.

'However, your ability to differentiate between Sayer's son and this reality indicates you are of reasonably sound mind, hence why you passed the test.' He pushed the worksheet and pen towards me. 'Please sign and date.' I obliged before handing them back to him. 'I'm sure you understand we were apprehensive about disclosing information about Sayer's family. It could have compromised the mission.'

'Is that why the debriefing was minimal?'

'Correct. Please, don't take it personally.'

'I won't.'

'Did you manage to spend some time with Sayer's son?' I nodded. He smiled sympathetically. 'Do you need a toilet break before we continue the mission?'

Suddenly, the thought of self-medicating consumed me. '…Yes.'

'Okay.' He gestured towards the door.

Exiting, I walked to the conference room where the director, Carroll and Penrose sat.

'I just need to freshen up,' I said timidly, entering the control room and exiting the main corridor.

I stood there for a moment. The door closed behind me. It was early morning. I saw a few agents walking around, about to start their shift.

I wondered what had happened since the nano-bombing yesterday morning. Had any survivors been found?

Julia.

I took out my phone—still no response. Frustrated, I turned off the screen and pocketed the device.

Walking into the toilets, I went into a cubicle and relieved myself. Hearing a cleaner coming in, I waited until they had finished their work. Minutes later, I walked out and approached the sink. Turning on the tap, I pressed the dispenser button, covering my hands with soap. Cleaning them under the water, I looked up at my reflection.

It was strange looking back at my true self. But something felt different.

Qubit's words echoed in my head—'Are you baseline?'

After washing my hands, I dried them off with a paper towel. Walking back to the sink, I placed my hands on either side, looking at my reflection in the mirror.

The impulse struck me. I reached into my trouser pocket and withdrew the bottle of Statera. Opening it—and realising I hadn't locked the toilet door—I knew I would have to be quick with medicating. I poured a few tablets onto the palm of my shaking hand, and as I reached upwards to throw them into my mouth, I looked myself in the eye.

'Are you baseline?'

Suddenly, I remembered seeing Ollie lying there unconscious and the sadness on Mimi's face.

I felt *her* suffering. I felt *Thom's* suffering.

Why was I subjecting myself to this? Why was I using these drugs to escape from my issues?

Voluntarily, my hand turned on its side. The tablets fell into the sink and rolled in the plughole, echoing.

Looking up at my reflection, I nodded before pouring the remaining contents of the bottle into the sink and brushing the tablets down the plughole.

I was no longer staring at my life at the bottom of an empty bottle.

It was time to let go.

Thirty-Eight

Everyone stood when I re-entered. The director ushered us into the operations room. Once there, we walked over to the quantum computer. Qubit brought up the database on the screen.

'We now have ninety minutes to stop Fielding's variant before he releases the nano-bombs,' the director explained. The veins on his temples were throbbing. 'We now know, for definite, that the agency nor your civilian variants exist in the terrorist's dimension.'

'Is there a way to stop Leveller from transmitting the nano-bomb?' I asked. 'Somehow remove that dimension from the quantum network?'

'That won't be possible,' the director admitted.

'There is only one option,' Qubit interjected.

'Which is?' Penrose asked.

'I have found that there are a few quantum computers in that dimension through which we can connect,' Qubit explained, 'but only a few of them have the capability for consciousness migration.'

'Why is that?'

'Because there must be a connection with a person's mind.'

'What kind of computers are they? Similar to the experiment Sayer was taking part in?'

'Not exactly,' the director replied. 'The devices are virtual reality headsets.'

'What, like a computer game?' I asked.

'Correct,' Qubit replied. 'It seems each device taps into the brain's neurology to access and manipulate the user's senses—a fully immersive experience.'

'And you are convinced that this can migrate consciousness?' Carroll asked.

'It is a risk we will have to take.' Qubit grimaced.

'Who is the vessel we will be traversing?' Penrose asked.

'It will be a stranger,' Qubit replied.

'But that means the computer will migrate our consciousnesses into completely different brains?!' I replied. 'Has this ever been done before?'

The director exchanged dubious looks with the technician. 'It has not.'

'There is a high probability that whoever traverses into that world might never return,' Qubit admitted.

I turned to Penrose and Carroll. We all exchanged disconcerted looks.

'I will go,' I said, facing the director.

'You are sure of this, Blake?' he replied.

'Yes.'

'If Blake traverses first, can he get other people to use the headset so we can join him?' Carroll asked.

Qubit stood there for a moment, pondering. 'That could work.'

'Are you sure about this?' I asked her.

'Of course.' She smiled.

Penrose stepped forward. 'We're a team, right?'

'What about your cat?'

'She's resourceful.'

I smiled, turning to face the director.

'Very well,' he said. 'Blake, take a seat and prepare to traverse.'

'Yes, sir.' I walked over to the seat and sat down. 'I don't suppose we know where Fielding's variant might be?'

'No,' Qubit replied, typing feverishly into the keyboard.

'Great,' I said dryly. 'Only ninety minutes to pull a miracle out of my arse.'

'Well, get pulling!' the director said.

For a moment, I thought he had a sense of humour.

'Not quite,' Qubit replied.

'What now?' I asked.

'Due to time dilation, it appears their dimension runs faster.'

'By how much?' the director asked.

'One of our hours is thirty minutes in their dimension.'

'We have forty-five minutes?!' Penrose exclaimed.

'Yes,' Qubit said timidly.

I eased myself under the brain scanner. Carroll brought forward the ECG electrode pads for me.

'The vessel is using the device. You must traverse now, Blake!'

'See you on the other side,' I said, closing my eyes.

Thirty-Nine

Sebastian Howler was standing in the middle of the green room. He was wearing a VR headset covering his eyes and ears. Across the inside of the device were many pads communicating with signals inside his brain.

From an outsider's perspective, seeing him standing there with his head and arms moving around, immersed in the experience, looked amusing. To his side, Clara and his manager were sitting on a sofa spectating.

'How real is it in there?' she asked, looking up at Howler.

'The graphics are life-like.'

'That seems kind of scary, Marvin,' she said.

'Why?'

'It might be hard to tell the difference between augmented reality and our own.'

He chuckled. 'Yeah, true!'

Suddenly, there was a knock at the door. Marvin stood, walked over and opened it. There in the doorway was Rufus Miller's assistant, Emilia.

'Hi, guys!' she said. 'Do you mind if I come in?'

'By all means,' Marvin said, standing back, allowing her inside.

Emilia walked into the room, looking at Sebastian using the device. 'It looks like he is having fun! Rufus thought it would be nice for his guests to experience this new technology.'

'I've never seen him look so content.' Marvin chuckled again.

Emilia closed the door. 'I'm just doing the rounds and wanted to ensure everything is ready for Sebastian's appearance and performance?'

'He's ready,' Marvin replied.

'Very good.'

'When does the show begin?'

'It started a few minutes ago!' Emilia replied.

She walked over to a screen mounted on a wall and turned it on. Collecting the remote control, she switched to the channel where the live show was playing. There on the screen was the host Rufus Miller. He was standing in front of the audience, saying his opening monologue.

Emilia checked her watch. 'One of the stagehands will come in fifteen minutes to collect Sebastian. Will he need last-minute make-up before going on?'

'No, I think he is ready,' Marvin replied.

'Excellent!' Emilia exclaimed. 'I heard the soundcheck earlier—they sounded *great!*'

'Hopefully, they won't blow the roof off,' Marvin joked.

'I will probably wear my earplugs, just in case,' Emilia giggled. Clara rolled her eyes. 'See you later!'

She went to the door, opened it and left.

'See you later,' Clara reiterated in a mock tone.

'Now come on, Clara, she isn't that bad!' Marvin said.

'Should we tell Sebastian that he needs to get ready?' Clara asked.

They both looked over to the musician. He had removed the headset, standing there with an awkward expression.

'Sebastian, are you okay?' Clara asked.

I was looking at a young woman and a middle-aged man. They looked amused by the expression on the vessel's face.

'Sebastian?' the woman asked.

'Yeah, I'm fine,' I replied. The vessel's voice sounded younger. His chest felt tighter—I suspected a smoker.

'Emilia just came in, saying the show has already started. They'll call for you soon,' the man explained.

'Oh, good.'

Averting my attention towards the screen, I saw a recognisable face. Walking forward, I stood gazing at the person, taking a few moments to process it—there on the screen was the variant of Fielding from the video transmission. He was sitting at a wooden desk on what appeared to be a stage, showered in studio lighting.

The man continued: 'I'm sure the interview will go well. And everyone is going to love your performance.'

Performance?

I turned to a wall-mounted mirror, seeing the vessel's appearance: young, tall, handsome, wearing a black top and leather trousers. Instantly, I knew the person was a musician.

Remembering Carroll and Penrose, I turned to the two strangers. 'Do you guys want to try this?'

'Sure, I will give it a quick go!' The man said excitedly, standing forward. I handed him the VR headset.

'The program is working. Just put it on, and off you go!'

He followed my instructions, placed the headset on, and marvelled at the experience. After a few minutes, I noticed a change in his facial expression. He abruptly withdrew the headset, looked at me and frowned analytically—like Carroll did.

She took a few moments to process the new environment before mouthing: 'Blake?'

'Yes,' I mouthed.

'What did you think?' The young woman stood forward.

'Oh, yeah—it was impressive,' Carroll replied sheepishly. 'Do you want a go?'

'I don't know.'

'Oh, come on!' I joked.

The young woman took the headset and put it on. Meanwhile, I exchanged baffled looks with Carroll. We returned our attention to the stranger. A few minutes later, she abruptly removed the headset and looked around.

'What the!' she expelled wide-eyed, looking down at her body. 'Wait, I have traversed into a woman's vessel?!'

'Welcome, Penrose.' I took the headset, placing it to the side.

'There is always a first time for everything!' Carroll patted him mockingly on the shoulder.

'Do you know where we are, Blake?' Penrose asked.

'In a television studio. I'm a musician. I don't know who you both are. I'm about to go on a talk show for an interview. And look at who by—'

I pointed at the screen where Miller was now interviewing his first guest.

'You are *kidding* me?!' Carroll exclaimed, looking at the screen.

'This is wild! Penrose added.

'The final member of Leveller has been leading a double life in this world?' Carroll asked.

'It seems that way,' I replied.

'How can we question Miller on a live broadcast?' Penrose asked.

'I will have to improvise,' I replied.

Suddenly, there was a knock at the door. We all turned to face it. I walked forward, opening it. Here stood a young woman wearing a microphone headset and holding a clipboard.

It was Elina Well's variant.

'Hi, Mr Howler! Are you ready to head down to the studio?'

'Sure!' I announced, masking my surprise, looking back at the other two.

'Please, follow me this way.' She stood back, ushering us away.

I stepped out, followed by Penrose and Carroll. The variant led us down the corridor. On either side were framed photographs of guests. In the distance, we could hear the muffled sound of the studio audience laughing and applauding.

I looked to the side. There was an open door with 'Studio Two' above it. Approaching, I peeked inside and noticed something familiar.

'Can we take a quick look inside there?' I asked.

Well's variant checked her watch, nodded, and directed us through the door and onto the sound stage.

Inside, at the centre of the room, was a three-walled wooden set illuminated by overhanging lights. It was a small dining room scene. Facing it was a studio camera.

'What is this?' I asked.

'Mr Miller comes here to record advertisements for the show and often records private video messages for fans.'

'*Video messages,*' I said, looking at Carroll and Penrose.

We all shook our heads, acknowledging that we had false clues about the location of Fielding's variant. Leveller had covered every aspect other than hiding the prototype software.

'You're on with Mr Miller in a few minutes.'

Well's variant ushered us into the corridor, shepherding us towards a double door. Above it was the sign 'Studio One.'

I exchanged disconcerted looks with Carroll and Penrose. Moments later, we went inside and stood beside the talk show set. Several metres away, Miller was sitting at his desk telling the audience an anecdote.

I could feel the vessel's heart rate increase.

Suddenly, brass band jazz music blared overhead. Miller stood to announce the arrival of his next guest.

I turned to Carroll and Penrose. 'Be prepared for anything.'

They nodded firmly.

The stage assistant gestured for me to walk on. I accepted, drawing forward onto the set. Above, hot, blinding lights engulfed me. The sound of the screaming audience was overwhelming.

Rufus Miller stood a few metres away. He walked from behind the desk, brandishing a big smile and extending a hand. I accepted this.

Our eyes met for the first time.

I had finally tracked down the remaining member of Leveller.

'Please, Sebastian, take a seat.' He gestured to the couch by his desk.

I accepted the offer, sat down, and looked at the vast studio audience—it was like multiple realities were staring at me.

Forty

The audience eventually stopped applauding. A few hysterical fans in the back rows screamed. I looked at Miller—he was laughing at their response.

What was I meant to do? I would have to work off whatever he said. But how long did I have left until he would unleash the nano-bombs? Less than thirty minutes? And how would he do that whilst on a live broadcast?'

The vessel was sweating. It felt weak—drug-fuelled. Experiencing this made me appreciate quitting the Statera.

'Now, settle down!' Miller said in a mock-authoritative tone towards the audience. Many laughed. He looked at me, smiling. 'This must be the norm for you?'

'You could say that, yeah,' I said casually.

The crowd settled.

'How are you, Sebastian?' he said warmly. 'It is a pleasure to have you finally on the show.'

'I'm very well. And thank you for inviting me on.' I smiled at the audience. There were a few more hysterical screams.

'Now, I have listened to the new album, and I must say—it is your *best yet*!' he exclaimed, turning to the audience. They started cheering.

'That's kind of you to say.' I nodded, looking out at the sea of people.

'You will be performing a song for us. Tell me, why have you chosen 'One Man Army'?

'I, ah, like the riff.' I laughed awkwardly. The audience chuckled.

'You can't argue with that! How did you find the recording process?'

I looked to the opposite side of the set. There was a stage. Upon this were various instruments ready to be played. I noticed Sebastian's full name was on the drum skin. 'It was an enjoyable time. My backing band did a great job.'

'And are you planning to go on tour?'

'Yes.'

The audience started cheering.

'Excellent. Well, I'm glad you have come on the show tonight to give a world-first exclusive performance.'

'It is my pleasure.'

His tone of voice changed. 'Now, if you don't mind—I wanted to talk to you about the recent incident.'

'Oh, yeah.' I shuffled in the chair.

'Yes, there has been a huge amount of press coverage and social media reaction to what happened when you assaulted that photographer. Would you feel comfortable talking about it?'

'I guess so.'

'I understand paparazzi were trying to photograph you and your girlfriend outside a restaurant. You threatened one of them. Eventually, you grabbed the camera and smashed it on the ground. Do you think that was necessary?'

'I…' Looking out at the audience, I suspected that Howler had a bad reputation. For his benefit, I would help: 'I overreacted. My actions were unacceptable.'

'The photographer was hospitalised.' I looked at Miller in shock but had to change my facial expression. 'You seem surprised by that? Surely you knew?'

'I just feel uncomfortable when you mention it.'

'Have you apologised to the photographer?'

'I have.'

'Why did you ridicule him in a recent interview?'

'It took me a while to accept that I'd done wrong. I now hold myself fully accountable.'

'Have you managed to curtail the drug abuse?' His eyebrow rose.

'I'm doing a lot better.' I nodded.

Miller sat there momentarily, analysing my face before turning to the audience. 'We all make mistakes in life and deserve a second chance, isn't that right?'

The audience cheered in response.

'Thank you.' I nodded encouragingly. 'That means a lot to me.'

Despite the talk show host's abrasive questioning, it only seemed like a journalistic technique. There was no indication Miller was trying to dig deeper to expose anything else.

But I considered how much time we had left, knowing it would not matter anymore, trying to disguise myself.

I looked to the side of the set. Carroll and Penrose were standing in the shadows. I hoped they understood what I was about to do.

It couldn't continue any longer.

I stood up abruptly, turning toward the camera operators. Everyone looked up at me with intrigue, seeing the frown on the vessel's face.

I was conscious of not ruining his life. Anyone outside of this studio couldn't witness whatever was about to happen.

'Stop the broadcast!' I shouted at the camera operators.

They looked out from behind the viewfinders, puzzled. I repeated the demand.

'Sebastian, whatever is the matter?' Miller asked, taken aback. I looked at the variant. He was half-stood, wide-eyed.

I turned to the camera operators. 'Turn off the cameras right now. This interview is *over!*'

I saw Carroll and Penrose walking forward from my periphery. They stood by the camera operators. To the unsuspecting eye, it would have appeared that the unhinged musician's entourage was coming to de-escalate the situation. They walked toward the camera operators, calmly instructing them to do as I said.

'Sebastian, will you please retake your seat,' Miller asked, this time with agitation and force in his tone. He looked out at the audience, letting out a nervous laugh.

Facing him, with my back turned to the cameras and audience, I said quietly, 'We have come to stop you.'

Miller looked up at me, one side of his face suddenly forming a smirk, before addressing the camera operators: 'Do as he says—turn off the cameras.'

He sat back down, placed a finger on an earpiece, and spoke into a microphone attached to his suit lapel. I suspected he was talking to his colleagues in the control room.

The operators turned off the cameras. I looked at the audience, noticing everyone sitting calmly with neutral expressions, unfazed by the outlandish behaviour.

Suddenly, I heard loud noises on either side of the set. Security guards now stood vigilantly by the exits. They had locked the doors.

I returned my focus to Carroll and Penrose standing by the camera operators. They looked unnerved, eyeing Miller. Following their trail of sight, I looked back at the talk-show host and became rigid.

Miller was standing at full height, holding a handgun, pointed straight at me.

Forty-One

'I must say, you made a remarkable effort walking down the yellow brick road to come here,' Miller said. 'And taking the risk to traverse into the vessel of a stranger! I'm aware that isn't typical branch procedure.'

'You went to great lengths to hide within this dimension. But this ends now!'

'That won't be possible. You see, not only are you held at gunpoint, but I also have protection in case something like this happens.'

'What protection?'

He pointed at the crew and audience. 'You see all those people out there? They are not civilians, but variants, also part of Leveller.'

Suddenly, the audience stood up in perfect formation, the collective sound perforating the silence. The crew also joined by standing forward in a line.

Hearing scuffling, I looked down at Carroll and Penrose. They were held at gunpoint by several of the variants.

'They are all hosts for variants of you?'

'Yes. Here to enjoy the spectacle.'

I looked at Miller. 'A little self-indulgent, don't you think?'

'They appreciate good-quality television.' Miller smirked, gesturing with the handgun. 'Please, take a seat.'

I edged back towards the sofa and sat down.

Miller retook his place behind the desk, holding the gun firmly. 'Now, let me guess—you are Jackson Blake?' I looked him intensely in the eye. Noticing this, he laughed. 'How fitting!'

I sat upright, clenched hands resting on the inside of each thigh, ready to engage. 'How d'you know my name?'

'I've been tracking your profile since you started traversing the quantum network.'

'Is that how Tate knew we were coming for him?'

'Correct.'

'Was he part of Leveller?'

'Not officially.'

'Why didn't you warn Braithwaite?'

'Because he was none the wiser to our operations.'

Agent Alexeyev was right.

'There was a possibility that someone could access the prototype and find you. If you removed this dimension from the quantum network, why not remove Braithwaite's?'

'I did. But your colleagues found it again once your variant appeared on the quantum network.'

Sayer, I owe you—again.

'Did Fielding source the prototype from Braithwaite to encrypt the video transmission?'

'As a matter of fact—*I did*.'

'What do you mean?'

'Did you think the founder and leader of Leveller would have risked being caught or killed in your reality whilst orchestrating this multi-dimensional plan?'

I sat for a moment, shocked. 'Are you…George Fielding?'

'A pleasure to meet you, Blake.' He addressed Carroll and Penrose in a sarcastic tone: 'Look who is pointing the gun *now*?'

'Is Rufus Miller being held captive in my reality?' I asked.

Fielding looked at me. 'Correct.'

'But when did you traverse here?'

'After I killed Doctor Aditi. Miller followed my instructions to remove vital information from his mind before conducting the nano-bombing of our London.'

'But why would he agree to do that on your behalf?'

'Because I showed him the truth. He understood the cause. Now that all dimensions are interconnected, it is a moral obligation.'

For a moment, I sat there digesting everything, my mind racing.

The realisation struck me: 'Was it your intention to draw us here?'

'Well done!' I exchanged stunned glances with Carroll and Penrose. 'I left the prototype with Braithwaite. It was no coincidence that quantum migrators and hosts are nearby for you to get here in time. I hoped you would find me. But I had to make you work for it.

'And now, I can humiliate all three of you in front of this audience. Then, the various organisations across the multiple dimensions would have to concede or face the consequences.'

'How many organisations are you targeting?'

'Sixty-seven.'

'Have any of them given in to your demands?'

'Not yet.'

I presumed all variants of the director must have been as stubborn as my own.

'How exactly can you transmit the files whilst presenting this talk show?'

'I have a computer connected to the quantum network programmed to automatically transfer the files once the time runs out for each dimension.'

'Has that happened yet?'

'For some, yes.'

The sound cut deep into my ears, making me shudder.

I looked back at Carroll and Penrose, horrified.

Despite our efforts, we were too late—billions of lives lost across multiple dimensions.

Forty-Two

I turned back to Fielding, swallowing hard. 'Why would you do such a terrible thing? You were once—'

'Part of the grand illusion?' he interjected. 'I understand what falsehoods the agencies have committed across multiple dimensions.'

'What do you mean?' I asked, exchanging confused glances with Carroll and Penrose.

'The agency you have risked your life to uphold is morally corrupt. You are brainwashed and submissive.

'Since the dawn of civilisation, hierarchies and institutions have been in place to maintain power for the few. In our original reality, we have what appears to be a prosperous world. Extreme poverty is decreasing. Living standards are, in general, improving. But we are witnessing the biggest wealth transfer to the super-rich in history. It is a rigged political-economic system based on infinite growth with finite resources. Unsustainable. The vast majority is powerless, preoccupied with distraction and hedonism, and polarised by cultural wars.

'And in the background, the agency upholds it all—squashing dissent, manipulating the narrative, promoting corruption. It has facilitated proxy wars, illegal wrongdoings, the spinning door of nepotism and cronyism, institutional racism, and misogyny. It could have influenced superpowers and international corporations from perpetuating climate change but has allowed it along with the consequential humanitarian crises and animal extinction.'

For a moment, I sat digesting his words—the uncomfortable truth. I had ignored it for too long.

It was no black-and-white situation.

'Why did you target those areas in our London?'

'Because of what they represent in our outdated system. Admittedly, I had to go to extremes. The loss of innocent lives will rest on my conscience.'

'The likes of Tate, Braithwaite and Miller represent exactly the thing you detest?'

'True. But sacrifices and compromises must be made. It is all for the greater good.'

'The greater good?'

'Do you know of the Convergence Protocol?'

'I do.'

'Imagine the infinite possibilities and wealth of knowledge you can plunder, traversing alternative dimensions. After discovering the quantum network, our director had grand ambitions in sight, setting up the experimental branch.

'I, with a handful of other agents, were brought in. We spent years exploring other realities, witnessing how they organised their worlds in far better ways than ours. I had conversations with the director about how we could change our world. But he was adamant about continuing this trajectory—unwavering, inflexible. Motivated by self-interest and short-sightedness, just like the elites.'

'What was his reason for sending you to alternative realities?'

'His goal was to assemble the best variants into our reality, to take down hostile nations in the way of the agency gaining global domination. It was all about power. But do you know what happened?'

'The technology fell into the wrong hands?'

'Told you this, did he?'

'Not everything.'

'Due to the director's negligence, other people gained access to quantum migrators. It caused chaos across the quantum network. The director had to sort out the colossal mess he had made. All agents in the branch would traverse realities to hunt down our enemies. We took orders to conduct horrific acts, resulting in countless civilian fatalities.

'The director wanted to extinguish all threats, levelling things out before destroying all quantum migrators.'

'This is the Convergence Protocol?'

'Correct. The blood is on my hands, just as it is for Carroll and Penrose.'

I looked at them. They looked ashamed.

'But why hold other directors and agencies accountable?'

'They are all part of the farce. D'you now see what happens when you follow orders without question? The truth will hit you between the eyes. Blink, and you will miss it.'

'You're stalling us whilst the time runs out for our dimension to meet your demands.'

'True, I am stalling you. But also telling the truth.'

'Are you willing to release nano-bombs, destroying other dimensions?'

Fielding started laughing. 'I wouldn't *dream* of such a thing!'

'What?'

'The nano-bomb threat was a *ploy*, forcing the agencies to humiliate themselves,' he said mockingly.

'Then what files are you transferring?'

'Damning, classified intelligence.'

'What are you going to do with it?'

'Send it to reliable journalists in each dimension. They can expose this farce.'

I exchanged disconcerted looks with Carroll and Penrose.

I turned to Fielding. He had a bemused expression. 'The wheels are already in motion. Do you realise that this is a no-win situation for you? Either the agencies give in to our demands, causing global scandals. Or, we release the files, which will do that for them. Or, you stop me but allow the agency to continue, unaffected, despite knowing the inconvenient truth. That last outcome is not going to happen.'

I sat there contemplating his words and, admittedly, accepting the impossibility of this situation.

It couldn't continue any further.

Standing up, I said, 'After all this time, I never thought it would amount to this. I always believed that we were fighting on the right side. But now you have shown me, opening my eyes.'

'You must ride the rising storm, Blake.'

'What should we do to assist you?' I asked, looking back at Penrose and Carroll. They maintained neutral expressions.

'You must allow for the inevitable process to unfold.' He looked at the watch in his free hand. 'In less than five minutes, the countdown will run out for your dimension. We will leak documents to the appropriate contact.'

'I understand,' I said, looking down at the ground in sorrow.

'Very good,' Fielding said sympathetically, lowering the handgun. He stood and walked forward, placing a free hand on my shoulder. 'I know that these truths are not easy to accept. It takes a person of strength to acknowledge deception.'

'It does.'

Without hesitation, I reached forward, grabbed the handgun from Fielding's grasp, spun it around, loaded and aimed it at his forehead.

And yet there was no reaction from the crew or audience—they remained eerily still and quiet.

'Now, now,' Fielding said anxiously, looking at the barrel. 'You wouldn't shoot an unarmed civilian?'

'You are a *terrorist*, Fielding!' I said, tightening my grip. '*Where* is the computer?'

'That, I cannot reveal.'

'Where *is it*?!' I pushed the barrel against his skin.

'I'm not going to reveal that to you, Blake,' he enunciated through gritted teeth. 'In a few minutes, our world is to become destabilised. Accept it for what it is. Don't fear change.'

Aiming the handgun at his kneecap, I pulled the trigger. But it didn't fire. I checked it was loaded and pressed the trigger again—nothing happened. I looked into his eyes. He glared at me.

'You didn't think I would bring a loaded weapon on set?' He swung forward, punching me hard in the face.

Due to the vessel being of medium stature and not accustomed to fighting, the impact sent me flying backwards, landing hard on the floor.

'Attack them!' I heard Fielding announce.

Disorientated, I quickly sat upright, watching Fielding run off the opposite side of the stage. Throwing the weapon aside, I got onto my feet, looking over at Carroll and Penrose. Unravelling themselves, they attacked the guards, disarmed them, and took their weapons. From behind, I could see a surge of audience members hurtling down the walkways, onto the studio floor, and in our direction.

'Blake, go after Fielding!' Carroll expelled, punching a stage assistant hard in the face. She recoiled in pain, wringing the hand, her vessel unfamiliar with violence.

'Don't kill any of these people—their vessels are innocent,' I said, launching forward, jumping off the stage toward the exit.

Meanwhile, Carroll and Penrose untangled themselves from the swarm of variants flooding upon them, tailing me.

Kicking the door wide open, before me was a long corridor. I could see Fielding in the distance.

With all my might, I started running after him.

Forty-Three

Behind me, I heard Carroll and Penrose entering the corridor, both panting heavily. I looked back at them whilst tailing Fielding.

'This guy *does not* look after himself,' Carroll heaved, bending over to catch her breath. She gasped with exhaustion.

Penrose slammed the side door shut. 'We need to keep on moving!'

'Yeah, okay.' Carroll stood to full height, put both hands on her hips, drew a breath through the nostrils, and recommenced her approach.

Looking forward, Fielding had reached the end of the corridor. There was a pair of double doors. He stopped momentarily, glanced back at us, and pushed through.

Ignoring the vessel's lack of stamina and spasms of nausea surfacing from the stomach, I kept pushing forward. Suddenly, I could hear the side door exploding open. I looked back to see a surge of Fielding's variants flooding the corridor, hurtling towards us.

Reaching the double doors, I kicked them wide open. Entering, I stopped to process this new space—a large room. To either side were rows of empty computer desks. Giant screens illuminated with news coverage covered the left wall.

In the distance, steps led up to a semi-circular office partitioned with a glass door and wall. Fielding had already entered. He was rummaging around near a desk.

I paced forward cautiously, taking large breaths to oxygenate the vessel. The heart was beating frantically. Sweat dripped from his brow.

Carroll and Penrose entered the room, both vocalising their surprise.

'What is this place?' Carroll asked.

'It looks like a newsroom,' I replied. 'Miller might be more than just a talk show host.'

'Perhaps it was his idea to leak classified intelligence to the journalists,' Penrose remarked.

'Today's news is tomorrow's fish and chip papers,' I said dryly.

'What?' Penrose exclaimed.

'It doesn't matter,' I replied.

'Here,' Carroll said.

I turned. Carroll threw me a spare handgun. As I caught it, suddenly, there was an explosion of noise from the opposite side of the newsroom. Looking towards the source, Fielding was standing at the top of the stairs bearing an assault rifle, firing in our direction.

Reacting, we all dived to either side of the room, taking cover behind desks. Checking that the handgun was loaded, I peeked over the top of the desk. Aiming the weapon, I emptied a few rounds in his direction. Sitting back, I looked to my left. The other two were trying to shoot at Fielding. Above me, a computer blew to pieces.

My gaze drifted towards the double doors. An idea arose.

Fielding had stopped firing—most likely to change the ammunition clip.

Standing up, I held my hands non-threateningly, walking out into the centre of the room. From the corner of my eye, Carroll and Penrose both looked puzzled.

'Please, Fielding, let's be civilised,' I said, walking towards him.

He aimed the rifle at me.

Suddenly, the variants burst through the double door, dispersing into the room. Carroll and Penrose aimed their weapons at the crowd, who instantly stood back.

Fielding stood there looking at his reflection. He wouldn't risk catching versions of himself in the crossfire.

In that moment of hesitation, I reached forward, aimed, and fired a few rounds.

Miller's body gyrated, peppered with bullets, crumbling to the ground.

Forty-Four

Without hesitation, I launched towards him with a finger still held firmly on the trigger. He lay there, arms and legs splayed out, looking up at me with mixed anger and fear, coughing, blood spilling out of his mouth and mushrooming around him on the floor.

Picking up the assault rifle, I looked back at Carroll and Penrose. They steadily approached me, weapons still trained on the crowd.

Mounting the steps, I opened the door and turned back to throw the assault rifle at Carroll. 'Hold them off whilst I stop the transmission.'

She nodded.

Entering the office, I closed the door, walked over to the desk, laid down the handgun, and inspected the room. On the desk was—what I hoped—the quantum computer. Lying next to the keyboard was another VR headset. I presumed it was how these variants traversed into this dimension.

I walked around and sat down at the computer. An interface for the quantum network illuminated the screen. It showed a long list of what appeared to be scheduled file transmissions, each detailing the dimensions and time to be forwarded. I noticed that these weren't being sent to quantum computers but directly to the journalists' email addresses. Until then, I was unaware that the quantum network could interact with the internet.

At the very top of the list was the configuration for my dimension. I recognised the recipient's name—Elina Wells.

Had she survived the London nano-bombing?

Without hesitation, I right-clicked on the file. It came up with a list of actions, including one to delete. I selected it. The file disappeared from the list. I proceeded to choose the rest, inputting the same command.

Eventually, there were none left.

I sat back, expelling a sigh.

Finally, we had done it. And yet, I felt an unavoidable discomfort. Despite the fact we had stopped Leveller, I was more confused than satisfied.

I needed to check what Fielding was sending out to the other dimensions. There was a possibility that I was about to release a nano-bomb. But I suspected he was telling the truth. I commanded the computer to make a transmission back to itself.

Moments later, a notification appeared on the screen. Warily, I opened the download folder. There was the file.

I looked up at Carroll and Penrose. They still stood outside, their weapons aimed at the variants gathered on the opposite side of the room.

I hoped they could understand why I had to do this.

Clicking on the file, it opened.

There was no burst of nanobots self-replicating inside the computer—just a folder of files. I started scrolling through. There were countless documents and photos.

I couldn't look at them—the sight made me feel unnerved.

Fielding's words still echoed in the back of my mind. I thought about the director and everything about this mission. The possibility that I had been used to preserve an organisation with malicious intent suddenly made me feel sickened.

Was it acceptable for the agency to operate this way? I thought about all of the great things it has done. There have to be compromises along the way. But at what cost?

Unable to exorcise these reasonable doubts, I decided to do something for future reference. Again, I commanded the computer to forward the classified documents and the file listing the journalist's email addresses. This time, I selected a dimension I had only been to recently—Sayer's world. The quantum network would deliver the files to Professor Everett's computer. He would be oblivious.

Moments later, the interface announced it had sent the files. I deleted the original classified documents folder and the email address list.

We had to work out how to get back into our original dimension. Picking up the VR headset, I clicked the power button. On the computer screen, a notification said the device was synchronised.

I stood, walked over to the door, and opened it.

Fielding lay dead.

Carroll and Penrose looked over their shoulders.

'Have you done it?' she asked.

'I stopped the files from being transmitted to most dimensions.'

'Well done, Blake,' Penrose exclaimed. 'Is it over?'

'Yes.'

'How are we going to get out of here?' Carroll asked.

'There is a VR headset. Hopefully, we can use it to traverse back home.'

'But what are we going to do about these vessels?' Carroll asked.

'They will have to deal with the repercussions,' I said remorsefully.

'And what about *those* variants?' Penrose asked.

'Let me handle this,' I said, walking between them to address the crowd. They all looked at me venomously. 'Leveller's plans have been foiled. We will traverse our original dimension, returning these vessels to their owners. Once this happens, please do not attack them because they didn't volunteer to participate—they're innocent civilians. I hope you can all use this VR headset to return to your realities.'

The crowd remained deathly quiet.

I turned around. 'Carroll, you go first.' I took the assault rifle from her and aimed it at the crowd.

She walked into the office, sat at the computer, surveyed the interface, and searched for our configuration. Moments later, she exclaimed: 'I found it!'

'Okay, get out of here!' Penrose said.

I looked back over my shoulder. Carroll put on the VR headset. 'Penrose, you had better go quickly because Carroll's vessel will start asking questions.'

'See you on the other side.' He nodded, walking into the office.

Over my shoulder, I heard Carroll's vessel vocalising his confusion. I looked back. Penrose quickly took the VR headset and put it on.

That was my signal to move.

I lowered the assault rifle, stepped back into the office, closed the door, and turned to face them. Carroll's vessel was looking around, evidently disorientated.

He looked at me. 'Sebastian, what are we doing here? And *what* are you doing with that weapon?!'

Ignoring him, I looked at Penrose's vessel, whose facial expression had changed. She removed the VR headset, looking around the room, perplexed.

I walked forward, grabbed the VR headset from her, laid the assault rifle down on the desk, and said to them, 'I am very sorry about this.'

Without hesitation, I pulled the VR headset onto the vessel's head.

Suddenly, everything went black.

Forty-Five

Opening my eyes, I was relieved to see the familiar sight inside the brain scanner. For a moment, I remained still, reluctant to engage with the others.

Instead of jubilation, I felt conflicted. It was the opposite feeling of what I anticipated after completing a mission of such scale and implausibility.

Qubit drew forward. 'Are you okay, Blake?'

I nodded.

He helped me to remove the endotracheal tube. Ripping the ECG electrode pads from my chest, I lowered from under the brain scanner. To my left, there stood the quantum computer. From behind, I could hear excitable chatter.

I stood up, placed the cable down, and turned to face the others. Carroll and Penrose stood with the director.

'Blake!' the director erupted, walking around to me. He extended a hand to shake mine. 'Exceptional work.'

I accepted his hand. He shook overzealously. 'Thank you, sir.'

'Carroll and Penrose gave me a brief overview of what happened. We can commence a full debriefing in the conference room. Are you ready, or do you need a minute?'

I looked towards the doorway. 'I will freshen up.'

'Very well.' He nodded.

I walked around the seats. Everyone beamed at me. I nodded, pacing towards the door. Passing through the control room, Okoro and Alejo congratulated me. Interacting with them suddenly made me aware of how exhausted I was—in every aspect.

I walked out of the secretive branch and into the corridor. There was a temperature change, a light breeze wafting from overhead air conditioning.

Getting out of there felt like a sense of release.

I walked down toward the toilet. But this time, I needed space for a different reason. Stepping inside the bathroom, one agent was cleaning his hands. Once finished, he nodded before walking out.

I closed the door, locked it, and walked over to the sink. Turning on the cold tap, I cupped my hands underneath it, collected water, and drenched it across my face. The sensation alleviated some of the disorientation.

I looked up into my eyes. They looked overly tired. Was I feeling the consequences of having traversed into a stranger's vessel? My body felt weak. Was this from exhaustion? Withdrawal symptoms from the Statera? But for once, despite the sleep deprivation, my mind didn't feel congested.

There was something different about how I felt: a sense of autonomy. Was I finally overcoming the urge to self-medicate?

The thought struck me—I had a new stubborn itch: the glaring realisation that I had spent the last twenty-four hours putting my life at risk doing something that made me question what I stood for.

Fielding had set off a charge in my mind.

I heard his voice: 'the greater good'.

Whose interests was I serving?

I closed my eyes, inhaling through my nostrils before brushing my fingers across my face to remove the last drops of water. Straightening up, I looked at my reflection before unlocking the door and walking back into the corridor.

Reentering the secretive branch, I walked to the conference room. Okoro walked in behind me. Carroll, Penrose and Qubit had taken seats on either side of the table. The director was standing at the front, looking incredibly pleased with himself.

'Blake,' he announced.

Everyone turned to face me.

'Shall I give a breakdown of what happened?' I asked, walking forward.

'Penrose and Carroll confirmed that the final member of Leveller was Fielding?' he replied, shocked.

I took a seat. 'Fielding was deceiving us the whole time. We fell into his trap.'

'It explains why our interrogation techniques were ineffective, especially if we captured Miller,' the director huffed.

I then explained everything about the host vessels, TV studio, misleading living room set, talk show and interview. All the while, the director sat wide-eyed.

'And sir,' Carroll said. 'Fielding claimed that the crew and audience were all variants.'

'What?!'

'Like us, they traversed into host vessels.'

'Which means Fielding was not the final member of Leveller?' he questioned.

'Apparently so,' Penrose said.

'What happened to all of these people?'

'We had to leave them there, sir,' I explained.

'Why? Terminating them all would have been the best option.' He said this with such conviction and lack of remorse. It reminded me of what Fielding told me about all the missions the director authorised, resulting in countless civilian casualties.

'Because the hosts were all civilians, sir,' I said sternly. 'Besides, Fielding might have called our bluff. None of them spoke.'

'Did they traverse that reality using the same quantum computer you used?' Qubit asked.

'Yes,' I replied.

Qubit addressed the director: 'We should monitor the quantum network to see if there is activity.'

'Good idea,' the director said.

Standing nearby, Okoro overheard this. She nodded and went to action the order.

The director looked at me. 'What did Fielding say to you?'

'Fielding explained that they never intended to release nano-bombs. Instead, they had gained access to classified intelligence. He intended to release it to expose the various organisations.'

'How was Leveller able to gain access?' Qubit asked.

'I'm not sure,' I said.

'Blake,' the director spoke, 'when you accessed the quantum computer, did you terminate all transmissions and delete the files?'

'Yes, sir.'

'But had they already been transmitted to other dimensions?' Qubit asked.

'Yes.'

'Are we going to help the other organisations to contain the leaks?' Carroll asked.

'No,' the director replied, his tone of voice lacking empathy.

As far as he was concerned, despite the London bombing, everything else had worked perfectly: We'd stopped Leveller. Fielding was dead. Our organisation would endure. And his reputation was intact.

Business as usual.

'You should all be immensely proud of yourselves,' the director said.

Should I have left it there, walked away and done my best to forget what happened?

The new stubborn itch.

I couldn't help it any longer.

Forty-Six

'Sir.'

He faced me. 'Yes, Blake?'

'Fielding went into detail about his past with the organisation. He mentioned the Convergence Protocol.'

His smile vanished. 'What about it?'

'Its true purpose.'

From the corner of my eye, Qubit looked mystified.

'What did he tell you?' the director questioned.

'That you are responsible for the other quantum migrators getting into the wrong hands.' I eyed him analytically. 'Is that true?'

'The Convergence Protocol was established to weed out all threats —'

'He said you set up this branch to rectify the situation. And you authorised missions conducted by him, Carroll, Penrose, and other agents, which resulted in countless deaths across other dimensions. Did you?'

The director kept a neutral expression. 'I had to do what was necessary to preserve the fragile balance in this world.'

'What do you define as balance?'

'Excuse me? Blake, I think it is time you went for an assessment with—'

'Please elaborate, because I'm confused by what has happened.'

'Leveller was supposedly planning to release a weapon of mass destruction capable of destroying the entire world. You saw what they did to the city centre!'

'I'm not justifying their actions. But Fielding felt compelled to expose this organisation—why?'

'Because he wanted to take over. He is a deranged psychopath!'

'Not because he realised that this organisation functions solely for the vested interest of the elites, operating morally bankrupt?'

The director stood there for a moment in silence, contemplating his answer. 'I will level with you.' His eyes squinted. 'For decades, this organisation has sought to provide safety and security—'

'But at what cost?'

'What cost?' he sneered. 'There is no cost.'

'The countless deaths in other dimensions? The breaking of international laws in this dimension. I pledged my allegiance to serve the people. Instead, I am contributing toward their oppression.'

'They live in blissful ignorance, Blake. This system functions because everyone knows their place within it.'

'But do they? Do you acknowledge that this is all about power?'

'It is about *stability*. Before, you didn't have a problem with how we operate? Now you're starting to sound like Fielding.'

'And you're sounding like you're *full of shit*, sir.' There was an uncomfortable silence. He looked taken aback by my comment. The typical trait of a bully—I doubt anyone dared to throw it back at him like this. 'You didn't listen to Fielding. And because he didn't align with your objective, you ordered his execution. It led to him setting up Leveller.'

'What are you implying, Blake?!'

I stood up, looking him fiercely in the eye. 'You are accountable for the terrorist attack!'

His face contorted. Temples on his forehead throbbing. Lower lip jittering. 'How dare you! If we have a problem here, there will be severe consequences!'

I could see the others watching, wide-eyed.

'Are you threatening me?'

'Don't push my patience,' he said through gritted teeth.

We stood there looking at each other, my heart racing, hands clenched.

Without hesitation, standing tall, the words fell out of my mouth: 'Sir, please consider this my verbal resignation with immediate effect.'

The others gasped.

'Accepted,' the director said bluntly.

I looked at the others individually. 'It has been an honour working with you.'

They nodded, perplexed.

'Qubit, I will not be taking part in an assessment,' I said before removing the work phone from my trouser pocket and placing it on the desk. 'I will remove my belongings from the flat. How can I return the keys and laptop?'

'Someone will come to collect them,' Qubit explained.

'Very well.' I nodded, turning to walk out of the conference room.

'*Blake!*' the director barked.

'Yes, sir.' I turned to face him.

'When you first joined this organisation, you signed a non-disclosure agreement. You are still contractually obliged when you leave. Do you understand?'

'Yes, sir.'

'Good, because we don't want what happened to Fielding to repeat.' He eyed me intensely.

'I am too fond of Carroll and Penrose to imagine facing them in armed combat, sir.'

'Wise.' He frowned.

I turned on my heels, leaving a lingering silence behind. Entering the control room, Okoro and Alejo turned on their chairs. Having heard the exchange, they looked up at me, shocked. Meanwhile, I kept my eyes trained on the door, not saying anything.

As the door closed, I stood momentarily, digesting what had happened. I finally felt a semblance of satisfaction.

Proceeding forward, I was now a free civilian walking amongst submissive servants. It was baffling that so much had happened over the past day, and none of these people knew about it.

Walking northwards until I reached an armed guard station, I passed through a biometric scanner and reciprocated nods with the security.

Eventually getting to ground level, I walked out onto Belvedere Road. It was a beautiful, sunny Saturday morning. Across the road stood the Jubilee Gardens and the London Eye. The whole area was quiet. It was haunting. On the opposite side of the Thames, I could see the decimated skyline and mounds of defective grey nanobots.

Seeing it in a new context made me more discomforted than before.

My thoughts drew to Julia. Despite the many possibilities, I had a sinking feeling. Once back at the flat, I would try to contact her again.

Pondering this, I could hear the distant noise of an engine. At first, I ignored it. But it became louder, drawing closer.

Suddenly, I heard the screeching of braking tires. I looked toward the source of the noise.

There was a grey van with blacked-out windows. The side door slid wide open. Two men, wearing balaclavas and overalls, launched forward, grabbing and pulling me inside.

Before I could retaliate, a hood drew over my head. The side door slammed shut. And the last thing I can remember was the sensation of an object smashing against the side of my head.

Part Three
Redemption

Forty-Seven

I remember the day it happened—opening my eyes for the first time.

But here I am, sitting within the confinement of these four walls. I still look at the single white feather lying on the floor. Delicate. Curved upwards and frayed at the edges.

Entranced, I had not paid attention to my surroundings, oblivious to the interrogators sitting across the table. Returning my focus to them, the woman removes documents from the beige folder.

'Mr Blake, do you know why you are here?' she repeats.

I want to question them. But I am cautious not to divulge any information.

Why was I thrown in the back of a van by masked men? Did the director have something to do with it? Perhaps these are other agents from the experimental branch attempting to frame me for the nano-bombing. Or, they might be from another department, trying to uncover our operations.

Looking at the two-way mirror, I contemplate who might be standing behind it watching this interrogation.

'Mr Blake, we are here to perform an assessment,' she says, revealing a document.

Assessment?

'I understand you might be feeling overwhelmed.' She looks around the room. 'This isn't exactly the most pleasant of places. Unfortunately, there have been funding cutbacks.'

Funding cutbacks?

'Why do you think you're here?' she asks, removing a pen inside her coat pocket, clicking the end cap, and scribbling on the document.

'You should not feel threatened, Mr Blake,' the man says in a friendly tone. 'We are only here to help you.'

I look down at the collection of documents. Amongst these are some I recognise—the forms from my assessments with Qubit. I look back at them.

'You see these documents?' she asks in a gentle tone. 'They were provided as part of your referral.'

Referral?

Although exhausted, I am irritable, becoming impatient, wanting to get out of this interrogation. I can't remember the last time I took the drugs. Withdrawal is making my skin itch; I feel cold. The over-hanging light causes my eyes to blur. This situation makes me want to give in and self-medicate again.

'Mr Blake,' she says. 'We only came here this morning to ask you some questions as part of your ongoing treatment.'

What treatment?

'You have received treatment for a long time now. But because of recent events, it was appropriate to bring you here. We can review your treatment and monitor your progress.'

What the *hell* is she talking about?

'Do you know where you are right now, Mr Blake?' she asks.

There is a protracted silence.

The man speaks: 'Once we received word you'd had another mental health relapse, we had to gain permission to have you sectioned.'

Mental health relapse? Sectioned?

'You are in a psychiatric hospital, Mr Blake,' she explains, looking up at me analytically. 'My name is Doctor Aqeel; I am a clinical psychologist.' She gestures toward the man. 'And this is Doctor Gamble.'

He smiles.

'You have a complex history of Post-Traumatic-Stress-Disorder and psychotic illusions,' she says, leaning back. Her jacket opens slightly, revealing a blue NHS lanyard hanging around her neck. 'We were made aware of this before today's assessment. I understand that you have stopped taking your anti-psychotic medication?'

What medication?

'You have taken medication for quite some time now,' Doctor Gamble says.

Wait, is he talking about the Statera?

My expression is no longer neutral. The interrogators deduce a reaction.

'What do you think the medication does, Mr Blake?' Doctor Gamble asks, waiting for a moment. 'Very well. The medication helps to quell psychotic delusions.'

What delusions?

'Mr Blake, we understand that after the tragic passing of your son, you had a mental breakdown and have since created an elaborate, multi-layered world you have retracted within to find refuge. To deal with the trauma, you escaped.'

The mention of Charlie triggers me. I can feel my body swell with stress and anguish. It's unbearable.

Involuntarily, I erupt: 'I don't know what you're talking about! My son, Charlie, died after being kidnapped!'

They react to my break in silence.

'Mr Blake, I know the tragic loss is tough to accept,' she smiles, nodding sympathetically. 'That is why we are here to help you.'

'I think there has been a misunderstanding here.'

'How so?'

'I don't take that medication because of psychosis; they were prescribed to me by—'

She stops writing. 'By whom?'

'What exactly is your intention? To extract intelligence by gaslighting me?'

'Who prescribed those drugs to you?'

I look down at the assessment papers. 'See for yourself.'

'Here?' She points at where my eyes are focused. I nod. She picks up the forms that Qubit completed.

'It will tell you who I work for. *Who* prescribed those drugs to me.'

As she reads, I realise that I should have instead attempted to escape. 'Ah, yes—the unnamed clandestine international agency?'

'Correct.' I eye them both suspiciously. 'How did you get hold of these documents?'

'Colleagues provided them for this assessment.'

I huff through my nostrils. 'On there, it will explain everything about whom I work for and what I have been doing.'

'What we have here, Mr Blake, is documentation of the elaborate story you concocted during a delusional episode.' Doctor Aqeel says.

'You're wrong.'

'The covert global organisation. A terrorism group. Inter-dimensional travel. You have a creative flare.'

'I didn't make this up! Those were assessments conducted by the branch technician after every part of the mission. I'm not lying. There is proof!'

'Mr Blake.' She then speaks gently: 'Charlie died drowning in that pond. There was no kidnapping. It was a freak accident. You are not to blame.' That last sentence hits me. My teeth grind. 'We understand you are an avid pop culture consumer and have researched various conspiracy theories. From this, you might have sourced inspiration for this spy world you have created around yourself.

'We are here to help you. As soon as you reconnect with reality, we can start making progress. All these things are make-believe, part of a meticulously thought-out fantasy you reside within.'

'Why would I do that?'

'To cope with the trauma of losing your son. It offers you comfort. A distraction.'

'Tell me, was there a nano-bombing?' I analyse her eyes.

'...No, there was not.'

'You hesitated. Why are you avoiding the truth?'

'Mr Blake, nothing happened,' Doctor Gamble interjects forcefully. 'We don't understand what bombing you are referring to.'

'It was an orchestrated attack made by the terrorism group called Leveller.'

The two doctors exchange side glances.

'I am afraid, Mr Blake, you are fabricating events.' As she says this, I have the impulse to lash out. 'I can see you are disturbed by what we are discussing. You must recommence the course of medication. We will then conduct another assessment to determine whether you have progressed.'

'And then what?'

'Then we can consider your release. But you are far away from that prospect.' Placing down the pen, she looks at me. 'Will you agree to recommence the course of medication?'

It dawns on me—what have the drugs done to my sense of judgement?

I lean over, looking her squarely in the eye. 'What do you think?!'

Doctor Gamble gently pushes back his seat, stands, and walks to the door. Opening it, he speaks to the guard, who was not bearing a weapon, as I had previously expected. Instead, there is a strap for a walkie-talkie on his left shoulder.

Doctor Aqeel says: 'Now, Mr Blake, I hope you will be compliant and won't present any hostility.'

'If you think you're going to lock me away, you have another thing coming!' I push back my seat. It falls to the floor. Standing with my fists clenched, I look at the guard speaking into the walkie-talkie.

Meanwhile, Doctor Aqeel remains seated, looking up at me with concern. 'Please, Mr Blake, we don't want to cause harm.'

I look down at her. She has already put the pen out of sight. I can't grab it to use as a weapon. Doctor Gamble leaves the room.

The guard enters with two accomplices. They walk to either side of the table, slowly edging toward me. All the while, I stand defensively, fists clenched, ready to engage.

One of the guards surges forward. I punch him hard in the side of the face. He stumbles to the side. The other two launch, grabbing both of my arms. One of them kicks at the back of my right knee. I tumble down. They hold me in place. The original guard gets to his feet.

Doctor Aqeel approaches bearing a filled syringe. She stabs the needle into my neck. I desperately try to pull myself away from their grasp, feeling the liquid sedative seeping into my body.

Moments later, my eyes lose focus. I fall unconscious.

Forty-Eight

Sebastian Howler was sitting in his flat looking vacantly out of the window. He had been in this position for a while, recollecting everything that had happened a few nights ago. A light rain fell. Morning sunlight spilt through cracks in the cloud line, painting the room with a dull, grey glow.

Clara walked into the room, taking a seat opposite.

'Couldn't sleep again?' she asked.

He looked at her. 'No.'

Nodding sympathetically, she, too, was feeling confused and exhausted.

'I keep on thinking about what happened,' he croaked. 'One minute, I was standing in the green room, putting on the VR headset, but something *changed*. And the next thing I knew, I removed the device and was standing in a random office!'

She shook her head. 'It doesn't make sense.'

'And there was that rifle, Miller's dead body, and all those people just standing there.' He leaned over, brushing both hands through his hair.

'All three of us had memory loss using that headset. It was like we were sleepwalking.'

'We were completely out of control!' He sat back. 'And Miller? What *happened* to him!'

Clara swallowed hard. 'Did you shoot him?'

'What?' Sebastian protested, his hands shaking.

'I remember you were holding the weapon and apologised for something before snatching the headset from me. Why did you do that? And then take off the headset again?'

'I don't remember any of it. It was like I was possessed or something.'

'And the crew and audience members?'

'They just came up to us and were so…calm….'

'And just told us to leave?'

Sebastian looked at her. 'When taken into custody, the police didn't mention anything about the weapon.'

'Do you think those people got rid of it?'

'They must have because the police didn't say anything about Miller's body, either.'

'I don't understand.'

'I don't know, Clara,' he sighed pensively. 'As far as I know, they suspect Miller has gone missing.'

'This is all so weird.'

'You don't say.'

'We should be okay. Marvin has brought in a good team of lawyers. As far as anyone outside of the studio is concerned, you stood up during the interview, demanding the end of the broadcast, and then Miller went missing. The cast and crew have given their statements. They were also oblivious to the live show—'

'Why? Were they possessed like us?'

'Possibly.'

'This just keeps on getting weirder and weirder.'

'I know.'

'Nothing has been mentioned about the rifle or Miller being dead?'

'We are in the clear.'

'But the police will eventually find out.'

'If things turn against us, we can plead that the VR headset is dangerous, and they need to remove it from the market immediately. Something happened to us when we used it.'

'Do you know how far-fetched that sounds? I could still face manslaughter.'

'I know, I know.' She leaned forward, rubbing his knee. 'But do you know what the good thing is about all of this?'

'What?'

'You *nailed* the interview.'

'How can you say that? I stood up, demanding they turned off the cameras!'

'True, you were dramatic, borderline nuts. But the controversy has done wonders.'

'How, Clara?'

'Reactions have spread like wildfire over social media. People think your display was a pre-planned publicity stunt. They think it was bold. You won everyone over with your apology for assaulting the photographer. Whatever was going on inside that brain of yours certainly helped us out!'

'You think so?'

'Yes! Marvin told me that record streams have increased. He has received countless emails offering endorsement deals. There have even been enquiries about film roles.'

'You are kidding me?!'

'Apparently, so.'

'Wow.' He smiled. 'This could work in my favour.'

'We just have to hope that the police don't uncover evidence leading to Miller's body.'

'Why did the crew and audience help us?'

'Perhaps because they love you, Sebastian. They don't want you to go to prison. Shall we get showered and go out for breakfast?'

'I like that idea.'

'Great.'

'Do you know what? I suddenly feel better about myself.'

Forty-Nine

I presume it is a side-effect of the sedatives because I cannot re-member how long I've been here in this psychiatric hospital. Or the time spent in this room since the interrogation.

Thankfully, I am not in a padded cell wearing a restraining jacket but in more civilised surroundings: a small room, electric blue, with a single bed, a side table with a lamp, a desk, and a cupboard. All edges are smooth. To my left is a triple-glazed, large window. It has plastic Venetian blinds hanging down. Through these are views overlooking a courtyard framed by other rooms. I am on the third floor. Above, I can see clear skies—a sign of freedom. The main door is reinforced and has a locking mechanism. I cannot break this without tools. The air is thick, tinged with my body odour and a clinical smell.

I've been lying on the bed looking up listlessly at the ceiling, think-ing about how to escape. The sheets are saturated. Despite my ex-haustion and mental fogginess, I try to remain focused.

I can feel waves of withdrawal—the urge to tear my skin off.

The only thing keeping me sane is the thought of Julia and Charlie.

From beyond the door, I hear the muffled sound of approaching footsteps and talking. Involuntarily, my body stiffens, sitting upright.

I suspect it is the doctor conducting her morning rounds.

There is metal clinking. The guard unlocks the door before opening it outwards. He steps in. It is the same person I had punched—there is a healthy bruise on his right temple. He looks at me cautiously, one eye bloodshot, proceeding forward before standing tall, clasping hands behind his back.

A side glance indicates that it is safe to enter. Doctor Aqeel enters the room with a large folder and a tub containing various medicine bottles.

'Good morning, Mr Blake,' she says in a friendly tone. 'How are you today?'

'I have felt better,' I say dryly.

'I can imagine. But hopefully, soon, you will feel a lot better.' The doctor walks over to the bedside table and places down the folder. 'Do you know why I am here?'

Somewhere, deep down, I am willing to accept the drugs. But I ignore the impulse. 'To force me to take those tablets?'

'"Force" is a powerful word, Mr Blake. As I explained in the assessment, we need you to comply with taking your medication to make progress.'

'And like I have told you before, I am *not* taking them!'

She sighs and opens the folder, flicking through various pages in plastic pockets before stopping on one that contains a record of my non-existent medication administration.

'If that is how you want to do this, Mr Blake, I have no alternative.'

'What do you mean?'

Suddenly, three more guards walk into the room. Along with their bruised colleague, they launch forward, surround the bed, and take hold of each of my limbs. They hold me down. I groan with retaliation, shifting frantically.

'I know this does not appear humane, Mr Blake, but what we are doing is for your benefit,' Doctor Aqeel says, opening a bottle. 'Once you have regained a reasonable perspective, we can discuss releasing you.'

'Tell them to get off me! Otherwise, I am going to *kill* them!' I protest through gritted teeth.

'We do not promote or tolerate violence in this hospital, Mr Blake.'

'What do you call this?!' I say, looking at the guards.

'Preventative measures.'

I look at the bottle she is holding. It has a similar label to the Statera I used. But these tablets contain a higher dosage of the drug.

'Why are you giving me something stronger than I have used before?'

She follows my eye trail. 'Because it's necessary to bring you back to baseline, Mr Blake.'

'I know you will not tell me why I am here. But I reiterate—you are making a *grave mistake*. Once my superiors know this, you will face the consequences.'

'But, from what you told me yesterday, Mr Blake, you handed in your resignation to the organisation?'

'Yes. Are you starting to believe me now?'

'Unfortunately, this is another fabrication and an example of your psychotic delusion.'

'How do you know that?'

'Because of years of assessments and documentation.'

'Whatever you have heard is a *lie*!'

'Please,' she says gently, easing forward, holding the opened medicine bottle in one hand and a small cup of water in the other, 'this will all be much easier if you just comply.'

I love you, Julia and Charlie.

Shaking my head defiantly, I say, 'I will not.'

She looks out of sight. Another guard enters the room. He reaches forward, tilts my head back, and clenches my mouth with both hands. The doctor leans forward, pours in a few tablets, and empties the glass of water into my mouth. The guard closes my mouth shut. Instantly, I have the gagging reflex—water spurts from my nostrils.

I start wriggling frantically, groaning, trying desperately to free myself from their restraint. But I am concerned that the water will enter my lungs. To prevent drowning, I swallow hard, feeling the tablets and water seeping into my stomach.

Satisfied that I have digested the medicine, the doctor tells the guards to release me. They remove their clasps. I fall back onto the bed, defenceless. I start panting, looking up at the ceiling.

'Mr Blake, I don't want to resort to this method, but you have left me with no other option. Your behaviour is life-threatening. What we are doing is for your benefit.' From the corner of my eye, I see Doctor Aqeel make a few notes on the medical record before replacing the sheet in the plastic pocket, closing the folder, and picking up the tub. The guards leave the room, leaving just the two of us. 'I will return this afternoon to see how you are getting on.'

And with that, she walks out of the room. The door closes momentarily.

I lie, looking up at the ceiling, catching my breath, feeling the tension in my cheeks and limbs. My stomach churns, reluctantly accepting these horrible drugs. It will not be long before they flood into my bloodstream, stimulating my senses and corroding my judgment.

Memories of my last Christmas with Julia and Charlie. Fairy lights. A crackling fire.

Instantly, I sit upright, turn onto my right-hand side, spread my feet onto the floor, and lean forward. Taking my right hand's index and middle finger, I insert them into my mouth and push them down into my throat, pressing against my tongue and tonsils. I start to gag, ignoring the impulse to stop. My stomach gyrates, I cough, and liquid spurts out of my stomach onto the floor. I continue to do this until a small puddle in front of me contains the tablets.

I can feel pressure in my head, tears seep down my cheeks, and my throat is sore from the stomach acid. Ringing out my two fingers, I sit upright, inhaling a large breath.

The disorientation subsides. I hear more footsteps nearing the door.

Did the doctor hear me making myself sick?

Brushing away the tears, I sit defiantly despite my body feeling weak.

Suddenly, the lock unlatches. The door slowly opens.

My stomach is turning in knots. A tension headache pulsates.

Two people in medical scrubs walk into the room, stop, and look down at me.

I can feel a cold shiver disperse across my body.

It is Carroll and Penrose.

Fifty

Seeing the puddle of vomit in front of me, Carroll comes forward, kneels to my side, puts a hand on my shoulder, and says, 'Jackson, are you okay?'

I am looking into her eyes, digesting this moment, perplexed.

Penrose enters the room and checks that the corridor is clear before slowly closing the door. He addresses Carroll: 'Is he all right?'

'Jackson?' she says in a disconcerted tone, her eyes searching mine.

I wipe a stream of saliva from my mouth. 'I don't know what happened.'

She nods sympathetically.

Penrose walks around the puddle, kneels on the other side, and inspects the collection of soaked tablets. He points at these. Carroll looks.

'They forced me to take them,' I explain, my throat burning.

'That is not standard medical procedure—they must be on the agency's payroll,' Penrose remarks.

'What are they?' Carroll asks.

'Statera,' I say.

'The performance enhancement drug?' Penrose asks.

'Yes. But I was told this is anti-psychotic medication.' They exchange concerned looks. 'What am I doing here?'

'I will explain soon,' Carroll says.

'How did you find me?'

'We can tell you everything after we get you out of here,' Penrose replies.

They both stand. Penrose walks towards the door, disappearing outside. Meanwhile, Carroll walks over to the cupboard, opens it, and pulls out a fresh cotton gown for me. She walks over.

'We need to change your clothing. Do you need help?'

'No, I should be okay.'

I accept the garment, place it on the bed, and stand up. Suddenly, the tension inside my head increases. I take a moment to stabilise. Carroll looks at me with concern. I pull off the vomit-covered gown and scrunch it up. She takes it, throwing it aside. I put on the new garment.

Penrose re-enters the room, pushing a wheelchair. He stops, puts on the brakes, and closes the door. Carroll assists me over to the wheel-chair. I sit down. She releases the brakes, taking hold of the handles.

Penrose walks into the corridor, ensuring the coast is clear before we edge outwards. He closes the door gently behind him.

I sit vigilantly, looking down the corridor, inspecting various personnel going about their day. Carroll eases me forward, Penrose flanking us. We all remain silent. They roll me through the hospital, the wheels squeaking, passing under strip lighting. There are various security cameras. Medical staff pass by, oblivious.

I anticipate seeing Doctor Aqeel.

We come to a set of double doors with a sign above it directing toward the hospital entrance. These open. Ahead of us is a lift. Penrose walks ahead and presses the button. Moments later, the doors open. It is empty. Carroll pushes me inside. She manoeuvres the chair to face back outwards whilst Penrose presses a button for the ground floor.

The doors close—we all vocalise our relief.

'I have to say, Jackson, I never thought we'd get into a situation like this,' Carroll jokes.

'It wasn't exactly what I had in mind after completing the mission,' I croak.

'You don't say,' Penrose adds.

The lift eventually reaches the ground floor, doors opening. Carroll rolls me out into the reception area. Psychiatric nurses are standing near the desk chatting. Some exchange glances with Carroll and Penrose. There are smiles and nods. But nobody rouses suspicion about a patient wheeling out of the hospital. It looks like a standard discharge.

We reach the entrance. The double doors open, revealing a filled car park and field in the background. Pushing over the threshold, Carroll increases her pace, leading me down a pathway until we reach a blacked-out, white NHS van. I hear a plane flying over.

Penrose walks forward, reveals keys from his trousers, and opens the locking mechanism. Carroll puts on the brakes. I stand up. She withdraws the wheelchair and pushes it to the side.

'Do you need assistance getting in?' Penrose asks.

'I can manage,' I say.

He opens the front passenger door and ushers me inside. I climb in, followed by Carroll. Penrose closes the door, walks to the other side, and jumps into the driver's seat.

'Did you see anyone tailing us?' Carroll asks.

'I think we are in the clear,' Penrose replies, closing his door and looking in the wing mirror.

'Where are we?'

'Near to Crawley in Sussex,' Penrose explains.

They remove fake identification lanyards.

Penrose turns on the engine, checks the mirrors, lifts off the handbrake, and eases the van out of the parking space. Driving through the winding car park, we reach the exit and turn onto a residential road.

Carroll opens the glove compartment, revealing a small hand-held device. 'Please show me your left forearm, under-turned.'

'What is that?'

'I need to remove the bio-tracker implanted when you first joined the agency.'

'I forgot about it.'

'This will only take a moment.' She places the device against my forearm, pressing a button. I see a red laser projecting onto my skin. There is a beeping sound. 'There you go.'

'Have you removed yours?'

'Yes.' She puts the device back into the glove compartment. 'And we also jammed all the security cameras inside the hospital to ensure no recordings.'

I smile. 'Nicely done.'

'All in a day's work.' She reaches inside the glove compartment and reveals a bottle of water. 'Here. You need to drink.'

'Thank you.' I accept the offering, open the cap, and squeeze the thin plastic. The liquid quenches my sore throat. I look at a small screen on the dashboard presenting camera footage on the rear—no one is following us.

'Well, that was easy enough,' Carroll says jubilantly.

'If only missions were that straightforward,' Penrose adds.

'Thank you both for rescuing me,' I say, swallowing the last drops of water.

'Of course, we couldn't leave you in that place!' Carroll replies.

'Do you know what happened to me?'

'After you gave in your resignation and left the headquarters, we overheard the director issuing an order for your detainment,' Penrose explains.

'He sent those men?'

'Yes,' Carroll answers. 'He gave the order while we were there in the conference room. A few days ago, we gained access to your records on Okoro's computer and were able to track you down.'

'Why didn't the masked men just bump me off?'

'It isn't malicious enough for the director.'

'I don't understand why they sectioned me into a psychiatric hospital?'

'It was the director's new method to remove anyone who could compromise his operations.'

'New method?' I ask.

'He sought to keep you locked up, out of sight, with no evidence to support your claims. Make you suffer.'

'The Statera—when did you start taking it?' Penrose asks.

'After my son, Charlie, disappeared. I was offered therapy and prescribed the medication.'

'Do you know not all agents take the drug?' Carroll asks.

'…No.'

'They wanted to make sure you were able to operate accordingly, to develop a dependence towards the drug, to keep you in line.'

'Why?' I ask impatiently.

'You were an experiment,' Penrose replies. 'They kept you tamed with the highly addictive drug, using everything documented in Qubit's assessments to create an elaborate story about you having a supposed mental health breakdown. Because there is no proof of the organisation existing, you would have been classified insane, numbed out, and locked away for the rest of your life.'

'That is a lot for me to process.' I sit for a while digesting this before asking: 'Why did you put yourselves at risk to save me?'

'We are both conflicted about our positions within the organisation,' Carroll explains. 'And couldn't allow this to happen to you.'

'This cannot continue,' I say.

They both look at me gravely.

'Now that you are free, what do you want to do?' Carroll asks.

'It is not safe here for you anymore,' Penrose says, turning a corner.

'I'll have to go into hiding.'

'But where?' Carroll asks. 'Despite removing the bio-tracker, the agency will soon know you escaped the hospital. And you know the organisation's surveillance capabilities.'

'I will have to go off the grid.'

'There is another option,' Penrose says.

'What?'

'We managed to find one of the quantum migrators.'

'How?'

'It was the next assignment. But we haven't told the director its whereabouts.'

'We found Fielding's hideout,' Carroll adds.

'How wasn't this discovered before?' I ask.

Penrose replies: 'The task force failed to find it because Fielding installed a remote satellite with an encrypted signal to gain connection to the internet and quantum network. We secretly used the prototype software to decrypt the signal and followed it to the location.'

'Where is the hideout?'

'In Ashdown Forest.'

In an assertive tone, Carroll says, 'Jackson, this is your opportunity. We can take you to the migrator. You can traverse into a new life. Remain anonymous. Start again.'

'But I don't feel comfortable taking over someone else's life,' I say, frowning.

'You don't have many other options,' Carroll replies. 'Once the director knows we have rescued you from the psychiatric hospital, he will pool all his resources to hunt us down.'

'What about you two?'

'We will also have to escape,' Penrose replies.

I sit there contemplating this, feeling ashamed, but eventually nod. 'Okay, take me to Fielding's hideout.'

Fifty-One

We drive for another thirty minutes through the countryside, passing farm fields and dense woodland—an ideal, unsuspecting place for Fielding to hide and orchestrate his inter-dimensional plans.

The van gyrates along a rough track, driving up a hill. Carroll taps my forearm, rousing me from a daydream. She points to the right-hand side. Further up the muddy trail is a large, closed wooden gate.

'This is it,' she says warily.

Penrose swerves onto a bank, puts on the brakes, pulls on the handbrake, and turns off the engine. 'Jackson, stay here whilst we check the place is clear.'

He removes his seat belt, opens the door, and jumps out. Carroll does the same. I look towards the gate but can't see where it leads. To either side are high stone walls.

Moments later, Carroll reopens her door. She has changed into combat attire, holding clothing in her arms, with a rifle slung over her shoulder.

'Here you go,' she says, handing me the clothes. 'It's a bit nippy out-side.'

'Thanks.' I receive these and put them on my lap.

'And take this.'

She reaches behind her back, unveils a handgun, and gives it to me. I load the weapon.

'We will be right back,' she says, closing the door.

Carroll withdraws the rifle from her shoulder, loads the weapon, holds it defensively, and starts edging toward the gate where Penrose is already waiting, dressed the same. Penrose signals. Carroll reaches forward to open the gate. They both proceed on, out of sight.

Laying the handgun down, I checked the wing mirror and the track ahead. No one. I push off the slippers, remove the gown and trousers, throw them into the foothold, and put on the underwear, jumper, jeans, and trainers.

Once done, I retake the handgun and wait for them to return.

The following few minutes seem to drag.

I cannot hear anything. The silence is unnerving.

Feeling restless, I shuffle across the seat, open the door, and jump onto the track. The trainers hit the muddy surface with a squishing sound. I look back down the hillside—there are no disturbances. Closing the door behind me, I edge toward the wooden gate, momentarily peering along the track to ensure no one is coming in the opposite direction.

Reaching the opened gate, I look beyond. A short track leads up the hillside to a derelict, two-storey house. The roof has holes; cracked, beige-coloured paintwork and boards cover all windows.

I see Carroll and Penrose circling the building before running back down the track towards me.

'All clear,' Carroll affirms, standing before me. 'When we first discovered this place, we had to disengage boobytraps. There is no indication of disturbances since we were last here. Come, we can drive up the track. Penrose will provide cover.'

I follow her back to the van. We get in. Holding the gun in my grasp, I sit tight. Carroll drives us up the track until we reach the house and park around the back, out of sight. She gets out and directs me towards a door leading into the kitchen. Opening it, she turns on a torch attached to her rifle.

Following her, I hold up the handgun and enter. Through the minimal light, I see the fixtures and furnishings have degraded. Dust covers everything. Cobwebs hang from the ceiling. There is a damp smell. And a distant, echoing, dripping water.

We walk through. The floorboards creak underneath our feet. We reach a large room. I suspect it was once the lounge. Carroll steps forward, opening a set of tardy curtains. Light spills through cracks in the boards, partially illuminating the room.

At the centre is a table. On this are three flat screens, a keyboard, and a mouse. Underneath is a large black tower. I presume the quantum computer. Lights are flashing along its surface. Various wires snake away from the room. In front of this is a single chair with a brain scanner harnessed above it. Behind is life support equipment.

'This is where he orchestrated everything?' I ask, walking forward.

'I know—very unassuming.' She says dryly, walking over to a switch and turning on the light.

My eyes adjust, looking around the room. To the side is a single camping bed with a sleeping bag. Across the walls are maps of various cities—London in other dimensions?

Penrose walks towards the screen and taps a few keys on the keyboard. The screen comes to life.

'I bet you can't guess the password?' she asks whimsically.

'That is not exactly the most subtle of choices,' I laugh.

'He covered his tracks to hide this place and laid all those boobytraps. Using the terrorism group's name wouldn't be too risky.'

Hearing footsteps approach, I raise the handgun and move towards the noise. It is Penrose. He walks into the kitchen, hands held up. Lowering the weapon, we enter the lounge.

'I've checked the perimeter,' he announces.

'Are you certain the migrator connects to the quantum network?' I ask.

Carroll looks up at me, nodding. 'We did notice something.'

'What was that?'

'The psi branch removed your profile,' she explains.

'Removed?'

'The director wanted to delete any trace of your connection. But I have located a new configuration.'

'Anything I might recognise?'

'Braithwaite's world. Your variant is connected.'

My mind's eye floods with images of the mission. Suddenly, I remember: 'I forwarded the leaked documents to that dimension.'

'What?' they both exclaim, looking at me.

'I did it in case something like this happened.'

'Your methods *are* unorthodox, Jackson,' Penrose laughs.

'Would you both be prepared to expose the agency?' I ask.

'By releasing the intelligence?' Carroll asks, exasperated.

'Yes.'

'You realise we would be doing Fielding's work for him?' Penrose questions, taken back.

'But what happens if we don't?' I protest.

There is a moment of silence.

'This could cause an international scandal, Jackson!' Carroll says. 'I know that things aren't perfect, but—'

I interject: 'We joined this organisation to serve the people. But instead, we are doing the complete opposite. Can we allow the director to continue? After what he has done!'

'But why expose the whole organisation because of one person and a single branch?' Penrose protests.

'How d'you not know that other directors aren't doing something similar?' I ask.

'I…don't.'

'The population must know the truth. It's the right thing to do. Especially because of what happened in London. And what happened in the other realities.' I eyed them both. 'I'm not blaming you for following orders in the past. But what now? Just leave it behind and escape to other realities?'

Another moment of silence.

Carroll nods. 'He's right.'

Penrose draws a large breath through his nostrils and sighs, stressed. 'If the organisation is exposed, it could create instability. And lead to World War Three!'

'That is conditioning speaking. Not your judgment,' I oppose. 'After the leak of the documents, I can come back. We can wait for the public uproar and lead the way to change the organisation.'

'Remove the director?' Carroll asks.

'Jackson, do you comprehend what we would face up against?!' Penrose protests. 'Even if the files reach the journalist, the agency might intercept them.'

'I'm sure Leveller considered this and might have found a way to bypass the system.'

'And what happens if the world does find out? Carroll adds. 'How can we face up against the combined strength of the global organisation?'

'Only time can tell,' I say. 'It isn't impossible. Look at what we achieved in that mission.'

'You seem pretty certain of this?' Penrose asks.

'There is no other choice unless we want to give up on our duty to the people.'

'And how do you think the world will respond, learning about the existence of alternative realities? Carroll asks.

'It is time to open their eyes. I know we are on the same wave function. But are we on the same wavelength?'

They both stand there looking at each other—my heart races, waiting to hear their decision.

Penrose turns to me, nodding.

'Sit down and prepare to traverse into Sayer's vessel,' Carroll says, turning back to input the command into the computer.

I walk over to the chair, easing myself onto it. Before positioning my head underneath the brain scanner, I look at them.

For a moment, I consider whether they will follow through with the whole plan. Whatever the case, I am going to expose the organisation.

I submerge my head underneath the brain scanner.

'This won't take too long,' I say, closing my eyes.

'See you on the other side,' Carroll says.

Fifty-Two

I open Sayer's eyes. There is an unexpected sight: a lounge. From recollection, it takes a few moments to realise that I am sitting in Sayer's flat.

But why?

I look down at the variant's body. It is reclining on an armchair. Reaching forward, I pat the vessel's weakened right leg.

Admittedly, it is good to be here.

I look around. The lounge and kitchen are clear.

Extracting the endotracheal tube and throwing it aside, I gently pull out the intravenous cannula, which also falls to the floor. As blood dribbles from the wound, I use the right index finger to apply pressure. After a few moments, I pull down Sayer's jumper sleeve and unwrap the heart-monitoring pad from the other arm—this, too, falls to the floor.

Easing from underneath the brain scanner, I look to my right-hand side. The quantum computer sits on a small table. To my left, the sofa, under the windows, is empty.

In front of me is a TV. It is on. The images draw my attention. It is news coverage—stock footage of Wallace Braithwaite. Brandished across the lower screen is a scandalous headline stating his arrest due to allegations of racketeering.

Lennox had received the files and uncovered his illegal dealings. She had followed my advice. I am immensely proud of her.

The screen changes. Footage of Braithwaite taken into custody, looking miserable.

At least his fake wife will be happy.

The screen changes again. Now, there is a television studio. Two presenters are sitting, talking into the camera. I can't distinguish what they are saying because the sound is off. The screen is too far away to lipread. There is a shot change—their guest—Lennox. She is sitting there, radiant, speaking confidently, owning it.

Looking up at her, I think of why I am here: to send incriminating files to her variant in my reality.

For a moment, I sit to listen for any movement in my periphery. But convinced I am alone, I ease from under the brain scanner. I take a walking stick, lean to the side, place my weight on it, and stand straight.

Walking towards the quantum computer, I sit at a chair in front of it and place the walking stick aside. Once again, I look around to make sure I'm alone. The screen shows images of the vessel's most recent brain activity before I took off the scanner.

I hold the mouse and command the computer to open the applications folder. Here, I find the hard-drive utility application. Opening it, I'm relieved to find the one named 'QN' is still there.

The tab opens, showing the list of quantum configurations, conversation box, upload function, and now something new: a received file.

I open it. A separate folder appears on the screen. It shows the classified documents and email address list I sent from Miller's dimension.

I feel relieved.

On the application, I click on the upload function. Like when I uploaded Brathwaite's prototype software, I selected the classified documents. When it asks me for a destination, I open the email address list, find that of Elina Wells, and paste it. Then, I type a message in the conversation box to the journalist explaining what she is receiving and what she must do. There is no sender email address.

The computer waits for me to activate the transfer.

I sit, accepting the magnitude of what I'm about to do: turning my back on everything I had worked for—but doing what is right despite the repercussions.

Now a whistleblower, am I as bad as the terrorists?

It might come to nothing. But I must try.

There is no going back from here—it is time to level things out.

I'm flush with excitement. Activating the transfer, I wait for the upload bar to complete. It slowly moves across the screen as Sayer's heart beats frantically.

The transfer ends. I quickly deleted the original file.

And now all I see is the list of quantum configurations—infinite possibilities—countless realities beyond the limits of my imagination: another life to start afresh.

Returning to my original dimension, would we stand a chance against the powers of the organisation? Perhaps Carroll and Penrose were right—I should walk away from my old life and traverse into someone else.

It is time, for once, to do what is right for me.

Sitting digesting everything, I have been oblivious to my surroundings. There is a sound coming down the corridor.

Feverishly, I reach for the mouse, close the hard-drive utility application, and sit back casually in the chair, looking listlessly at the image of Sayer's brain activity.

'Thom?' I hear from behind—a familiar voice. Turning in the chair, Professor Everett is looking at me, perplexed. 'Has it happened again?!'

'I am afraid so, professor,' I enunciate with concern, forcing a frown.

He walks forward, leans over to look at the scan reading, and back at the vessel. 'Did you wake up prematurely again?'

'Yes.'

Everett stands up straight, rubbing his bearded chin. 'I don't understand how that is possible! This time, I increased the dosage of the anaesthetic. You should have been out for hours.' Leaning down, he places a hand on my shoulder. 'Tell me, how are you feeling?'

'A bit disorientated.'

'Can you remember your full name?'

'Thom Sayer.'

'And why were you in the induced coma?'

'Because you have been monitoring my brain activity to understand where consciousness goes in a comatose state.'

'Well, yes, but not quite.'

I try to conceal my intrigue. Instead, maintaining a look of concern. 'Professor, why are we experimenting here in my flat?'

'It appears you have short-term memory loss again, Thom. When you woke up from the last session, you could not recall sleep-walking through a few days of freelancing work in Italy. Because of this, I suggested monitoring you at home. Today's session is to look into your mind and see what happened to you. Do you remember any of this?'

For Sayer's future sake, what was I meant to say?

'I, I, don't know. Have I been in a bad place?'

'Mimi told me that the past few weeks have been tough.'

Suddenly, I am awash with guilt.

He leans in closer, smiling. 'But I know something that might change how you feel.'

'…What do you mean?'

There is a moment of silence. I can see the professor trying to process what he is about to say.

'Ollie, he is *awake*.'

I feel a cold shiver wash over Sayer's body. Something so revitalising. So pure. I haven't felt this way in a very long time.

The vessel's hands are shaking—*my* hands are shaking.

Tears start to well.

'What?' I utter.

'Thom, your son has woken up from the coma.'

Typically, the response would be to celebrate the news. But I remain. Static. I should put the brain scanner back on and traverse to my actual reality. But I sit here, the professor's words still echoing around me.

Is it wrong to interrupt this vital moment in Sayer's life?

'Are you okay?' the professor says, stirring me to the present from my thoughts.

'Yes,' I nod, smiling.

'Come.' The professor stands upright, offering support.

I reach around, take hold of the walking stick, and stand.

He walks by my side from the lounge. We go onto the landing and walk up the stairs towards Ollie's room.

Fifty-Three

We stand on the top landing. At the end is Ollie's room.

My depth perception—the door looms back and forth toward me. It is disorientating.

What am I doing? I should turn back. Leave.

But suddenly, there are flashes of memories: Charlie's birth, taking him home, changing his nappy for the first time, him crying at night, no sleep, patting his back, his infectious laugh, the fragmented utterances of words, reading bedtime stories, first steps, playing with dinosaur toys, his crayon drawings on the walls, birthday cakes, tantrums, wiping away his crocodile tears, trips to the seaside, cuddles, him running around screaming happily.

If only I could see him again.

I remember Qubit's analogy of the sets of ripples upon the pond's surface. Perhaps I can find a version of Charlie someplace else?

Professor Everett walks ahead of me, pushing the door open. The room is no longer dimly lit. Sunlight emits through open curtains.

Sayer, I am sorry for ruining this moment for you. I, I need this.

The professor stands aside, allowing me to walk in.

In front of me is Sayer's son—*my* son—sitting upright in bed. He looks sleepy and confused. A heart monitor beeps by his side.

To his left sits Mimi, smiling at me. She hasn't looked this happy in years.

I walk up to the end of the bed; every footstep is heavy. Sayer's lungs are holding in a breath. Tears fall onto the torso.

'Dad?' he croaks. His voice is familiar. But different. It has matured since I last saw Charlie.

The sound resonates—a warm, comforting sensation overwhelms me.

Our eyes connect. We smile at each other.

It all floods back to me—that fateful day: walking in the park, looking at the birds by the pond, and losing him.

His kidnapping. Not his drowning.

Instead of resisting what happened, I am embracing it—accepting what went wrong—forgiving myself—because I'm finally reuniting with a version of my son.

Suddenly, the crippling guilt I have been bearing for years lifts.

My mission is complete.

I know I must leave this place—this perfect moment. But is it wrong to stay a bit longer?

Standing here, looking down at my son, I am transfixed.

But an impulse arises. I don't know why. My eyes avert to the right-hand corner of the bedroom.

There, I see something on the floor. Familiar. A single white feather. Delicate. Curved upwards and frayed at the edges. Identical.

Everything is in its right place.

Reviews help to draw an audience to the book. Please leave an honest comment. I would appreciate it.

Amazon:

GoodReads:

Acknowledgements

The story began with a thought experiment: what if you could amend mistakes—and have unrestrained free will—by switching realities? I wanted to incorporate this within a spy context, letting the idea simmer in my mind for years. Other elements slowly drew into focus. And one night, I dreamt about trying to find a lost child—an emotional anchor. The jigsaw fell into place.

Despite many (possibly) untestable ideas, I wanted to ground the story in hard science. I am indebted to professors Prateek Agrawal, Jonathan J. Halliwell, Amihay Hanany, Arttu Rajantie and Simon Saunders for answering my questions about theoretical physics.

I would also like to thank Timothy Barrett for his military advice, Peter Lyon for his language consultation, my mum for her medical knowledge, my dad for always being the first person to read my work, and Jamie Harris, Lorna Gribbin, Tom Pritchard, Alic Joy, Ian Gaughran, Wendy Murphy and David Tuchman for your invaluable feedback.

And finally, Z. You have tolerated my obsessing over this book. Thanks for joining me on this wild journey.

Printed in Great Britain
by Amazon

43577563R00172